THE DRAGONWITCH TALES
AN UNEXPECTED
BEGINNING

THE DRAGONWITCH TALES
AN UNEXPECTED
BEGINNING

SHANNON M. HARRIS

SAPPHIRE BOOKS

SALINAS, CALIFORNIA

Acknowledgment

A few people deserve my thanks for seeing this book to completion. Chris and everyone at Sapphire Books for believing in me enough to publish this, my fourth book. Heather, who was an amazing editor and a pleasure to work with. Ann, for creating a fantastic cover, Lori for tidying everything up. Also, a shout out to Candi, who continues to be an awesome beta reader and everyone else behind the scenes. Thank you.

Paisley stood with her back plastered against the wall leading into the kitchen, her eyes fixed on the scene in front of her. She blinked a few times to make sure she wasn't having a stroke, but every time she opened her eyes, nothing had changed. One minute, she was sitting on the couch with her cat Jynx watching a *Golden Girls* marathon, and the next she found herself in her current predicament. If she was asked, she would deny it, but at the moment *she* appeared in her living room, she peed herself a little. Anyone in her situation would have. Anyone.

The woman in front of her was floating a few inches above the floor, with her arms crossed across her chest. It was the craziest thing she had ever seen, and she had seen some crazy stuff in her thirty-two years. The woman looked like she had just stepped off the cover of a romance novel, and even though she was freaking out on the inside, Paisley couldn't help but be in awe of her sudden appearance.

The stranger was staring at her with an expression crossed between annoyance and amusement written across the sharp plains of her chiseled face. Long legs were encased in black leather pants and a pair of well-worn brown leather boots adorned her feet. A simple, long-sleeved gray tunic lay beneath a sleeveless red jerkin that was unbuttoned. A symbol she didn't recognize was stitched onto the right shoulder of the woman's shirt.

Brown leather cuffs wrapped each of her wrists, and a silver chain hung around her neck that disappeared inside her shirt. Paisley finally raised her head enough to lock eyes with the woman and gasped at the intensity with which the other woman was looking at her. It scared her and she tried to take a step back, realizing too late that she couldn't go back any farther.

Paisley gulped and took in the woman's short, shaggy black hair and brown eyes. Out of habit, she reached up and fiddled with her glasses. It was a nervous tick that she had tried for years to ignore, but after a while she'd decided to just roll with it. She was who she was, and saw no reason to apologize for that.

As the woman lowered herself to the floor, Paisley's eyes surveyed the room, looking for an escape route. If the woman could appear on a whim, Paisley's escape seemed slim. The stranger was the most beautiful and frightening woman she had ever seen. She counted to ten, then had to remind herself to breathe. *I can do this.* Whatever *this* was.

As taken with her as she was, she couldn't get over the fact that the woman had started to glow. Light literally was pouring from her slim frame. Paisley squinted as the light continued to seep out of her, and for some reason she couldn't look away from it. If she hadn't been so tired from work, she probably would have questioned everything that was happening. She wasn't exactly book smart, however she had common sense, and things weren't adding up.

As the woman's eyes continued to assess Paisley's body, she shivered and was starting to feel a bit self-conscious from her attention. The woman's gaze never wavered from its appraisal of her, and Paisley tensed when the woman's eyes locked with hers. She decided that enough was enough. Who the hell did she think she was, breaking into her home—because that was essentially what she had done—and ogling her? She could only take so much. "What do you want and why are you here?" When she didn't answer, only smirked at her, Paisley started to lose what sanity she had left. "Look—" Her words were cut off when her cell phone started ringing. She wished now she would have assigned distinct ringtones for different people. She was just moving to grab it when the woman reached toward the coffee table, picked it up, and answered it.

"Hello." Paisley bit her lip and backed up against the wall once more. The woman's voice, she knew, could melt butter. It was smooth, smoky, and sexy. Her knees wobbled a bit when the woman looked her way with a knowing smirk on her face. Paisley frowned and mentally gave herself a pep talk to stand her ground. When she held the phone out to her, Paisley did debate whether or not to take it, but the woman spoke again and waved the phone in the air. "Paisley, it's for you."

Considering it was her phone, she'd figured as much. She pushed away from the wall on shaky legs, stepped as close as she dared to the stranger, snatched the phone from her hands, and hightailed it back to her wall. "Hello."

"P.J., honey," her mom said. "Stay calm, and don't run. We'll be there in a few minutes."

Her mom hung up before she could answer. Knowing that her mom, and probably her grams, was on the way gave Paisley's confidence a boost. "That was my mom. She's on her way, so if anything happens to me, she knows you're here." The woman didn't acknowledge her words, only continued to smile at her. It was at that moment Paisley realized she had stopped glowing.

"What's that supposed to be?" She pointed to a

small table that sat across from the couch with just a hint of amusement in her voice.

Paisley narrowed her eyes at the question. A bit curious, she glanced to where she was pointing. "What's what?" Even though the woman seemed to be able to perform magic, which should be impossible, she still hoped she wasn't dealing with a weirdo. They came in all kinds of packages, even ones wrapped in form-fitting leather. "That's a table."

The woman rolled her eyes and sat down on the tan couch that took up most of the small living room, and continued to point at the table. "What's that underneath?"

As Paisley glanced once more at the table, she noticed a black and white tail sticking out from under it. Paisley shook her head and walked to the table, knelt, and scooped Jynx into her arms. She had wondered where the little coward had run off to. If she knew she could have squeezed under there, she would have joined Jynx. "You must be stupid if you don't know what a cat is."

Before she even had a chance to turn around, the woman had taken Jynx from her arms and left one of her leather bracelets around Paisley's wrist. "What… How did you do that?" It was like she had super speed. She tugged on the bracelet but it didn't budge. It had somehow molded to her skin. Paisley tamped down the nausea that rose and took several deep breaths to calm her racing heart. "What did you put on my wrist?"

"You must be stupid if you don't know what a bracelet is."

Paisley squirmed at her voice. "Touché." She walked slowly toward and around the couch, still messing with the cuff, then sat down on the edge of the matching recliner. Jynx was curled up in the she-devil's lap, fast asleep. "Traitor," she mumbled and fiddled with her glasses. Where was her mother?

"You're not exactly what I was expecting."

Her tone wasn't one of disappointment, just resignation. *Well, screw her.* No one asked her for her opinion anyway, and she was the one who came in uninvited. Paisley knew she wasn't up to supermodel standards, but none of her previous girlfriends had ever complained. Her complexion was a bit pale, but it paired nicely with her shoulder-length chestnut hair and her green eyes, which she inherited from her grams. Her glasses were also almost a genetic trait, but there was no way she would ever be able to wear contacts, and over the years, her glasses had become a part of her. "Sorry you're disappointed. I didn't invite you here." She waved her hand in the air. "You may leave any time you want to."

The woman leaned back on the couch and looked up at the ceiling. Paisley could swear she heard her count backward from ten. After a few moments, she sat up. "I can't leave whenever I want, and if I did, you would be coming with me."

She had some nerve. "I don't know who the hell you think—" Paisley whipped her head around when she heard tires screech outside her house. Not a minute later her mother and grandmother burst through the front door. They looked at the scene before them, then at each other. It would have been comical, except for the expression on their faces.

"Well," Grams said. "This isn't exactly what I was expecting."

"I would say not," her mother said, pointing to the couch. "For one thing, that's a woman."

Paisley looked between them, then finally found her voice, breaking the silence that had descended on them. "So. Could someone please explain to me what's going on here?" She hoped her voice sounded as calm as she tried to project it, but when her mother walked across the room, sat down on the arm of the chair, and wrapped her arm around her shoulders, she figured she had failed. She watched, her unease growing, when Grams sat down on the couch.

"So," Grams said. "What's your name and what are you doing in my granddaughter's house?" You could always count on Grams to get straight to the point.

The woman turned to her. "My name is Lana." Grams gasped, stood up from the couch, and started pacing. From the way her mother was gripping her shoulder, Paisley deduced this couldn't be good news.

"Mom, my shoulder."

"Sorry, dear." She jumped up from the chair and grabbed Paisley's wrist, disbelief written across her face.

"What?" Paisley forced down the panic that started to rise in her chest.

"P.J., what have you done?" Grams accused, her voice rising.

If they were freaked out maybe she should be, too. *Play it cool. Play it cool.* It was the mantra that was playing on a loop in her mind. "It's just a cuff. Although, it is a bit suspicious that I can't get it off." *Play it cool.*

"Honey," her mom said. "You won't be able to get it off."

Without warning the entire exchange hit Paisley the wrong way and she glared at Lana. "It's all her fault!" She would take the blame for most of this. "One minute she's floating, looking all evil, and the next thing I know, she grabs Jynx from my arms and leaves this cuff in her place." She shoved the cuff toward her mom's face, then pointed at Lana. "You don't look so scary without your light show and all the theatrics." Lana sat there, unmoving, with that damned sexy smile on her face.

"Kate," Grams said, addressing her daughter. "This is out of our hands. All we can do now is explain everything to P.J., since Lana couldn't, or wouldn't, take the time to."

Lana fidgeted on the couch, and it was the first time since she had appeared that she looked uncomfortable. "Well. I think I should be going. Ladies, I will leave you three to talk. Paisley." She stood up, sat Jynx on the couch, lifted Paisley's hand, and placed a tender kiss on the palm. "I'll see you later." She winked, then disappeared. *Disappeared.* Paisley clutched her offending hand to her chest and took several breaths to calm her racing heart. After her heart rate returned to normal, she looked at her mom and grandma, who didn't look fazed in the least about what had just happened. *What the hell?* She stood up, then quickly sat back down.

"Paisley," her mom said. "We need to talk."

※ ※ ※ ※

Paisley ran her hand through her hair and regarded the two of the three most important women in her life, the absent one being K.G. "How can you two be so calm? Do you realize what just happened? It's not possible. I mean really, this is crazy. Not crazy good, or crazy bad, just crazy." She waved her hand in the spot that Lana had disappeared from. She took off her glasses and rubbed her eyes before replacing them on her face. Her hands were shaking so badly she slipped them beneath her legs.

"P.J.," her mom said.

She shook her head, stood up, and glared at them. "I'm not done yet." She stuffed her hands in the pockets of her lounge pants. "First some scary, sexy woman just appears in my living room unannounced—and out of thin air, I might add. Who. Was. Glowing." She started pacing. "I mean. Who does that? Light was literally pouring from her. Then she puts this cuff on my wrist, and apparently, by the way you two are acting, I should be even more freaked out about it than I am. Then"— she held up her hand to ward off their questions—"she just vanishes. Poof. Gone. But you two don't seem bothered by *that* at all. Tell me, how many people do you know that can just disappear and appear on a whim, hmm?" She stalked back to the recliner, flopped down, only to miss the chair completely and land with a thud on the floor. Mustering whatever dignity she had left, she hauled herself up off the floor and settled back down on the chair. She was having one weird-ass day. Stranger than usual. She sighed. "What does this cuff mean?" She sniffled, and shot them both a glare she hoped told them to stay where they were.

Grams bit her lip. "Sweetheart, we have a lot to talk about. We probably should have had this conversation a long time ago. We just never thought...I mean...you never showed any sort of ability whatsoever."

Paisley furrowed her brow and frowned. "Ability?" She scratched her nose. "I think I need a drink." She stood up before they could protest and headed to the kitchen, returning shortly with three bottles of water, handing one to each of them before she sat back down.

"Honey," her mom said. "I think we need to talk about what you consider a drink."

Paisley ignored her and took a long swallow. "I have one question for now. Just one." They both nodded for her to continue. "What does this cuff have to do with anything and what does it mean? I can't get it off."

Grams smiled sadly. "It's meant to form a bond between both wearers."

"Ooo-kay. What kind of bond are we talking about? What does that mean for this…Lana person and me?" Was this really happening? Maybe she was dreaming. She pinched her arm, and hissed when it stung. Her mom coughed and she swung her gaze back to them.

"Well—"

"It's like this, honey—"

Paisley clinched her fists. "Just spit it out!"

"It means you're married."

"She's your wife."

It took her a minute to absorb what they had said, and even when the words registered they still didn't make sense. She had to have misunderstood, but when she looked between them and saw the look on both their faces, she knew she had heard correctly. *Play it cool.* After all, it was just a bracelet. That she couldn't get off. But still. "Okay. Maybe we got ahead of ourselves. Maybe, just a bit. Let's start over." She scrunched her nose up trying to remember something Grams had said. "You said something about an ability. What was that about? And for the record, I don't know why it was such a big deal that she was a woman. You know I'm gay."

"I can't believe you're joking about all of this," Grams said.

She giggled, then quickly tamped it down. "I'm freaking out on the inside." Neither one looked convinced.

Her mother eyed her intently, then spoke. "Promise not to interrupt us."

"Yes."

"I'll let your grandmother start."

"P.J., you have to understand what we're about to tell you is the truth. No matter what we say. It is the truth. If nothing else, please believe and remember that."

Paisley gripped the arms of the recliner. "Okay." From the look on Grams's face, this was going to be even wilder than Lana appearing in her living room.

Grams smiled. "Let me start by saying that I loved your grandfather, and I know Kate loves your father. All our marriages and the marriages of every other female in our line were predetermined. Arranged, if you will. We never knew who our husbands were going to be, or when they would come to us. And there is a reason we never got to pick our husbands. From as far back as our line has been written, every female in our family has been blessed with an ability of some sort. Powers. Your great-grandmother had the ability to heal the human body. Her mother, your great-great-grandmother, had the ability of a seer. As for myself, I can be in several places at a time, a sort of cloning effect. Our abilities are rare and varied, and must be maintained. Because of the need to nourish our powers our marriages have to be with men who can guarantee our offspring will enhance, or at the very least carry on, the abilities we have been given." She rubbed her palms on her pants. "I say men, because that is the way it has always been. As much as the world has progressed, it is still not possible for two women to have a biological child of their own."

Powers. Paisley ran her hands through her hair. What the hell was going on? How in the span of an hour could her whole world be turned on its end? It was her first instinct to believe they were playing an elaborate trick on her, but that thought was squished by the look in her grandmother's eyes. This was happening. "That's why you were both surprised when you saw Lana?"

"Yes. This is where things will get tricky, and you must suspend your belief in the reality you've always known just a bit. We knew our husbands would come from another realm, one where magic is commonplace, we've just never been there ourselves. We are not allowed to cross the barrier between worlds. Only the women of Dangor—the other realm—are allowed to travel freely through the barrier. But the men...once they come through, they can't go back. The men who agree to wed us give up their lives and their families in Dangor to have another one with us in this world. That is the reason we were shocked to see a woman."

"But, you spoke to her on the phone."

"To be honest, that didn't even dawn on us. We still expected a man until we laid eyes on her. Lana will be able to come and go through the barrier as she sees fit. That also means that you will be able to go with her. The only way she could have come through to claim you is with the King's Council's approval. This is the first I have heard about a same-sex union."

Paisley adjusted her glasses. "Wait. If the cuff forms a bond, why aren't you two wearing one?"

Her mom smiled. "When we got married, we forfeited the cuff for a wedding band. The cuff is the tradition in Dangor, rings are the tradition in our world."

Paisley shook her head. She loved them dearly, but how could they really expect her to believe everything they were saying? They'd never mentioned any of this before, nor had Paisley ever witnessed anything odd concerning them. "Let's just assume, for the sake of discussion, that I believe all this arranged-marriage-from-another-realm stuff. A same-sex union...that's not the only reason you were shocked by Lana. What is it?"

"If I'm not mistaken, Lana is the name of King Perry's second born, and his only daughter. From time to time we get progress reports on the happenings in Dangor," Grams said.

Kate wrung her hands. "I don't mean this the wrong way, P.J., but what in the world would Lana want with you? Never in our line have we ever been matched with royalty, and to be frank, she has to be at least ten years younger than you."

Well, hell. What could you say to that reasoning? It hadn't escaped her notice that Lana did look young. She knew she should have been offended by her mother's words, but she didn't know why she would have been chosen either. "Surely, if she wanted to, she could take the cuff off and pick someone else." All three shared nervous glances. "Right?" *Play it cool.*

Her mom shook her head. "That's not the way it works, P.J. Once the bond has been made, it cannot be broken."

"No." She shook her head. "That doesn't make sense. Don't I have to agree to this before the bond can be made? Where is my consent in this entire debacle?" She hadn't been selective in her dating choices to just throw her life away to a stranger.

"Your bond would have been made a long time ago," Grams said. "Bonds are not made on a whim. They are divinely done. It is destined from your birth who will become your partner. Some bonds are made for the good of the people, some are made for the good of the few, and some bonds are made for the good of the two people involved. In your case, I'm not sure what the bond was made for. But I do know this: no matter if you both wanted to, that bond is secure and no one will be able to break it."

"So, that's it then? I'm stuck with her?" How could everything suddenly go bat-shit crazy? She took a deep breath. "I don't understand how this can be happening. I don't have any sort of ability. I'm just me: Paisley Jane. And both of you know I would never agree to marry a man, no matter what happened. I always thought I would marry for love."

"Actually..." Lana said from behind Paisley, making her jump in her chair.

Paisley glared at her and grabbed her chest. "Don't do that. You just can't appear and disappear on a whim." *Holy hell.*

Grams pushed off the couch and stood up. "What do you mean, 'actually'?"

Lana stepped around the recliner and leaned against it. "Paisley probably doesn't even realize she has any power. At least not until we go back to Dangor. There, her powers can be realized." She grinned down at her.

"She may have powers and not even know it?"

"Yes, she could. Look, I know I've probably upended everything, but I didn't have a choice. This way she is protected. Now she has the protection of the Royal Elite Guards."

Grams's eyes widened. "Why would she need their protection?"

"There are a lot of tales in my world. Some are true and some are simply myths. However, there is one story everyone seems to agree on because it has never been discounted. It is said a woman will be the one to bring the kingdom into turmoil, and this woman will hold power unknown to many." At the same time Lana sat down on the arm of Paisley's chair, Paisley stood up and moved away from her. Being so close to her was putting Paisley on edge. Lana smirked at her but continued with her story. "Some are aware of her and will never stop hunting her, while others couldn't care less about her existence. The Brotherhood of the Realm is among those hunting her. What I want to do is teach Paisley of her abilities and allow her to grow in her powers."

Paisley's mom stood up. "That's all well and good, but how do you know Paisley is that woman?"

"Kate," Grams said.

"Mom is right. How do you know that that's me?"

Lana seemed to be choosing her words carefully. "To be fair, we don't know it's you. But rumor has it that this woman will come from a different land, and since I am your chosen partner, it all has sort of fallen into place."

The story kept getting crazier by the minute. Paisley adjusted her glasses and bit her lip. At this point in time, she would have to consider every angle.

"Okay." She sighed. "Honestly, do you three realize how insane this sounds?" When no one answered her, she threw her hands in the air. So, that's how they were going to play it? Whatever. She couldn't fully trust Lana, but she didn't know that she wasn't telling the truth. Nor could she fully trust her family. She turned toward her mother to get the attention off herself. "Mom, you never told me what your ability is." Changing the subject was an ability she had mastered a long time ago.

"I don't have one."

Lana cocked her head. "You don't?"

"No. That's why we always figured P.J. never showed any signs."

"It could be that her and your abilities just haven't been realized yet," Lana said.

Grams waved her hand in the air. "I thought it was just dormant in them. That has been known to happen."

Lana shrugged, walked to the couch, and sat down. "I'm not really sure then." She grabbed Paisley's arm and pulled her down beside her.

Paisley debated jumping up, but Lana smelled amazing, like a combination of honey and vanilla. Lana seemed to sense her struggle and slipped an arm around her shoulders to hold her in place. The hand rubbing her shoulder sent shivers down Paisley's spine. As soon as Paisley leaned closer to Lana, she received a glare from her mom and promptly pulled away from her a bit. "So, what happens now?" Paisley asked.

"You'll come home with me of course," Lana stated matter-of-factly.

"No," Mom and Grams said at the same time.

Paisley ignored them. Her house wasn't a dump,

but it was older and small. An upgrade could be nice… Maybe Lana had an appealing alternative. It never hurt to listen to all possibilities before making an informed decision. "Where do you live?"

Lana's whole face lit up. "I have a house on Dangor Lake. It's not big, but it's home. Imagine waking up with a view of the Matek Mountains every morning. It's breathtaking."

Paisley grinned right along with her. That sounded nice. A lake view and a view of the mountains. She could imagine the multitude of colors that would splatter the morning sky. She scrunched her nose when it hit her that Illinois didn't have any mountains, and for the life of her she couldn't recall ever hearing about the Matek Mountains. She searched her memory for a clue when something Grams had said pulled at the forefront of her memory. *Another realm.* She pulled away from Lana and looked her in the eye. "Where are the Matek Mountains located?" When Lana's eyes widened, she looked to the other two women, but neither one was looking at her. Paisley stood up. "Well?"

"The Matek Mountains are in Dangor. My home country. You do know where Dangor is, don't you?"

"No, I don't recall." Paisley's words were clipped. She ran her shaking hands through her hair. None of this could be real. How could it? Everything seemed to click into place. "I need to sit down." Before she could sit back down on the couch, her mom grabbed her arm and settled her down in the recliner. "Where is Dangor again?"

Lana jumped up. "She doesn't know?" Kate shook her head and Lana turned toward Paisley. "I think I'll really take my leave now and let the three of you discuss matters." She took a step toward Paisley. "I will be back later." She placed a chaste kiss on Paisley's cheek and promptly disappeared.

She could feel the kiss all the way to her toes and felt certain her cheek shouldn't be tingling where Lana's lips had been. This was a nightmare. "This is really happening?" She had some crazy shit happen in her life. K.G., her ex and best friend, was one of them, but what was happening now took crazy to a whole other level. "Dangor?" She wasn't sure she wanted to know, but she needed all the facts.

Her mom started. "We should have told you years ago about what was happening and what could happen. I am so sorry we didn't. It was my responsibility to inform you, and I have failed you. And yes, this is really happening."

"The Realm," Grams said, "is another dimension that the men in our family, and now Lana, of course, are able to travel through. The men who cross over can never go back. I see questions behind those captivating green eyes of yours. I don't know why our family was chosen for such extraordinary gifts, but it has always been this way and we have never taken them for granted. Your grandpa once told me that traveling through to our world was the scariest thing he had ever done in his life, but that he wouldn't trade it for anything."

Paisley wiped a tear away. His death last year of a heart attack had shocked everyone, and they were still dealing with his passing in their own way. "What did Lana mean when she said I would go home with her?" Moving didn't faze her, but moving to another realm did seem a bit excessive, even for her standards.

They both fidgeted. "I can only reason that she wants you to go back with her."

Paisley rolled her eyes. "Yes, Grams, I got that, but what does it mean?"

Kate tilted her head. "We don't know. You'll probably want to ask her that. It might ultimately mean you will be living with her. The men come to the women they are betrothed to, so I can only assume that you will go with her."

By their words and their actions, they were stuffing everything into a neat and tidy box. This wasn't a story they were retelling; this was her life. "What happens if I don't want to accompany her back? What if I refuse?"

"I...don't know," Grams said. "No one has ever refused a joining before. It's part of who we are. It makes up our lifeblood. We should have told you earlier to help you get used to the idea, but over the years no one came for you. It's obvious now that the reason she didn't come earlier is because she's at least ten years younger than you. She simply hadn't been born yet. As the years passed, we just figured no one was coming for you. Even your father had started to wonder. You should talk to him as soon as possible."

"Honey," her mom said. "You seem to be taking all of this rather well." She smiled, but the tone of her voice conveyed an entirely different meaning.

How was she supposed to act given the circumstances? They'd had years to adjust to everything, and now they expected her to take in everything in a matter of hours. What she wouldn't give to go back in time and continue to watch *The Golden Girls* with Jynx on the couch. She glanced at the clock. "It's late and I think I should sleep on all of this. Maybe by tomorrow morning my brain will have caught up with everything that was discussed. After everything that's happened, I wouldn't say no to dinner, either."

When they hesitated to leave, Paisley stood up, kissed them each on the cheek, and pushed them toward the door. "Really, I'll be fine." She closed the door after they had walked through, then leaned back against it and let her body slide to the floor with a thud. After a few minutes of silence, she lay down on the floor and traced the patterns on the ceiling with her eyes. She smiled when Jynx licked her face then settled her weight on her chest. "Jynx, remember when I said we needed more excitement in our lives? I lied."

❧ ❧ ❧ ❧

Beep…Beep…Beep

Paisley burrowed deeper into the covers and pretended that the alarm wasn't going off. She snuggled under the warm blanket and closed her eyes in anticipation of a few more minutes' sleep.

Beep…Beep…Beep

She sighed and rolled over, pulling the covers from her face, and blinked at the red numbers taunting her on the alarm clock and frowned. Now, she knew she was still dreaming, because that couldn't possibly be the right time. She lay still staring at the blinking numbers until her brain finally caught up with what her eyes were seeing. It couldn't possibly be a quarter to nine in the morning. "Shit."

She flung the covers off and jumped out of bed. She could have sworn she set it for seven. She hopped around on one foot until both legs were in her jeans, and pulled them up and over her pink boy shorts. She fumbled with the zipper and looked from her legs to the bed, then back to her matching pink bra. Wait a minute. How did she get into bed with all her clothes off? The last thing she remembered was falling asleep on the living room floor. *What the what? Play it cool. Play it cool.*

She grabbed her white T-shirt that she normally wore to work and pulled it on over her head. The RiversEdge was one of only two bed and breakfasts in her small town. The hours where decent and the pay was good, and since she only worked four days a week it was the perfect combination for her. She flung her door open and was halfway down the hallway when she skidded to a stop and sniffed the air. Bacon. Considering she didn't have any bacon in the house it was quite odd, but she figured maybe her mother had come to fix her breakfast. But, no, that wouldn't be right. Her mother would have woken her up for work.

She couldn't find any fault with someone cooking bacon for her, until she stepped into the kitchen and came to a complete stop. Lana stood at the stove in a pair of tight, black leather pants and a brown and red long-sleeved shirt. The sleeves were pushed up her forearms. Today her short hair was put up into a small ponytail and it all looked so domestic. Paisley frowned when Lana turned around to greet her.

Lana pointed her spatula at the table. "Sit down. Breakfast is almost done." She turned back to the stove.

Paisley noticed she was flipping hash browns, and licked her lips. She loved hash browns. Why did her life have to be so complicated suddenly? "Why didn't you wake me? I have to work. I don't even know you. You need to stop coming into my home unannounced. It's rude and that's not even considering that it's against the law."

Lana picked up a piece of bacon and nibbled on

it. "You're not hungry?"

At that moment, Paisley's stomach decided to show its displeasure and Lana grinned at her. Paisley eyed the plate of bacon and eggs Lana set in front of her. When she reached for the plate, Lana's smile was almost blinding but before she could say anything, Paisley picked the plate up and headed toward the back door. "See you later."

She walked as fast as she could, without disturbing her plate, and slid into her car. Setting the plate on the passenger seat, she flung the car into reverse and spun out of the driveway. She was tempted to look in the rearview mirror, but she couldn't care less whether Lana was following her or not. Bonding bracelet or not, she didn't know Lana and she wasn't sure she wanted to.

The events from the day before were still hard to fathom. Truth be told, she would have never believed a story like that from her mom and grams if Lana hadn't appeared in her home beforehand. She loved her family, but the story was beyond far-fetched, even by her standards. Add to that the fact that she was supposedly married, and it was almost too much for her to handle. She would try to reserve judgement until she had a chance to talk with her family in more depth. She hoped they showed a little bit more concern for her well-being instead of just throwing facts at her.

It wasn't until she was halfway to work and had finished most of the bacon that she realized it was Monday. She didn't work on Mondays. At the next stop sign she turned left toward her parents' neighborhood. As she neared their house, she noticed Uncle Cliff's camper parked beside her dad's Jeep in the driveway. That was odd, considering he and her father shouldn't have been home from their annual fishing trip until Saturday.

She pulled into the drive, killed the engine, and ate the rest of her breakfast. She moaned when the first bite of eggs passed her lips. They were cooked to perfection, as was the bacon. It made her sick to think how perfect Lana seemed. She knew looks could be deceiving, but she bet the hash browns tasted amazing as well.

Paisley frowned when her mother pulled back the living room curtain for the third time, and with a groan she stepped out of her car before her mom came out and got her. Bracing herself for whatever would come, she climbed the porch steps and walked to the front door. Deep in her gut she knew that what would happen inside the house would be life-changing, even more so than what had already occurred the previous day. Before her hand touched the doorknob, the door swung open, and her mother grabbed her and drew her into a hug.

"Sweetheart, how are you this morning?" She pushed her to arm's length and ran her eyes along Paisley's body. When she was satisfied, she pulled Paisley through the open door and deposited her on the couch beside her grandmother.

Paisley adjusted her glasses, then scratched her nose. "I slept okay, all things considered, and Lana made me breakfast." At Lana's name, they both frowned.

Grams patted her knee. "Well, that was nice of her. So, she came back after we left?"

Paisley shrugged and bit her lip. How much should she tell them? "I don't know when she came back or if she even left. The last thing I remember is falling asleep on the living room floor. When I woke up, I was in my bed." She decided to leave out that she was practically naked.

"That's nice, dear."

Paisley regarded her grandmother. "Dad and Uncle Cliff came back early?"

Her mom sat down on the recliner across from the couch. "I called your dad last night and they both insisted on coming back early. They're not here now, though. I asked them to give us today to talk to you and they both agreed. But, your dad has a lot he wants to talk to you about." She stood abruptly and headed out of the room only to return a few minutes later carrying a wood box, roughly the size of a shoe box. When she set it on the coffee table, Paisley leaned forward to get a closer look. Numerous, differently shaped squares and circles were cut into the surface of the wood. She wasn't a hundred percent sure but it looked like cherry wood. Honeysuckle vines lined the edges of the box and wrapped around the lid. Again, looks could be deceiving, but by the wear and rust on the hinges, the box was old.

Paisley looked from her mom to the box, when her mom pulled her necklace off. A small key dangled from the simple silver chain. Ever since she could remember her mom had always worn the key around her neck and she had never seen her use it before. It always held an air of mystery to her, and now she wished she never had to know what the key was for and she wasn't at all sure she was ready for what was in the box. She took several deep breaths when her mom placed the key in the lock on the box and opened the lid. Paisley squinted and tensed, but when nothing happened she felt a bit let down.

A hardback-sized, black leather book and several different pieces of jewelry were nestled inside the box. Grams reached into the box and lifted out a necklace that had a square-shaped ruby dangling from the silver chain. Paisley eyed the stone, then the hands that held it, and couldn't help the sadness that overcame her. She reached for her grams's hand and ran her fingers over her palm. Where had the years gone? Her grandmother was eighty-five. Every inch of skin was wrinkled and weathered, but still as soft as ever. Grams wrapped her fingers around Paisley's hand and tapped her chin, then smiled. When hundreds of memories flooded her mind it suddenly hit Paisley: what would she do if she went to Dangor and something happened to her grandmother? She didn't think she would be able to survive that.

"Sweetheart," Grams said. "I know what you're thinking and you need to stop right now. Life is a cycle. A cycle that doesn't end for anyone and life is meant to end. But rest assured, I am not done living yet. We have plenty of time."

Paisley sucked in a breath and held the tears at bay, but smiled and kissed Grams's palm before pointing to the necklace. "What are you going to do with that?"

"It's for you. Here." She handed it over. "Put it on."

Paisley accepted the necklace and slipped it over her head. When nothing happened, she looked up. "Was something supposed to happen?"

Mom shook her head. "We weren't sure if it would. The necklace is one that has been passed from generation to generation. There is more power in that pendant than any of us combined could ever create."

Paisley laughed to ease the tension that suddenly flared up in her. Good grief, if it held that much power, why would they give it to her to begin with? "So, I guess I shouldn't lose it then? Huh."

"It would be best not to, dear." Grams winked.

"I'll guard it with my life, Grams." Kate pulled the book out of the box, closed the lid, then set the book on top of the box. The leather was weathered, but looked to be in good shape, and had the same honeysuckle patterns that were etched onto the box. Something told her this wasn't an ordinary box or book. She was quite confident she could have been Sherlock in another life.

Her mom opened the book and flipped through the pages until she found the one she was looking for. "Paisley, this book is our heritage. It contains everything that has ever been written about our family and the abilities they have received. This is not a joke and something you must always take seriously. No one, and I mean no one, outside of this family should ever be allowed to see this book. Do I make myself clear?"

It was the first time she had ever heard such passion in her mother's voice. She pointed to the book and her mom nodded. She flipped through the pages and frowned. All the pages were blank. "I don't understand?"

"You will." Grams handed her a pen. "On that page, I need you to write your full name, age, birthdate, your parents' full names, your grandfather's full name, and mine. Underneath that you need to write Lana's name, then a short biography about yourself. It only needs to be a couple of paragraphs."

"Okay." Paisley bit her lip and accepted the pen her grandmother handed her. Her hand hovered above the pages. For some reason, it felt wrong to be writing in the book, but she shook off the nerves and wrote down what they asked her to. When she reached the biography, she hesitated. It would have helped if she could read what others had written about themselves. She didn't want to write the wrong things down. She scribbled a few things, then handed the pen to her mom, but as soon as her mom took the pen, she grabbed Paisley's hand and without warning produced a knife and slid the blade across her palm. Paisley hissed in pain as the blade tore her flesh.

Her mom turned her hand over and allowed the blood to drip onto the page she had just written on. The blood soaked the paper and spread out, devouring her words. *Good grief.* Paisley yanked her hand back and squinted at her mom. This was some weird shit. What had she gotten herself into?

As she traced the wound with her fingertip, it started to heal. Where once there was a deep, angry gash, one would have to look closely to even see the faint scar that now dotted her palm. "How?" Her mom winked and closed the book, only to reopen it a second later to the first page, then started flipping through it. Every page was filled with writing and pictures of different women. Some of the languages she recognized, others she didn't.

"This is our heritage," Grams said. "The book will only reveal itself, or its secrets, through a blood sacrifice from our line."

Paisley glared at them. "You could have warned me." All of a sudden, this felt too real.

Her mom waved her hand in the air. "You're fine."

"Whatever." Paisley slumped back on the couch and glanced out the window. There was no turning back now. If she had any reservations before, they had all been thrown out the door. She still wasn't sure what it all meant. Sure, she knew that magic existed now, but that still didn't explain so many things. She was a nobody. There wasn't anything special about her. What she did know was that she was…a witch. In a long line of witches, including her mom and grandma. *Holy shit. Play it cool.* She fiddled with her glasses before pushing them back up the bridge of her nose, then turned and faced them both. She needed more answers. "Not to worry. I'm good. I just needed a minute." She pointed to the book. "What does all this mean? What is to be expected of me?" Those two questions seemed straightforward enough. Dozens more lingered on her tongue, but they could wait.

"P.J., your grandma and I were talking last night and we don't want keep anything else from you."

"Okay." That didn't sound good at all.

"If you had shown signs of your powers before now this wouldn't be so difficult. As it is, I don't know anybody in our line that has come into their powers at the age of thirty-two." Her mom waved her hand in the air and took a deep breath. "We think Lana may be right about your powers manifesting themselves in Dangor. As much as it pains me to say this, we believe your best chance will be to go back with her. Learn from the people there and learn from her. She has the means to protect you that we never will. Let her protect you."

"Just like that?" How could they be so nonchalant about everything? They may have had years to become comfortable with their purpose in life, but she'd only found out about hers the day before. She needed her family right now, not some stranger, and she needed them to be on her side. Instead, it felt like they were throwing her to the wolves. Granted, Lana was an attractive wolf, but she was still a wolf.

"Lee."

Paisley jerked her head up at Grams's voice. Only her grandpa had ever called her Lee, and to hear it coming out of Grams's mouth felt wrong, but it also meant that whatever she was about to tell her was important. She was glad she was sitting down. Grams slipped her hand into hers and squeezed.

"Sweetheart, you are a part of something. Something far bigger than any of us. You are part of a legacy and as such you will show only respect to it. Do not do anything to draw disrespect upon it or our family. Once you wrote in the book, you signed your fate. You cannot turn away from your powers, and you cannot run away from this. If you have any questions do not hesitate to ask me or your mother. We will gladly answer them." She squeezed once more, then released her hand.

She loved both her grams and her mom, but just like Lana, they had also sealed her life to something without asking her permission first. She wasn't sure how she felt about that. Fate. That was only a word she read in books. It shouldn't have any bearing on real life. At least not her life. How did everything get so screwed up? She dug her fingernails in to the couch cushion before she said something she would regret. She loved them both too much to do that. "May I look at the book?"

Mom held up her finger. "Hold that thought." She then walked out of the room.

"Grams, what if I can't do this? What if I fail? What then?" She choked back a sob and rested her head in her hands.

"Oh, Paisley. That won't happen. For one, you're too smart to allow that to happen. For two, you come from a long line of strong women, magic notwithstanding. Draw from them, and as much as I hate to admit it, draw from Lana. I am sure she is a fine woman, but first and foremost you have been and always will be my girl." Paisley raised up and grabbed her into a hug, only pulling back when her mom walked back into the living room carrying a container filled with chocolate cupcakes.

"I made these for you last night. Take them and the book home. Eat and read. Trust me, P.J. It's what you need right now and if Lana is there, share the cupcakes with her." She winked.

"What about the book? May she see it?"

"You can let her look at the book, because you are bonded to her, but all she will see is blank pages. Only one that has sacrificed blood can see what has been written."

"So, if she was to let her blood soak into the pages, she would be able to read them too?"

"Well, no," her mom said.

"Oh. Okay. That's awesome." Awesome and frightening at the same time. They both laughed, but Paisley couldn't even muster up a smile. She picked up the tray of cupcakes and the book.

"When you get home, take a shower, eat, and read. It will do you some good." She let her fingers linger on Paisley's cheek. "I love you."

"I love you, too, but I won't be able to read most of what is written."

"Not now, but you will be able to. In time."

Paisley readjusted the items in her arms. "What

do you mean?"

"Over the coming days, you will start to adjust to the different languages. Your brain will decipher them for you." Her mom patted her on the back. "Call us tomorrow."

"All right. Shower, eat, and read. I can do that." She hugged them both before stepping out of the house and walking toward her car. She set her belongings on the passenger seat letting her finger linger along the spine of the book, then jerked her finger back and grabbed the pendant around her neck when it felt like it was getting warmer. She pulled it out of her shirt and let it rest against the fabric. She shook her head, backed out of the driveway, and headed toward her house. What the hell had she gotten herself into?

❧❧❧❧

Instead of going home right away, Paisley drove to the nearest park. She needed a moment to herself, and the water always had a calming effect on her. Her mom never understood the appeal, but her dad had her in the water only a few months after she was born. Next summer they had planned to learn to surf together. It was going to be the first family vacation they'd had together in years. She'd even convinced K.G. to take a week off work and go with them. The plans were made, and the hotel and surf lessons were booked. Those plans were shot to hell now. This time next year she would probably be in Dangor.

After pulling into an open spot and turning the car off, she grabbed the book off the seat beside her and walked toward the hill overlooking the river. She took a moment to appreciate the stillness of the water before sitting down at an empty picnic table. Her fingers lightly thumped against the cover of the book, but she couldn't bring herself to open it. The women inside the pages were special, and had something unique to offer the world. Paisley wasn't sure she would ever measure up to their standards. Did her mom and grams even realize the pressure they were putting on her? Did they even care?

Her family had always been supportive of her, and she guessed that's why it felt now like they were abandoning her to a life she never asked for. Without taking her feelings or concerns into account they'd decided what was best for her. They just expected her to go along with everything that was happening. Her life wasn't anything fancy, or exciting, but it was her own life, to do with as she wished, with whomever she wished. Now all that had changed, in what amounted to a blink of an eye.

She closed her eyes and enjoyed the cool breeze that whispered through the trees, only to snap her eyes open a moment later when the sound of giggling reached her ears. A mother and a small boy were perched on the picnic table near hers eating ice cream. The carefree looks on both their faces caused a deep ache to grow in her chest. She'd always wanted kids, but now she didn't know if that would be possible, or if she would even want kids with Lana. Lana who was a stranger, a princess, and according to everyone, her wife.

She traced around the edge of the cuff with the tip of her finger. On one hand, it felt like it had always been there. On the other hand, she wanted to grab a knife and try to cut it away. This would have been a vastly different situation if she would have been asked, or at the very least, told what would happen when it was slapped on her wrist. Who knew all it took was a nondescript piece of jewelry to flip the switch on someone's life?

She took several deep breaths, breathing in the freshly mowed grass, trying to slow the pounding of her heart. Besides being married, she was a witch. A legacy witch, at that. *Jesus.* This stuff wasn't real. How could it be? What she needed was someone to talk to, but she knew K.G. was still at work and she was the only person she would be able to talk things over with who wouldn't think she was crazy. Because crazy was exactly how she felt. She slipped her glasses off and rubbed her eyes. After a few minutes of staring at the blurry water, she put her glasses back on and opened the book. No time like the present to delve into an unknown world.

Every page had a woman's picture on it, and she wondered if someday her picture would grace these pages as well. She steered clear of her mom and grandma's section. The last thing she wanted was to learn any more about them right now. She skimmed the biographies and skipped over the languages she couldn't read, before coming to a stop on a page that held a photo of a woman who looked like her. Emily Harger was the name printed at the top of the page. Her great-great-great-great grandmother. Except for Paisley's glasses, the resemblance was uncanny and a bit eerie.

Emily was ninety-two when she died, and had two children. Her powers were manifested by her emotions and she had a knack for creating power orbs. Paisley frowned. Whatever they were. She tore her eyes away from her picture and skipped down to her biography and read.

I refused to write my biography when I was first approached to do so. I was a scared fifteen-year-old whose mother thrust her into this crazy life. And yes, I do mean crazy. Now I am twenty-four and still don't completely grasp what is expected of me and what my powers fully are. I was hesitant when I first learned of my family's secrets and what that would mean for me, and I still am. I don't fully embrace the fate I was given, but I also will not throw it away. It is a gift that very few are allowed, and I would be a fool to not try and make it work.

My suitor came through the barrier when I was eighteen. I've known him for six years and we've finally gotten into a groove with our lives. We love each other but aren't in love—and I'm not sure we ever will be— but he is a good man and a wonderful father to our two little girls. This life was pushed on him as much as it was me. We both knew what was at stake and decided to stick it out. I think we'll be okay. At least it feels that way. Falling in love never really appealed to me, so I'm not bothered by our situation. Others might be and I can't speak for them. I can only urge you to consider all your options before making a decision concerning your future. This life isn't for everyone, even if that's what they tell you.

My mentor told me I should try and give anyone reading this a piece of advice. I don't feel I am qualified for that, but I will heed her wisdom. Don't be afraid of this new world or adventure, but take everything with a grain of salt. No two witches are alike and no two fates will ever mirror the other. Wherever or whenever you learn of your destiny, you don't have to like it or even want it, but think long and hard before you turn your back on it. A few witches have done just that and lived to regret it. I learned the hard way that those closest to you don't always take your feelings into consideration. My mentor has been an amazing friend and has led me through every obstacle I have ever encountered, unlike my mother. Find someone who will stand in your corner and wish for your success. Good luck; you're going to need it. But remember, you're exactly where you should be and what the world needs right now.

Paisley shut the book and rested her forehead atop it. She wasn't sure she was as strong as Emily to live in a loveless marriage. She knew it would be wasteful to throw the gift she'd been given away, but so far, she had never showed any signs of being anything other than normal. For her, that's what was making everything so hard to believe. How could she accept the fact that she was a witch when she didn't feel any different than she did a couple of days ago? Maybe if she would exhibit some ability it would make it a bit easier for her to tolerate. Fully accepting what was happening, without any proof of what she was capable of, was a tall order. And that wasn't even taking Lana into consideration.

She groaned, then stood up, glancing once more at the woman and young boy, who had settled down on top of the picnic table and were looking up at the sky. Her dad used to bring her to the park and do the exact same thing. It was hard to believe she would never have that. She was only thirty-two and it felt like her life was ending instead of beginning, and that was not how she wanted to live. She wasn't sure she would ever, could ever, accept being thrown into this world without a safety net, but given how everything had happened so far, she wasn't sure she had a choice.

From now on, she would listen to her family and try to see it from their point of view, try being nicer to Lana, and make a point to visit K.G. in the coming days. They had both been so busy lately, but a K.G. hug was exactly what she needed right now, and if she did have to go to Dangor, she wanted to spend as much time with her best friend as possible. As she started the car and pulled out of the parking spot, she hoped that if Lana was still at her house, she'd at least made dinner. She was starving, and while she could make a meal out of the cupcakes, she hoped she wouldn't have to.

☙☙☙☙

Paisley didn't realize how late it had gotten until she was halfway home and noticed the streetlights had started to come on. No wonder she was so hungry. She'd given in and eaten two cupcakes on the way home, but they didn't curb her appetite one bit. She didn't know whether to be freaked out or relived when she pulled into the drive and saw a shadow pass by her living room window. What was one more heart-to-heart for the day? She should probably just get it over with. As soon as she closed the back door, her stomach growled when several different spices wafted toward her. Lana was leaning against the kitchen counter, grinning at her.

Lana pointed to the slow cooker. "I made dinner."

Paisley took a deep breath and nodded, relieved. She wasn't ready to confront her issues with Lana after all, at least not right now. All she wanted was to eat her dinner with as little fanfare as possible. "Good. I'm hungry." Lana's smile slipped, but motioned for her to take a seat. Paisley deposited her book and the cupcakes on the table, then she spotted a woman standing in the far corner of the room, wearing some type of uniform. She shook her head, then sat down at the table. Lana placed a big bowl of what looked and smelled like beef stew and a large piece of crusty bread in front of her. "I'm impressed. Everything looks good and if it tastes as good as it looks, I might have to keep you around."

Lana rolled her eyes and sat down across from her. She pointed to the solider. "Addison is from Dangor, and she will be your personal guard while we are here. Once we reach Dangor, you will be assigned a permanent guard." She held up her hand. "Please, don't argue with me."

Paisley sighed and pushed her spoon around in her bowl. "I don't agree, but I won't argue." She looked at Addison, pushed the chair out beside her, and indicated that Addison should sit down. She hesitated, but after Lana nodded, she sat down and Lana stood up and fixed her a bowl.

Paisley squeezed her palm, then picked up her spoon and took a bite of the stew. The flavors danced on her tongue and she hummed in pleasure. *Wow.* She would have never guessed Lana knew her way around the kitchen. They ate in silence with Lana continually looking between her and Addison. After she swiped the last bit of gravy up with herr bread, she poured a glass of milk and carried it along with the book and the cupcakes into the living room. "You both are welcome to a cupcake. My mom made them for me last night." She plopped down on the couch and lifted her legs to rest her feet on the coffee table. Jynx ran over, jumped onto the couch, and settled down beside her.

Lana sat down at the far end of the couch and eyed her. "Paisley, is everything all right? You're quiet."

She slipped her glasses off and pinched the bridge of her nose before slipping them back on and turning to face her. "I have had a weird-ass couple of days, and the weirdness doesn't seem to be ending anytime soon. It's a lot to take in. You appear, then I find out we're married." She held her wrist up. "Then I find out I come from a long line of witches, and on top of that, I am supposed to go to Dangor with you. Which, by the way, is in another realm. On top off all that..." She picked up the book. "This is my legacy and I am supposed to read it, but I can't read half of what is written."

She sat the book down and picked up a cupcake. "You know. Just any other day. Addison, help yourself to a cupcake. They're good. If you want one, grab it now, before I eat them all." Addison looked to Lana for permission, and only when it was given did she pick one up. Well, that wouldn't do. "If Addison is my guard then she shouldn't have to look to you for permission to do something. I assume you trust her or she wouldn't be here. If I am to continue to accept this—and her—she has to be allowed to make her own choices."

Lana frowned, then picked up a cupcake. "Fine. Addison, if it doesn't interfere with your duties, you may do as Paisley wishes."

"Yes, your Highness."

Paisley finished her cupcake, then groaned. It had completely slipped her mind that Lana was a princess. "Since we're married, does that make me royalty, too?"

"Yes."

She drank the last of her milk, then swung her legs off the coffee table and slipped them underneath her. She turned to Lana. "Tell me about the Brotherhood of the Realm."

"What do you want to know?"

"Everything." She winked at Addison when she picked up another cupcake.

"The Brotherhood of the Realm is a powerful organization that has been around for hundreds, if not thousands, of years. They're not necessarily against the royal family—my family—but they do wish to limit our power and our reach. If they stay in line, my father will leave them be. But, the whole situation involving you has him rethinking their stance in our country. And they don't agree with our union."

"Why? Because were both women?"

"No, because they feel you are the one mentioned in the tale. But the public reason they give is because we can't have a baby together to carry on the royal line. A small group of select members have formed a more radical group and my father has sent out a handful of Elite Guards to keep an eye on them. The fact remains, we cannot identify all members. A lot of them keep their identity secret. There is always that one that gets through."

Wow. If they didn't know who the members were, how would they be able to protect her? She shook her head. It didn't make any sense. She picked up another cupcake, mindlessly peeled back the paper, and took a bite. "What happens now?"

"Well." Lana stood up and moved to sit on the coffee table. "You'll come home with me and we'll try and get into some sort of routine. I know it won't be easy, but I think we can make it work. Of course, we will have to deal with the Brotherhood, but I am confident of my soldiers' abilities to protect you."

Paisley sat up and put her feet on the floor. On impulse, she leaned forward and kissed Lana on the cheek, then pointed to the rest of the cupcakes. "You both are welcome to finish them." She picked up the book, put it under her arm, and scooped Jynx up, hugging her to her chest. "Good night." They didn't protest when she walked out of the living room and into her bedroom. Jynx jumped from her arms and onto the bed, and Paisley figured she had the right idea, so she fell onto the bed beside her and swiped at the tears running down her cheeks. How could two days change her life completely? There was no turning back now. Whatever happened she would be right in the middle of it. Maybe a good night's sleep would put everything into perspective, but she wasn't holding out hope.

❧❧❧❧

After everything that had happened the previous day, Paisley didn't even want to get out of bed. She stilled her movements when she heard an unfamiliar sound in her room. Lana was the last person she wanted to see right now. She wasn't sure what possessed her to kiss her cheek last night. There was no reason to give her false hope. Time to face the music. She flung the covers off, sat up in bed, and cracked one eye open. She was pleasantly surprised to see Addison standing in the corner of the room. "What are you doing in here?"

"Guarding you."

Paisley rolled her eyes and mumbled, "I guess this is what my life has come to."

"Pardon?"

She waved her off. "Never mind. Could you at least step out while I get dressed?" It wasn't until after the door closed behind her that Paisley relaxed. She grabbed a pair of jeans from the closet, along with a *Star Wars* T-shirt. She had a feeling she would need the Force today. After putting her socks and sneakers on, she grabbed the door handle, flung the door open, and walked out into an empty hallway. She half expected to see them both standing there, waiting for her, but her heart lifted with the unexpected reprieve.

As she crept down the hall, she couldn't help but feel like her old self. Maybe, just maybe, this was all a dream, but as soon as she entered the kitchen her dream bubble popped. Addison was standing beside the table, but she didn't see Lana anywhere. "Where's Lana?"

"She had some things she had to take care of."

She tried to hide her relief, but if Addison's smirk was any indication, she wasn't successful. "She's gone?"

"Yes."

She resisted the urge to dance around the kitchen. It felt a bit like Christmas morning. She bit her lip and eyed Addison. She sure didn't say much. "Let's go."

"Wait." She held her hand out to stop her.

"No. No waiting. Let's pick up breakfast and visit K.G. I don't want any arguments. Lana isn't here. Let's go." She didn't wait for an answer and held back a smirk when she heard the door shut behind her. They settled into the car, drove to the café on the corner, and in fewer than thirty minutes they were pulling into K.G.'s driveway. Paisley grabbed the two bags with their food and only gave the car parked on the curb a quick glance. She had known K.G. for twenty years and for two of those they had dated, so she didn't bother knocking and opened the door that led directly into the kitchen.

As soon as she set the bags down on the counter, she heard K.G. scream from somewhere in the house. Without waiting for Addison, she took off running down the hall until she reached K.G.'s bedroom. Skidding to a stop outside the shut door, she debated whether to knock when K.G. screamed again. She pushed the door open with such force that both occupants in the room jerked their heads in her direction. She half stepped, half fell into the room. K.G. was sitting up in the middle of the bed, naked, and a woman she didn't recognize stood in the corner of the room with only a button-up shirt on—unbuttoned—and holding a book in her hand. If it wasn't for the sheer terror on K.G.'s face, she would have thought it was some sort of weird sex game gone wrong. The woman sneered at her, lifted her finger, and wagged it at her.

"Get out," the woman screeched, and started chanting in an unfamiliar language. It was a bit creepy, but not unusual for the last couple of days she'd had.

"I don't think so."

The woman took a step toward her. "You really don't know who you're dealing with. If you leave now, I will let you live."

"Paisley," K.G. squeaked from the bed.

She turned from K.G. and ran past Addison out of the room and down the hall until she reached the spare bedroom. After scanning the room, her eyes landed on her prize, and she picked up the hockey stick and ran back toward K.G.'s bedroom. As soon as she crossed into the room, she raised the hockey stick and swung it toward the woman, knocking the book out of her hand. The woman jerked her head toward Paisley and her steps faltered when her gaze drifted toward Paisley's chest. Clamping her mouth shut, she grabbed her book from the floor and walked out of the room, keeping her distance from Paisley.

"Addison, make sure she leaves." Paisley looked down and noticed her necklace had slipped from the confines of her shirt. Did the woman seeing her necklace make her run for it? She turned back to K.G., who was still seated in the middle of the bed. When she opened her mouth to talk, Paisley held up her hand. "Get dressed. I brought breakfast. Meet us in the kitchen. It looks like we both have a lot to talk about." She left before K.G. could say anything, headed to the kitchen, and started to unpack their food.

Addison helped her arrange the food on the table. "She got in the car by the curb and drove off."

"Good." She glanced up when K.G. walked into the kitchen dressed in a pair of plaid shorts and a black T-shirt. Her short blond hair needed to be cut by the way it hung on her forehead. Paisley reached up and pushed it out of her eyes. "Let's eat first, then we'll talk." K.G. frowned and walked to the window. "Yes, she's gone, and that's Addison." When K.G. didn't attempt to flirt with Addison, Paisley knew she was still freaked out. Over breakfast K.G. started to loosen up, and by the time they threw their trash away she seemed back to her old self, although Paisley could still see a bit of fear beneath her tough exterior.

"So," K.G. said and took a sip of her coffee. "Who wants to go first?" She looked between Paisley and Addison.

Paisley laughed and adjusted her glasses. "I

think, in this instance, your story will probably be a lot shorter than mine and make more sense."

She cocked her head and grinned. "I met her at a bar last night. We came back here. Everything was fine until this morning when she started to act weird. I didn't think anything about it." She shrugged. "I mean, I've been with some weird women, but this was different. I started to get suspicious when she slipped her shirt on and started pacing around the room. I tried to talk to her to no avail. Then she picked up her book and started chanting. A lot."

"Why were you screaming?"

She looked embarrassed for a moment, then sobered. "She was standing in the corner of the room, but I could have sworn someone was touching my shoulder. It freaked me out. I am so glad you decided to come over today. Right before you made your grand entrance, she said something about a blood sacrifice and that I was worthy. Creepy, right? I mean who does that shit? Then she mumbled something about being a witch."

Paisley clamped her mouth shut and averted her gaze. If that was true, then who was she and did she really want a sacrifice? Any other time she would have thought K.G. was crazy, up until her own ordeal started. Now, she knew anything was possible. "That's an interesting story."

"You don't believe me? Paisley, look, I swear, it's the truth."

She grabbed K.G.'s hand across the table and ran her thumb over her knuckles. "I do believe you. It's just after the last two days I've had, I am not sure if you're going to believe my story."

"Does it have something to do with her?" She

jerked her head in Addison's direction.

"Yes." She nodded.

K.G. grinned. "I can't wait to hear this." Paisley started from the beginning and told her everything, from Lana's first appearance until that morning. K.G. didn't try to interrupt her speech, but she didn't look skeptical either. When she was finished, K.G. ran her hands through her hair. "Well, fuck me. Seriously?" She stood up and topped off her coffee cup. "And here I thought I had a whacked-out morning."

Paisley stood up. "You believe me?"

"Sure." She shrugged. "Why not?"

Paisley flung her hands in the air. "Witches, other realms, kings, queens, powers…"

"Paisley, I've known you a long time, and in all that time I have never known you to lie to me. I love you and I would never discredit you or make fun of you just because your story sounds like a book I read last week. Just because we can't see something or experience it doesn't mean it isn't real."

"Why did we break up again?"

"I was a lousy girlfriend, but an exceptional best friend. I will always love you, you know that." She winked at her.

Paisley plucked the cup from her hand and sat it on the kitchen counter before wrapping her arms around K.G. and sinking into the hug. She leaned up and kissed her on the cheek. "I love you, too." She pulled away from her and wiped at her eyes before sitting back down.

K.G. pointed to Addison. "You have your own bodyguard. That is so cool. I could have used one of those this morning. So, Addison, amaze us with your battle stories." Addison regaled them with a few interesting tales, and before they knew it, it was lunchtime and they ordered pizza.

It felt good to be relaxed for once. Paisley wasn't sure how long she would get to feel that way. The encounter with the woman that morning felt off somehow. She shook her head and decided not to worry about it, instead throwing herself into their conversation. It was late afternoon and they were getting ready to leave when K.G. asked them to stay for dinner. Paisley readily agreed because it had been far too long since they had spent an entire day together.

She kissed her good night after an enjoyable meal of grilled chicken and vegetables. Paisley and Addison were laughing when they walked through the back door of her house only to come to a complete stop when Lana glared at them.

"Where have you been? It's eleven o'clock. You have no business running around town." She planted her hands on her hips and glared at them. "And you." She pointed at Addison, who stiffened beside her. She was about to walk around Paisley when Paisley put her arm out to stop her.

"You need to watch your tone with me." Paisley huffed. "I am a grown woman and I will do what I want, when I want, and with whomever I want. You may think you have a place in my life, but you are wrong. I don't even know you, so watch the attitude. And as for Addison, she was doing what she was supposed to do. I never thought for a second that she wouldn't be able to protect me if something were to happen. Don't you dare question her or reprimand her. She is my guard, not yours. Do I make myself clear?"

Lana bit her lip, and after a few tense moments, nodded and sighed. "I was just worried."

"I was perfectly safe. Isn't it a bit early in our relationship for you to be worried about me?"

"You're my wife. I am going to worry about your safety."

It was Paisley's turn to nod. "Still, I am not going to be locked up in my own home just because you feel it's where I should be." She patted Addison on the arm. "Let's go to bed." She ignored Lana as they walked past her and down the hallway. The last thing she wanted was Lana telling her what to do, and she would be damned if she treated her like she was a possession. She didn't belong to anyone, and that was the way she intended for it to stay.

⁂

Paisley accepted the cookie that Helen, her boss, handed her and wished her a good day before walking out the front door of The RiversEdge. Work had been pleasant and time flew by. That morning she had managed to leave the house without running into Lana. Thank goodness for small miracles. Addison had mentioned that she left before the alarm went off. At this point, she couldn't see their relationship working out. Just because she had on a bonding bracelet didn't mean she would give in to anything Lana wanted. Granted, she was a looker, but looks had never swayed her in the past, and they wouldn't start now. When Addison squirmed beside her, she figured they should get going.

"Are we going back to your house?"

Once they were on the street, she answered her. "No. I promised my mom I would stop by and talk to my dad. I don't know what the hell I am in for with his speech."

"Does it change the way you see him, knowing now where he was born?"

Paisley shook her head. "Of course not. I love my dad and would do absolutely anything for him. Even though he and my uncle Cliff take a fishing trip every year, me and my dad, we fish a couple of times a month, even in winter. I love my mom, but me and my dad have so much more in common. I know that sounds weird now, knowing that I am a witch that takes after my mom's side of the family."

"If I were you, I would be more freaked out."

"Speaking of that, don't you find this world strange compared to yours? I mean, I don't know what your world is like, but considering the clothes you and Lana wear, I could only guess that it's not as modern as the world we're in now."

"It's not, but I love it. We don't have cars or any modern luxuries. No electricity, but most houses do have a water and sewage system. And to answer your other question, I have been coming to this world for years, along with Lana and a few of the other female guards. They wanted us to become acclimated to it, if the need ever arose that we would be needed to fulfill our duties here."

"That makes sense." She eased to a stop, then turned into her parents' driveway. She took a deep breath and ran her hands along her pants. After a few minutes, Addison touched her arm and they got out of the car. Once inside, she introduced Addison to her mom and grandma, who readily accepted her, then they directed her to the basement where her dad was waiting to talk to her. Paisley rocked back on her heels and fiddled with her glasses.

"Paisley," Grams said. "Why are you so nervous?"

She shook out her hands. "I don't know."

Her mom patted her shoulder, gave her a tray of cookies, then steered her in the direction of the basement door.

Even though she had just finished eating a cookie in the car, she somehow managed to eat another three by the time she made it down the stairs. Her dad was sitting in the middle of the couch, with his back to her and his arms spread out on the back of it, looking up at the T.V. that hung above the fireplace. On unsteady feet, she walked toward him, set the tray on the coffee table, then plopped down beside him. As soon as he pulled her against his side she started crying. Everything that she had allowed to build up over the last few days came crashing down around her. She snuggled into his side, inhaling his aftershave, and allowed him to comfort her like he did when she was younger. After her tears dried up he handed her a box of tissues and they both were content to let the drama play out on the cooking show. "What are they doing?" She sniffed. "For them to be professionals they put way too many red pepper flakes on that salad."

He nodded and squeezed her shoulder. "I know. Idiots. The first thing the judges are going to say is it was too hot." Her father had always been her hero and always larger than life to her. As she grew older, her hero worship turned into a friendship that she wouldn't trade for anything. Although she and her mother got along, she was always a daddy's girl and always would be.

They shared a bond that her mother was often jealous of, and now Paisley had a good idea why. She supposed that because her mother passed on the gifts of her family line, she should have been closer to her, but that wasn't the case. Growing up, her father often indulged in her hobbies, always encouraging her and taking part whenever possible. In the last few years, they had gotten into a routine of fishing a couple of times a month, binge watching cooking shows, and scouring the flea markets looking for their next treasure. He was her rock, and she hoped that after their talk nothing would change.

After the credits had rolled, he picked up the remote and turned the T.V. off, but he didn't make a move to get up and neither did she. After a few moments of silence, he spoke. "I grew up on a small farm that was situated outside of the city limits. My dad's family had always been farmers and my mother's had always been into trade of some sort. Furs, canned goods, you name it, they would make it or find a way to get it. When I took an interest in the Elite Guards, my family was surprised but supported me a hundred percent. I was just as shocked as anybody when I was chosen for marriage with someone I had never met." He squeezed her shoulder. "I won't get into that process just yet, so let's put that question on the back burner. My mother's name is Lucinda, and my father's is Richard. When I left, I had two brothers and three sisters: Malcom, Richard Jr., Olivia, Becky, and Abigail. My maternal grandmother's name was Paisley. She was an amazing woman, and someone I looked up to my whole life. I knew when I held you, you would be just as extraordinary as she was."

"I don't know. This is all so overwhelming."

"You'll get the hang of it."

"I'm not sure I want to stay married to Lana," she blurted out.

He was quiet for so long she thought she had said something wrong. She was leaning forward to stand up when he pulled her back down to his side. "Because of the rules and laws of Dangor, where I came from, I should tell you that you shouldn't let doubt creep into what fate has deemed an acceptable pairing. But I am your dad and all I want is for you to be happy." He raised up and tapped Paisley's chin. "I love you and the last thing I want is for you to be unhappy. Don't repeat what I am about to tell you to anyone. I mean anyone, Paisley."

"Okay."

"You only get one life and I would never want you to stay with someone you didn't love just for the greater good. You're my greater good. So, no matter what happens, or what people tell you, stay true to who you are. Don't stay with her because it's something that you think you should do. If you grow to love her that's wonderful, but if not, find someone who does make you happy. I am not saying it will be easy, because it won't. It will be an uphill battle, but you do have something going for you: you are your mother's daughter, as well as mine. You are no ordinary woman, and the sooner you realize that and accept it, the sooner you can accept who you were always meant to be." He pulled her to him and she cuddled into his side.

A weight was lifted off her shoulders from his words. She knew her mother would never tell her that. She was a stickler for the rules. "I love you, and I will try not to disappoint you."

"You'll never disappoint me and I will love you until the day I die. Even beyond that." He took a sip of his water, then handed her a piece of paper. It had names and different addresses on it. "This is a list of all my family members and where they lived the last time I was in Dangor. I know it was a long time ago, but I am sure if you ask around someone will be able to point you in the right direction."

"Okay." She didn't have to ask him if he missed it; it was written all over his face.

"I know what you're thinking, and no, I don't regret my decision to come here. At the time, I was convinced I was doing a duty for my kingdom, but once here, I quickly fell in love with your mother and not long after that you came into our lives. I have lived an amazing life and wouldn't trade it for anything."

"What's Dangor like? Mom and Grams said I should go back with Lana."

He sighed. "Before we get into that there is something I need to tell you. Uncle Cliff isn't actually your uncle."

She pulled away from him and sat up straighter. "What?" She should have known that from the list of names he gave her, but her mind wasn't working on all cylinders at the moment.

"He's not really my brother. He was a fellow solider with me and I saved his life in battle once. He pledged to always stay by my side and protect me. When I was chosen, he threw a fit until he was allowed to come thorough the portal with me."

That wasn't something she expected to hear. She adjusted her glasses. "One revelation after another. It doesn't make any difference to me. I love him as much as I love you. Nothing will change that."

"Good, because he loves you like you were his own, and I know he would feel lost if you saw him differently."

"Not going to happen."

He leaned forward and rested his elbows on his legs. "Your mother and grandmother will have a lot to tell you, on top of what they have already said. I know your heritage and who you are to them, but my blood also runs through your veins and I have just as much to teach you as they do. We still don't know what kind of powers you have or how powerful they are, but what I can teach you now is practical and could save your life. You can't always rely on your powers because they may not always be able to save your life. We should have started years ago, but we really didn't think you had any powers and with you being gay we weren't sure anyone would come for you." He raised up and leaned back into the couch.

"So, what do you have to teach me?" To her knowledge, he had been a landscaper his entire life, so she couldn't wait to hear what he had to say. She frowned when it finally dawned on her what he had said earlier. "You were a solider with the Elite Guards?"

A faraway look crossed his features. "I was a damn fine one. It was only my second year in when I was chosen to come here." He patted my arm. "I am going to teach you to fight. We'll start with hand-to-hand combat then move on from there. I am not sure when you will have to go to Dangor, but we will get in as much training as possible. It could save your life one day." He tapped her nose.

"Okay." If it wasn't one thing it was another. Not only was she a witch, but now he wanted her to learn to fight.

He laughed and stood up. "Honey, don't act so enthused." She jumped up and wrapped her arms around him. He gave her a gentle squeeze then pushed her to arm's length. "Always stay true to who you are.

Don't let other people define you. What one person wants for you may not be in your best interests. All I care about is your best interests. I don't know what awaits you in Dangor, but I know there will always be allies for you there. You may not be able to trust them a hundred percent but they'll be loyal to you. I don't care who they are, but if you find yourself drawn to someone, don't fight it. Other people's opinions are just that—their opinions. Listen to me. I cannot stress this enough. Always, always, trust your gut instinct. I love you and I don't want anything to happen to you. Even if everyone is fighting against you, all you need is that one person who will stand with you. At this point, I don't know if that person is Lana."

He was freaking her out with his pep talk, but if allowing him to teach her to fight eased his mind, she would do it. She kissed him on the cheek. "I will be back tomorrow and we can start on my training. I don't have any other plans."

He nodded and placed a kiss on the top of her head. "Tomorrow for your training, but there's something I need to show you now."

※ ※ ※ ※

Paisley tried not to let her surprise show when he turned and walked to the corner of the basement, beckoning her to follow him. They stopped in front of a locked door, and he pulled a key out of his pants pocket that was attached to a piece of twine. The room had always been locked, and neither she nor her mom had ever been allowed inside it. That he was allowing her now didn't bode well. "Wait, Dad." She stopped him with his hand on the knob. "Are you sure?"

"Yes, but you must never speak about what's inside this room. Not even to your mother or Lana or Addison. This will be between me, you, and your uncle Cliff." Without waiting for her response, he turned the handle and stepped into the room.

Paisley took a deep breath and stepped inside. When the door shut behind her, Paisley jumped as the lock clicked into place. After her initial apprehension faded, she looked around the room. It was a lot bigger than she would have first thought. A large couch and recliner were positioned against one wall, and the other wall had floor to ceiling built-in bookcases filled with hundreds of books. A table sat in the middle of the room with a place for a six-chair setting, although there were only two chairs present. At the wall opposite the door sat a large desk with several papers scattered on top of it. Even without a window, the room was well lit.

Her gaze flittered to the wall above the desk where several maps were tacked onto a corkboard. Her dad didn't stop her, instead encouraging her to look at them. One word, in the corner of every map stood out amongst the rest: Dangor. As realization dawned at what she was looking at, her pulse quickened, but a reassuring hand on her shoulder instantly calmed her. Several maps were starting to show signs of their age, but a couple of them looked new. This room was her dad's connection to his past. "Wow."

"Let's sit. There is a lot we need to go over." They each took one end of the couch, and Paisley drew one leg underneath her and waited for him to start. "Thirty years ago, your uncle Cliff and I were fishing when we received an unexpected visitor from Dangor. All three of us went to school together." He ran his fingers through his hair. "We were friends and it was surreal when she came to us. You must understand, we had been without information for three years. We talked for hours, catching up. She was always close with my family and she filled me in on what was going on in their lives."

"That's amazing."

He nodded. "Over the years, she not only brought information about my family, but also about the state of the country itself. She kept us in the loop, and it was nice to have a connection to my past, besides Cliff, if only once a year."

"Wait." Paisley fiddled with her glasses. "Your annual fishing trip really isn't a fishing trip after all?"

"No, it is. We fish, but she also shares information with us, and occasionally, she brings other things." He pointed to the bookshelf and the maps. "Her information has been invaluable to us. Just getting a glimpse into my family has kept me sane."

It was apparent to her, from the look on her dad's face, that the woman meant a great deal to him. "You love her?"

"Yes, but not in the way you're thinking. She's like a sister to me. We do share a bond and it would bother me if it was ever broken or I never saw her again." He shrugged. "But, I think that time is coming, sooner rather than later, when she won't show back up. There is unrest in Dangor. The exchange of power has switched hands so many times over the years, it's hard to tell who holds it now. Others will tell you different, but I don't believe you have anything to worry about with the Brotherhood. They're all talk, and she also thinks so."

"She's knows about my situation? How could

she? I just found out."

"She doesn't even know you exist. She has other business here besides me, but I have never told her of your existence and I don't believe she knows, but I wouldn't put it past her. I only have ever wanted to protect you, but I see now I should have trusted you more. For that, I am sorry."

"It's okay." This was a lot to take in. "I take it Mom doesn't know about her?"

"I've never told her and she has never asked. I love your mother, Paisley, and would never be unfaithful to her."

"I believe you."

He handed her a key and she took it. "Feel free to come in here and look around. It wouldn't hurt for you to study the maps. Get a feel for the country."

She tightened her fist around the key. "I'll do that."

"Now you need to get home. Get some rest." He pulled her off the couch and pecked her on the top of her head. "I love you. Go." He pointed to the door.

"I love you, too." After everything that had happened, she couldn't help but feel that there was much more her family was keeping from her. It was not a comforting feeling. As she passed by the coffee table, she grabbed a handful of cookies for her and Addison on the ride home.

⚜ ⚜ ⚜ ⚜

As she turned the car onto her street, her heart sped up and her stomach dropped when she spied K.G.'s car parked at the curb. After parking, she tapped her fingers on the steering wheel, unsure if she wanted to go in her house. She knew K.G. could hold her own, but Lana did have the ability to perform magic. She bit her lip, took the key out of the ignition, and turned to Addison. "Ready?"

She looked uncertain. "I guess."

"Let's do this." With more courage than she felt, she opened the back door and entered the kitchen. She paused by the doorway leading into the living room, but didn't hear any fighting or shouting. In fact, she didn't hear anything at all. The house was too quiet.

She motioned for Addison to go ahead of her. As she crept around the corner, K.G.'s body came into view, then Lana's. Lana stood on one side of the coffee table and K.G. on the other. Paisley couldn't read the look on Lana's face, but as she moved along the wall she saw the look on K.G.'s. She knew that look all too well. She was pissed and held a snoring Jynx in her arms. "Isn't this nice." When she didn't receive an answer, she walked closer to K.G.

She slipped her hand under the back of K.G.'s white shirt and started rubbing her hand along the small of her back. Lana tensed and frowned when she noticed where Paisley's hand had disappeared to. Paisley leaned up and whispered in K.G.'s ear. "Please calm down. Please." She continued to rub her back, and after a few minutes she felt her start to relax into her touch. Paisley smiled and kissed her cheek, then turned to Lana who snarled at them. *Good grief.* She and Lana hadn't known each other long enough for her to be jealous. "Have you two been properly introduced yet?"

Lana waved her hand in the air. "I don't care who she is, but she needs to leave."

"Listen, bitch," K.G. said. "I have more of a right

to be here than you."

"Wait. Wait." Paisley held her hands up. "Please don't fight. Lana, don't make me choose, because you won't like the outcome." She smacked K.G. on the arm when she smirked.

"Quit touching her. You're married, Paisley, and even though you may be friends, that doesn't change the fact that you are my wife."

Paisley groaned, then stepped away from K.G and ran her hands through her hair. Why did things have to be so complicated? All she wanted was five minutes of peace in her own home. Just five. "All right. Yes, according to you, I am your wife, but this is my life and I am sorry if this hurts, but K.G. has a part of my heart and she always will. I love her and I don't even know you. Lana, you have to see how crazy this whole thing is." She waved her arms in the air. "You have to."

Lana grunted. "I do, Paisley. I really do, but what do you want me to do when you have your hands all over her?" She glared and pointed at K.G. "If the woman you were married to suddenly started grabbing and kissing her ex, would that make you upset?"

K.G. shook her head. "Yes, it would, but I don't know you. You just appeared. How do I know you can be trustworthy? We don't know anything about you."

"I am a princess and her wife. That's all you need to know."

"Look, we are not getting anywhere. K.G., love, did you come by for anything particular?"

She cuddled Jynx to her chest and smiled at Paisley. "I just wanted to check on you."

Paisley's heart melted at the two of them. It would have been so much easier if they had made it as a couple. "Have you been here long?"

K.G. eyed the clock above the T.V. "Maybe an hour."

"I was at my parents'. I talked to my dad."

"How'd it go?"

"Lana, could you give us a few minutes alone?" She looked ready to protest, but at the last second seemed to think better of it and walked out of the room. K.G. sat Jynx on the floor, then flopped onto the couch and pulled Paisley onto her lap. She could understand Lana's point, but K.G. was her soft place to land and she would be damned if she was made to feel uncomfortable in her own home. Paisley leaned into her and sighed. "It went all right. He told me that I should follow my heart and if that didn't lead me to Lana, then I should find someone who did capture it." She played with K.G.'s hand that rested on her knee.

"I agree. Your dad is a wise man."

"Please don't tell anybody I just told you that. I don't know. It's a mess. They want me to go home with her. To her country. In another realm. How crazy is that?" K.G. hugged her tighter.

"It is crazy, but I think you should at least give it a chance. She seems capable of keeping you safe, and from what you told me yesterday, you need to be protected. I don't want anything to happen to you and if that means going to Dangor..." she hesitated, "then you should go."

Paisley sniffled. "I am going to miss you and everyone. This is my home."

"I know. I am going to miss you, too." She grew quiet. "You'll be back. Won't you?"

Paisley raised up and sucked in a breath when she saw K.G. fighting back tears. She leaned forward and kissed her on the lips before pulling away and resting her forehead against K.G.'s. "Yes, I will be back. I have to figure out what my power is and then I will be back. Nothing and no one is going to keep me from coming home. I promise you that." She ran her fingers down K.G.'s cheek, then kissed the tip of her nose.

K.G. pulled her tighter and rested her head in the crook of Paisley's neck. "This feels like good-bye."

"No. Never. Me and you against the world. We have too much shit we still haven't gotten into yet."

She laughed and kissed Paisley's neck. "You got that right."

She pulled away and reached for the tissue, and handed K.G. some. At this rate, she should buy stock in them. "Look at us. We're falling apart." She laughed, then blew her nose.

K.G. closed her eyes, then sucked in a breath before opening them again. "I should go."

"Okay, but you are always welcome here."

"I know." She stood up and patted Jynx on the head before they both walked to the front door and stepped out onto the porch. She took hold of Paisley's hands and cradled them between hers. "If you need anything, anything at all, all you have to do is ask. I don't care what it is, what time it is. I don't care. We will find a way to take care of it. Together."

Paisley slipped her arms around her neck and sighed. She couldn't shake the feeling that something was wrong. She felt it deep in her gut, but couldn't pinpoint what exactly it was. "I love you."

"I love you, too." She kissed her on the cheek, winked at her, then headed down the steps to her car. Paisley heard the door open behind her but ignored it and watched K.G. wave at her then settle into the driver's seat. When she started the car and pulled into the street, Paisley turned back toward the front door, only to whirl around a second later when something compelled her to do so.

Without thinking, she ran off the porch toward K.G.'s car that was getting ready to turn left, when suddenly Lana grabbed her from behind and Addison ran into the road. Time stood still as a scream ripped from Paisley's throat and they watched in disbelief as K.G.'s car exploded by the stop sign. Lana flung them both to the ground and covered Paisley's body with her own as parts of the car flew in all directions.

Paisley elbowed her in the stomach, scrambled up, and raced toward the burning car. Her chest heaved as the flames grew higher and hotter. She skidded to a stop and fell to the ground, scraping her knees. The flames raced toward the sky, and then everything, including what was left of the car, disappeared. She turned her head in circles, but there wasn't a trace of anything left. She gulped in deep breaths, digging her hands into the few ashes that were left on the ground, and sobbed. She fell forward, her hands smacking the road to keep her head from hitting the pavement, then grabbed her chest when a sharp pain raced from her head to her feet. She didn't have the strength to fight when someone picked her up and carried her into the house.

"Paisley. Paisley." Paisley couldn't stop the tears, and she buried her head in Lana's chest. Lana pulled her tighter drand rested her chin on the top of Paisley's head. "Addison," Lana said. "Did you get a sample of the ashes?"

"Yes."

"Paisley." Lana wiped the tears running down her cheeks. "We have to get you out of here. Okay?"

Paisley nodded, not exactly sure what she was agreeing to, but accepted Jynx when someone placed her in her arms. "Addison, are you ready?" Lana knelt and took Paisley's hand. One minute they were in her own living room, and the next they were in her parents'.

"Kate!" Her dad screamed for her mom, who came running into the living room, followed closely by Grams. He knelt next to Paisley and she fell into him and cried on his shoulder. "What the hell happened?" He glared at Lana as he pulled Paisley into his arms.

"Lana," Kate said. "What happened? Answer me now."

"K.G. came to see her and when she left her car exploded, then disappeared. Everything disappeared."

"What? K.G. is dead?"

"Yes."

When her words registered, Paisley pushed her dad away, stood up, and started pacing. "No." She ran her hands through her hair and shook her head. "No. She cannot be dead. I was just talking to her!" She grabbed handfuls of Lana's shirt, then pushed her away. She stumbled over the coffee table but was able to right herself.

Lana held her hands up. "Paisley, I am sorry."

Paisley screamed. "No, you're not. You didn't even like her. Did you do this? Did you do this?"

"I didn't do this. I may not have liked her, but I never would have killed her, and to be honest I don't believe the Brotherhood would either." She held a small cup out to Kate. "These are some of the ashes that were left from the car when it blew up. It's all that was left. After it exploded, it disappeared." She shook her head. "I've never seen anything like it. Everything disappeared."

Grams took the cup from Kate and peered at its contents. Paisley bit back a sob when she shook her head and looked at Paisley. "No, Grams. Please tell me this isn't happening."

"P.J., I can't do that." She gave the cup back to Kate, left the room, only to come back a short time later carrying a small black box. She handed Paisley and Addison each a necklace with a small clear stone hanging from it. Paisley didn't ask her what it was for, but she did allow Lana to clasp it around her neck.

"Did the Witches of the Fellowship do this?" Lana asked.

"Who the hell are they?" Paisley fingered the necklace, then fell back onto the couch beside her dad.

"They are a group of thousands of witches that have banded together and formed an alliance of sorts. Each fellowship appoints leaders and they answer to the governing body of the main Fellowship." Kate shook her head. "I don't believe they would have done this. They wouldn't have a reason to. It doesn't make sense, but if it wasn't the Brotherhood... I don't know." She dumped the ashes on the coffee table, then sucked in a breath.

Paisley jumped up from the couch. "What?"

"I don't know how, but there is a lot of magic in these ashes. I don't understand why a witch would want to take K.G. out of the picture."

Paisley turned away from them and caught Addison's eye. She blinked at her then looked away. "Yesterday," she said in disbelief.

"Sweetheart," her mom said. "You have to speak up."

She blew out a breath. "Yesterday when Addison and I went to K.G.'s house there was a woman there.

She was chanting and holding a book. I knocked the book out of her hand, and when she saw my necklace she picked the book up and left. When we sat down for breakfast, K.G. told us that before we walked in the woman told her she was a witch." She rounded her shoulders and gasped in a breath when the ruby around her neck felt like it was vibrating. "I never thought she was a real witch." She glared at her mom. "You didn't tell me there were other witches out there besides us."

"Paisley, this isn't our fault and it isn't yours."

"Whatever." She flicked her fingers. "If it's the last thing I do, I will make whoever did this pay."

"Paisley, no," Grams said. "No. Revenge isn't the option."

She turned and looked out the window. That might be their choice, but it wasn't hers. There was no way she could live with herself if she didn't avenge K.G.'s death. She took off her glasses and sobbed into her hands, ignoring the voices around her. All she could see was K.G. winking at her, then the flames. She shook her head when her eyes started to blur. How could this have happened? She didn't fight it when arms wrapped around her waist. "Is she really dead?" she choked out.

"Yes," Lana whispered in her ear.

"I want to go to bed." She allowed Lana to take her hand and lead her down the hallway to her childhood bedroom. She fell onto the bed, and Lana slipped her shoes off before climbing up beside her and wrapping her in her arms. Paisley settled down and laid her head on Lana's chest. The steady rhythm of her heartbeat calmed her instantly and she closed her eyes.

❦ ❦ ❦ ❦

Paisley groaned and kept her eyes shut as the sun filtered through the window. Whoever had opened the curtains would pay. She stretched under the covers, then stilled when the memories from yesterday slammed into the forefront of her mind. She fought back the tears and slowly opened her eyes until they become accustomed to the light.

The spot next to her was empty and cold. So much for Lana staying and comforting her. When her eyes adjusted, she threw the covers off and sat up in bed. *Fuck.* Lana had undressed her again last night. They would have to have a talk about personal space. She crawled out of bed and grabbed the jeans and shirt that were laid out at the foot of the bed and put them on. The familiar feel of her dad's twenty-year-old cotton T-shirt comforted her more than she would ever admit.

She paused at the door when voices drifted her way. A lot of voices. When she rounded the corner into the living room, she stopped. Standing in the middle of the room were her parents, along with her grandma, Lana, Addison, and two strangers. The older woman she didn't recognize, but when the other woman turned around, her stomach dropped and her heart started pounding in her chest. An anger like she had never known before consumed her. It was the same woman that had been in K.G.'s bedroom two days before.

Without realizing what she was doing and not fighting the urge, she ran to the couch, grabbed the back of it, and catapulted herself over, landing in a crouch in front of the coffee table and directly in front of the woman. Her dad grabbed her arm as soon as she stood up.

"What do you think you're doing?" Paisley threw his hand off and, out of the corner of her eye, saw Addison come up beside her. Her dad touched her arm. "Answer my question!"

"Paisley," Grams said. "This is Gloria and her mother Catherine. They are from the Myers Fellowship."

Gloria laughed. "If I had known at the time what a novice you were, I would never have run that day. Pathetic." She shook her hands out. "You're a joke."

"Gloria," Catherine said. "That's enough. Keep your mouth shut."

Paisley didn't even try too tame the anger that manifested within her. She bit her lip and considered her words. She weighed the odds of killing her outright, but needed answers. "Why did you do it? Why did you kill K.G., and what are you doing here?"

Catherine looked between them. "It was an unfortunate accident. She was only trying to scare her, but the magic developed a life of its own. It was too much for her to handle."

Paisley snapped her eyes to her. An ache started in her chest and moved outward toward her fingers. She bit her lip and rounded her shoulders to try to dampen the energy that was buzzing inside her head and shooting up her arms. If this is what her power felt like, it didn't scare her as much as she thought it would. K.G. was an accident. An unfortunate accident. "If she didn't know how to control the magic," she bit out carefully, "then why was she using it to begin with?"

"Paisley," her mom said. "Please. It was an accident." But even as she heard the words, Paisley saw the look in Gloria's eyes. Cold indifference. Accident or not, she wasn't sorry K.G. was dead. But she would be. The ruby pendant around her neck vibrated and started to heat her skin where it lay nestled against her chest. Tingles started in the tips of her fingertips and she shook her hands out to try and stem the power coursing through her veins. She knew she should probably fight it, but she didn't want to. "Paisley," her mom said. "Please wait in the kitchen. There is a lot at stake here."

How could her mom be so calm? Paisley slowly turned from Gloria to her mom, her movements more robotic than fluid. Was she really taking their side over K.G.'s? Over hers? Her mom's words bounced around in her head and she tried to hold her temper back, but it was taking every ounce of self-control she had to stay calm. She glared at Gloria, pushed past her, and walked around the coffee table toward the kitchen. As she stepped past her mother, she stopped cold when Gloria's words reached her ears.

"I don't know what the big deal is. She's just another dead dyke."

Paisley bit her lip and counted to ten under her breath before slowly turning around and facing Gloria.

"Paisley, get in the kitchen," her dad said, but she ignored his words and kept her eyes trained on Gloria, who was still smirking at her. The blood pounded in her ears and instead of trying to rein in the fire racing through her veins, she let it loose. She blinked to clear the fuzziness that suddenly overtook her, closed her eyes, then snapped them open when the air around her changed. She was standing directly behind Gloria.

"Boo," she whispered in Gloria's ear, and snickered when Gloria jumped and took a step away from her, then turned and faced her. "How about another dead witch." She sneered. "Would that be a big deal?" She didn't stop and question her actions when she grabbed the front of Gloria's shirt, twisted her fingers in the fabric, and lifted her body of the floor before throwing it toward the plate glass window that made up half the wall of the living room. The glass shattered and Paisley jumped through the window, paying no attention as the glass ripped into her palms. She landed with a thud on the ground beside Gloria's body. Gloria narrowed her eyes and attempted to stand but fell back to the ground, grimacing in pain.

"Paisley, stop!"

"Paisley, no!"

"Someone stop her."

Paisley drowned out their words and was standing when Gloria winked at her and spoke so low only Paisley would be able to hear her. "It wasn't an accident. I killed her on purpose."

Paisley growled from deep within her, positioned her hands by Gloria's head, then twisted them in the air without touching her. She felt a deep satisfaction when Gloria's neck snapped and her head fell back to the ground. "That wasn't an accident either." She spit on her body.

Catherine screamed and fell to the ground beside her daughter, and all Paisley could focus on was the surprised look etched onto Gloria's face. Catherine sobbed and cradled Gloria's body against her chest. "What have you done?"

Paisley rounded her neck and blue flames licked at the tips of her fingers. She squeezed her eyes shut, stood up, then took a step back from them. She squinted over Catherine's head when a man and woman suddenly appeared out of thin air. Her eyes were trained on the man's brown loafers as they came closer and closer to where she stood. He clicked his tongue and reached out to raise her chin. His eyes locked with hers, and he leaned forward and blew in her face.

Paisley coughed, lost her balance, and fell backward. The blood rushed to her head and pounded in her ears, and Gloria's lifeless eyes bore into hers. She clawed at the ground and grabbed fistfuls of grass to try to calm her racing heart and the piercing noise that echoed inside her head. She closed her eyes and focused on the sound of her beating heart until it slowed to a steady pace. When she opened her eyes, everyone was looking at her. How did she get outside? "What happened?" Her gaze landed on the dead body on the ground.

"Sweetheart, what's the last thing you remember?"

Paisley gulped. "I remember walking into the living room and everyone was talking." She wasn't sure what to think when everyone around her grew quiet. What the hell had happened between then and now? Surely she didn't kill her? Could she be capable of that? She lifted her hands and noticed for the first time the cuts and the blood and grass covering them. She sucked in a breath when the pain shot from her hands up her arms.

She allowed Lana to pull her up, then looked from the broken window, to her hands, then to Gloria. Suddenly everything that happened flooded her mind, and when she started to sway, Lana steadied her. "No. I wanted her dead, for what she did to K.G., but I would never have killed her. I'm not capable of that. Am I?" She sought out her mother's eyes and for once everything her mother was thinking was written on her face. Paisley didn't fight when Lana pulled her back into her arms and wrapped her arms around her waist.

"What is going to happen to her?" Catherine pointed at Paisley, but she was speaking to the two strangers. "She deserves a just fate." The man waved his hand, and Catherine and Gloria's body disappeared.

Paisley bent forward, rested her elbows on her knees, and promptly emptied her stomach. She gagged and accepted the bottle of water someone handed her. After rinsing out her mouth, she stood up and eyed the people gathered around. Who were the strangers and what would they do to her?

Her mind kept replaying what had happened since she entered the living room, and she quickly came to the realization that she didn't regret doing it, but by the looks of everyone's faces around her, maybe she should have. She wasn't scared or disgusted by her actions, at least not as much as she had expected to be. For the time being, she would keep that tidbit of information to herself. But what did that make her? A killer. She frowned. That didn't feel right. Gloria deserved what happened to her, and if it hadn't been by her hand it would have been by somebody else's, eventually. She held her hands up and watched the blood drip from the cuts onto the grass at her feet.

The man reached for her hands and waved his own over them. It felt surreal to watch the bits of glass fly out of her palms and for the wounds to heal themselves. "My name is Jeffrey and I am a member of the Governing Fellowship. This is Anita." He pointed at the woman who had accompanied him. "Paisley, I completely understand what happened here. You just came into your powers and after what happened yesterday, I can't fault you for them overpowering you. You have never been taught to use them. I can guarantee that you won't have any problems with the Governing

Fellowship because of your actions today, but whether you meant to or not, you have started something this morning. As much power as the Fellowship has, I fear there will be repercussions from other alliances within the Fellowship. Do you understand?"

"I am not a child, don't treat me like one." She was ready for this to be over.

He nodded, snapped his fingers, and he and Anita disappeared as quickly as they had appeared. Paisley ran her hands through her hair, bit her lip, looked at her hands, then the living room window. She waved her hand in the air and all the pieces of broken glass rose from the ground and flew back to the window, repairing it, good as new. She ignored everyone as she walked past them, entered the house, and settled down on the couch. Clutching a pillow to her chest, she waited for the lecture she was sure she was about to get. She didn't react when her dad started rubbing her back. "How after all these years could my powers just manifest themselves and be so strong?"

"Well," Grams said. "It's a combination of things. You've had a lot to deal with in the last few days. We shouldn't have thrown everything at you at once. It all escalated with K.G.'s death."

Paisley kept her face buried in the pillow. "If that bitch hadn't taunted me…" She let the words hang in the air and could feel the ruby pendant beneath her shirt growing warmer. She flung the pillow across the room and jumped up. "K.G.'s dead and I killed someone. Just another normal morning. Or at least another normal morning the way my week has been going." She chuckled and rubbed her hands down her face. If this was to be her life, she hoped she would be able to deal with it.

Lana reached for her, but she slapped her hand away. With that one gesture, her anger spiked, and she closed her eyes and tried to push it back as far as she could. If it flared up unexpectedly all the time, it would be hard to control it. She needed someone to teach her. As it was, the pendant was helping, but it was still taking everything within her to temper it and not snap Lana's neck like she did Gloria's. She opened her eyes and balled her fists, shaking. Lana held her hands up in surrender and took a step back. Paisley jabbed a finger in her direction. "This is all your fault." She growled and took a step in her direction. "I wish you had never came into my life."

Lana bit her lip and nodded. "I will be back in two weeks for you. Make sure you are packed and ready to go." She waved her hand in the air and disappeared.

Paisley shook her head and walked toward her childhood bedroom. She grabbed ahold of the doorframe and took several deep breaths, trying to calm her racing heart, before she turned and addressed everyone else. "I would like to be alone. Please don't bother me." Without waiting for an answer, she walked back to her bedroom, shut the door, and fell onto the bed. Jynx jumped up beside her, and she grabbed her cat gently and cuddled her into her chest. For the rest of her life she would never forget the haunted look in her family's eyes. She didn't fight her tears and let them fall freely into Jynx's fur. She knew, if her family turned on her, Jynx would always be there to offer comfort. Even if it was a lick on the cheek.

≈≈≈≈

Paisley stepped into the shower the next morning

and relaxed as the hot water beat down on her neck and back. She flexed her fingers under the spray and watched in amazement as they started to glow silver in color. She would have to find out what that meant. The sharp tingles that swept up her fingers and into her hand didn't scare her. Instead it helped to calm her and wash her in a sense of peace. After the events of yesterday, she wasn't sure how she would feel waking up, but surprisingly everything felt normal. Besides the looks on the faces of her family, she didn't regret anything that had happened. The feelings of disgust, shame, and pain never came. If she was honest with herself, the only thing she felt was hunger pain.

She shook her hands out and the silver dulled. After drying herself off, she dressed in a pair of jeans and a long-sleeved, light blue Henley. She pulled on a pair of Doctor Who crew socks, then slipped her feet into a pair of blue sneakers. After grabbing her glasses off the nightstand, she put them on, ran her fingers through her hair, and headed out of the room. The one thing she knew for sure was that she had slept the rest of the day yesterday and all through the night. She would have to remember that doing that type of magic would drain her.

Fretting in the hallway wouldn't solve any of her problems. Jynx walked beside her, and at the end of the hallway, Addison stood waiting. She smiled to herself when Addison started walking behind her. At least one person was loyal to her. She held her head high as she continued into the living room. Her dad was sitting on the couch reading a book and her mom stood by the window talking with someone on the phone.

Paisley turned around when she felt eyes on her. Grams stood by the kitchen sink and motioned for her to join her. She accepted the cup of tea Grams handed her and took a small sip. The first taste on her tongue worked its magic to center her. She leaned back and relaxed against the counter. They both were lost in their own thoughts staring into the living room.

"Dear, we need to talk about what happened yesterday."

Her words were sure and solid, and Paisley dared a look at her and almost broke down when she saw only love reflected back at her. "You're not afraid of me?"

"What?" She set her cup on the counter then took Paisley's out of her hands and set it down beside hers. She lifted her chin and looked into her eyes. "Listen to me. I will only say this once." Paisley nodded. "I have never been, nor will I ever be, afraid of you. Nothing you could ever do would ever make me afraid of you. This is partially our fault. We should have prepared you better for all of this. It broke my heart yesterday to see you so deflated."

"When everyone looked at me…" She shook her head and took a deep breath.

"No, Paisley." Her dad walked over from his perch on the couch and slipped his arm around her shoulders. She laid her head against his chest. "We weren't afraid of you. We were afraid for you. Your powers are quite strong." He squeezed her. "I ditto your grandma's words. We could never be afraid of you. Never."

"We do need to talk though, Paisley."

"Mom, I know." She accepted the tissue and wiped her nose. She picked her cup up and took a sip, then followed her grandmother and father into the living room. After everyone settled down on the couch, she sat down in the recliner opposite the couch, and Addison took up position beside her chair. When Jynx jumped into her lap, she waited until she was settled before running her fingers through the soft fur.

"It seems that your powers are controlled by emotion. While that will make you, with training, a powerful witch, it also means your powers will be unpredictable as well. Great powers come with great responsibility. What happened yesterday must not ever happen again. I know that you were overwhelmed and you didn't know what you were doing. I know you still don't know what you were doing, but at least now you know not to let go and have your powers control you. You must control your powers. If not, they will overtake you. I have seen it happen a few times and it is not something I ever want to witness, especially with my granddaughter."

Her mom scooted forward on the couch. "How did you feel the moment before you appeared behind Gloria? Why did you appear behind her? What happened to cause you to snap on her?"

Paisley jerked her head up. "What do you mean what happened? You heard what she said." What were they playing at?

"Paisley," her dad said. "What who said?"

"Gloria." They looked as confused as she felt.

"Gloria didn't say anything."

Paisley bit her lip and swallowed the lump that had suddenly formed in her throat. She knew what she had heard. "I was coping until I heard her say that K.G. was just another dead dyke. I felt something pass through me and I didn't fight it. A calmness settled over me and I wished that I was standing behind her. Then I was." She shrugged like it was an everyday occurrence.

They eyed each other, then Grams took her hand. "We didn't hear her. She must have been projecting only to you."

"I couldn't figure out why no one else did or said anything." It made sense now. "When I appeared behind her, I let everything that I was feeling wash over me and I knew what I had to do. I didn't fight it."

"You broke her neck. Without touching her," her mom said in disbelief.

"She told me K.G.'s death wasn't an accident. I did what I needed to do and I won't apologize for that. I would do it the exact same way again."

"Okay," Grams said. "I understand where you were coming from now. Let's move on."

"We are not moving on. We need to discuss this."

Grams held up her hand. "Kate, that matter is closed. I love you, Kate, but you have never felt the burden of power, and from what I saw yesterday, Paisley is powerful. To be honest, I'm surprised she didn't do more damage, and to be fair, she did fix your broken window. We are moving on from this subject, and I don't want it brought up again."

"I don't agree, but I will abide by your wishes." Paisley almost whooped at the way her grandma had shut her mom down, but kept her excitement at bay.

Paisley looked down at her hand when something was placed in it. It was another necklace. This one had a small butterfly pendant attached to the simple silver chain. "It's beautiful."

"It is, but it serves a purpose. It will dull your powers, to a manageable level, even for you. Slip it on." She did as she was asked. "It will not erase your powers, so if you feel anything different overcome you, you will still need to control it. If you don't keep your emotions in check, innocents could suffer the consequences."

"I understand." And she did. The last thing she wanted was to hurt more people or kill them. She now had three necklaces on and a cuff that was welded to her skin, and she didn't even like jewelry. The clear pendant didn't seem to make much of a difference. She felt the same, but maybe it only worked when her powers flared up.

Her dad stood up and started pacing in front of the window before he stopped abruptly and looked at her. "Now on to the next matter. Gloria. I agree with your grandma, the subject of her death will be dropped, but there will be consequences to her death. We will not be able to turn a blind eye to it."

"No, we won't," Grams said. "For right now, I believe the issue will be set aside, but Catherine, Gloria's mother, will not let the matter drop and neither will the others in her coven. I'm afraid that they will try to avenge her death." She smirked. "I am not sure they, yet, understand what they will come up against, but they will come."

"I could say that if I knew the outcome I would change what happened, but I'd be lying. When the time comes, I will be ready and I won't let anything happen to any of you." Paisley shut up when they looked at each other. They grew quiet and she looked between them. "What's going on?"

"Paisley."

She knew that tone of voice. Grams only used that voice when they had something important to tell her. She stood up and put Jynx down in the chair. Whatever they were about to say, she was sure she wouldn't like it. "Don't 'Paisley' me. Spit it out." They were starting to freak her out, and compared to the week she had experienced, that was saying something.

Her mom stood up and approached her. "We've talked, and for your safety and for you to learn your craft and get a handle on your powers, we feel it is in your best interest…"

She drowned out the rest of what she her mom said and crouched on the floor with her head in her hands. She knew what she was going to say. How could they do this to her? After everything. Why? She was still holding out hope, even after everything that had happened, that she wouldn't have to go. They were supposed to be on her side.

She took several deep breaths and glanced at her hands. The silver had returned. Her entire body was tingling, but she didn't have the overwhelming urge to attack anyone. She shook her hands out, and closed her eyes and searched her memories until she landed on one a few months ago.

She and Grams had gone to the local library book sale, and Grams had been so excited when she found a book she had been searching months for. She smiled, remembering taking her out to lunch, then enjoying a quite night in. Just the two of them. She flinched but kept her eyes closed when someone touched her hand. Getting her bearings, she opened her eyes into Addison's concerned ones. Paisley smiled, stood up, and shook her hands out. The silver was gone. "So, Dangor, huh?" Her voice was calm, but she was fighting the emotions swirling inside of her, so she kept the day with Grams planted at the forefront of her mind. At least she had learned one thing today. To counteract her heightened emotions, she only had to think of happy memories.

Grams scrutinized Paisley's face, then smiled. "Yes, Dangor."

Paisley reached up and adjusted her glasses. "Lana isn't my favorite person right now." Addison snorted.

"I would imagine she isn't," her dad said. "And if there was another option we would take it, but there isn't. I am well aware that you will be facing, according to Lana, danger in Dangor, but she has people that can protect you. I'm not sure what is going to happen here. You will be safer there."

"What about you three? Who is going to keep you safe?"

"Paisley, we can handle ourselves. I promise."

Paisley crossed her arms and scuffed her toe on the carpet. "I would hate to come back here and find you all dead." It was her biggest fear and it would break her. She couldn't imagine life without them in it. She liked Addison, tolerated Lana, but in Dangor she wouldn't know anyone else. She essentially would be alone. She and Lana might be married in the eyes of Dangor, but she wasn't sure she could ever fully accept her as anything other than the woman who forced her into a marriage she never wanted to begin with. "What happens now? Lana said she would be back in two weeks."

Her dad slapped her on the shoulder. "Now, you'll come with me. It's time we started your training. Uncle Cliff is waiting in the backyard for us. Get something to eat, then meet us in thirty minutes."

"Dad, not today."

"Paisley, I wasn't asking. You will meet me in the backyard in thirty minutes. Keep an eye on the clock. Don't be late." He squeezed her hand, then walked out the back door.

She looked around the room before her eyes landed on her mom. "I guess I'm going to start my training today."

"It looks like it."

She bit her lip and sighed. It was going to be a long day.

⁂

Paisley stepped out the back door and paused before slowly descending the four steps off the porch. Her dad and uncle stood in the middle of the yard, dressed in what she could only describe as costumes in a bad fantasy movie. They were both barefoot and had on a pair of loose, brown cotton pants that tied at the waist. Their chests were bare, and for the first time she noticed they both had a series of small tattoos littering their abs. Upon closer inspection, the tattoos were all weapons: sword, knife, spear, arrow, and others she didn't recognize. Her dad saw her staring and explained that each tattoo represented a weapon that the wearer had trained with.

She nodded, and brushed the hairs that had come loose from her ponytail behind her ears and slipped on her ball cap. Uncle Cliff looked unsure and avoided her gaze. That wouldn't do. Without prompting, she threw her arms around his neck and kissed his cheek when he wrapped his arms around her. After a few moments, she slid out of his embrace. "Do we have to do this right now?"

"Yes, we do. We should have done this before now," Cliff said. "We should have started when you were younger. We should have done a lot of things differently." Her dad squeezed Cliff's shoulder before stepping forward.

"We only have two weeks and I fear that will not be enough time. We will train from nine in the morning until two in the afternoon, from now until Lana comes back for you."

That wouldn't be possible. "I have work."

"Paisley, I called your boss this morning and informed her you wouldn't be returning. You have far more important things to worry about."

Paisley threw his hand off and started pacing. "You did what? How dare you. After everything I've been through. I thought out of everyone you knew how I felt about making my own decisions. I thought you were different from them." She gulped and held her tears at bay, but jerked around when her uncle grabbed her arm and she looked on in disbelief as he clipped a metal cuff onto her wrist.

As soon as the cold metal touched her skin, she fell to her knees and screamed. Fire raced up her arm and she slumped to the ground, too weak to fight whatever had hold of her. An immense pressure built up in her chest, and she gulped in air as she tried to get her breathing under control. She attempted to stand, but fell back to her knees. She closed her eyes and focused on a happy memory until her breathing evened out. When she opened her eyes, Cliff was crouched down beside her. Out of the corner of her eye, she noticed Addison had her dad pinned against the nearest tree. Addison had a cut on her head and blood was running down her face, but she was holding her own.

Paisley shook her head to clear the fuzziness, attempted to stand, but fell back to the ground again. She cursed her life, her luck, and at this moment, her family. She clamped her eyes shut when the trees started to spin around her. There was an energy buzzing under her skin, but she couldn't concentrate long enough to grasp it. Her magic was boiling beneath the surface. She licked her lips and focused on Cliff. "Why?" Why did they keep doing this to her? "Why?"

"You have to learn to fight without your powers interfering. I am not sorry for what happened." He pointed to the cuff. "That's your first lesson. Never let anyone get close enough to you to be able to do something like that. You have to protect yourself."

She caught Addison's eye and motioned for her to help her up. She would be damned if she accepted Cliff's outstretched hand. Addison grasped her arms and helped her to stand. "Go get cleaned up." When she hesitated, Paisley made it an order. She pushed her dad back when he reached out to touch her, and he stumbled. She pointed back to the house. "Do not ever touch Addison like that again. You had no right. It is her job to protect me. You're both lucky she didn't kill you. I will make sure the next time she doesn't hold back." Bile rose in her throat but she pushed it back and glared at the cuff on her wrist. "This cuff better be able to be removed."

"After practice, I will take it off, but at the start of each session we will have to put it on. You must learn without your powers. There may be times you can't rely on them; you have to rely on yourself. We are here to make sure you are ready for that," Uncle Cliff said.

"Paisley," her dad said. "I can see the indecision in your eyes. You may not like what's happening to you, but it is happening and you need to embrace it. If not, it could kill you. You don't belong in this world; you belong in Dangor. You have a life waiting for you there, and you need to accept that, because you don't have another choice. This will happen whether you're a willing participant or not." He pointed to a chair set against the fence. "Have a seat. You won't be training today, but you will sit and watch us. We'll go through several different formats and bring out several different weapons. Watch us carefully. At the end of today, you will be choosing a weapon to train with."

"Fine." There wasn't any point in arguing. She took a seat, and a few minutes later Addison walked out of the house and headed in her direction. The last thing she wanted was to watch them, but she sat quietly and tried to focus on their movements.

They stood across from each other and started bouncing on their feet to a rhythm only they could hear. Even though she kept her eyes glued to the scene in front of her, they were moving so fast at times, their limbs were a blur. After an hour of explaining the different movements, they stopped, bowed to each other, and walked to a table that had been set up by the fence. Her dad picked up a spear, tested its weight, and when he seemed satisfied he stepped back into the yard and waited until Cliff chose his spear as well. After a series of exercises, they moved on to the next weapon on the table.

After the fourth weapon, she sat up straighter when they each picked up a small dagger, a weapon she hadn't even noticed on the table. Cliff held his firmly, but her dad slipped his into a sheath that rested on his hip. Their movements were sure and steady, and it looked initially like Cliff had the advantage because he held his dagger, but after a few minutes her dad lunged forward. He brought his forearm across Cliff's arm that held the dagger, crouched, swung his leg out, and knocked Cliff off his feet. Her dad let his body fall and held his knee on Cliff's chest, slipped his dagger out, and held it to his throat. When Cliff laughed, her dad moved the dagger, clapped him on the shoulder, and they both stood up. Before they could pick another weapon, Paisley jumped up and joined them.

"Paisley?"

She plucked the dagger out of her dad's grasp and turned it over in her hands, marveling at the craftsmanship of it before looking back at them. "I want to train with this."

Her dad looked unsure, but Cliff grinned. "It's a fine weapon. I think you'll catch on quickly," Cliff assured her.

"I hope so." She handed it back and rocked on her heels. "I know you wanted to show me more, but I'm hungry. So, can we wrap this up and get started in the morning? Please, I'm only asking for the rest of the day." They eyed each other, then Cliff reached for her wrist and the cuff slipped off. Her knees buckled, but Addison caught her as a surge of energy raced through her body. She gritted her teeth and held her ground. After tempering her magic, she faced both men. The haunted look on her dad's face didn't bother her as much as she thought it would. He had to have known what her reaction would be to being forced to participate. The last thing she wanted right now was his comfort. If everyone in her life was going to make her decisions for her, they couldn't be upset with how she would react to those decisions.

❧ ❧ ❧ ❧

Paisley stretched and cringed when the muscles in

her back and shoulders pulled. Muscles she didn't even know she had. For the past three days, her dad and Cliff had worked with her and Addison on several different fighting techniques, some even Addison wasn't aware of. Paisley didn't quite have the moves down, but she had mastered the basics, and was confident she could scrap her way out of a fight.

The dagger, after only a few practices, came easy to her, which surprised both men. She slipped her feet into her sneakers and eyed the clock: half past seven. Her dad didn't know it, but neither she nor Addison would be practicing today. She'd had enough training for the week. The Hendricks Potato Festival had started the day before and she would be damned if she missed it. She went every year, and since it was Saturday, she was taking a day off.

She sidestepped Jynx and walked out of the bedroom, where Addison was waiting for her. "We're getting out of here today. If I have to spend one more day in this house, I will go crazy." She hadn't been back to her house since K.G. had died and didn't know if she ever would be able to go back. She slipped her hand through Addison's arm and guided her down the hall and into the living room. Surprisingly, everyone was up, including Cliff. "Good morning, everyone."

"Good morning, dear," Grams said. "We saved some breakfast for both of you."

She fiddled with her glasses. "Actually, Addison and I are getting out of here for the day. We're going to the Potato Festival. We'll grab breakfast on the way." She waited for to the anticipated blow-up, but they didn't say anything. "Okay?"

Her dad nodded. "Okay."

"Really?" She eyed him skeptically.

He laughed. "Really. Go have fun. I know all of this is overwhelming, but you need this. So, go. Have fun."

She patted Addison on the arm and walked farther into the room. "I also thought, since Hendricks has that Medieval shop, I would pick up some things to wear in Dangor. I don't know how long I will be there, so I figured I should buy more practical clothing. I've been saving for a while."

Uncle Cliff nodded. "I think that's a good idea. Get some sensible pants and shirts. Get a cloak and some nice boots, but also buy a few dresses. Besides that, have fun."

"I will also be bringing some jeans and T-shirts. I don't care what anyone says, they are coming with me." She leaned down and picked Jynx up, cradling her to her chest. "We'll get you fixed up, too." She noticed the looks everyone was giving her. "What?"

"Honey, Jynx can stay here with us. We'll take good care of her."

"No matter what I have to do, Jynx is coming with me. I'll swing by the vet's and see what types of shots she should get for traveling. Everyone here, besides Addison but including Lana, feels the need to dictate every facet of my life, but I draw the line at this. If I have to, I'll put a protection spell around her. There is such a thing, right Grams?"

Her grandmother studied her so long she started to squirm under her gaze. "There are a few things we can do."

"Good." She kissed Jynx's belly then set her back on the floor. "We're going to head out. Don't wait up for us. I don't know what time we'll be back."

"Be careful."

"Don't worry. We'll be fine." She settled into the driver's seat and waited while Addison slipped her seat belt on. "Ready for this?"

"Of course. I love potatoes." Paisley chuckled and put the car in gear. It took them under two hours to reach Hendricks. It was just after nine and all the shops downtown had started to open. They decided on Knight and Day, the boutique that sold Medieval clothing. Paisley grinned and didn't know where she should look. The store was amazing. Along the far wall were racks of pants and tunics, and spaced out in the middle of the store were mannequins draped in the most beautiful dresses she had ever seen. Near the back of the store were shoes and accessories. She eyed the dresses but decided to check out the pants first. There were so many options she didn't know where to start. She picked up a random pair of cotton pants.

"May I help you?"

She turned to the associate, and although she usually liked to shop on her own, she was at a loss in this instance. "What would you recommend for someone who is getting ready to travel to another realm that is more like Medieval period for an undisclosed amount of time because she has found herself married to a princess? Price isn't an option."

The saleswoman didn't even miss a beat when she picked up several pairs of pants ranging from leather to plain cotton to wool. After that, she pulled a few different lengths and colors of tunics. When Paisley pointed out that she liked the sleeveless ones, she went into the back room and returned with additional options that were more detailed and of finer quality.

The saleslady picked out two different cloaks, one of a thin material and one that was made of wool and leather. Footwear was next, and she recommended a pair of thick-soled boots and two pairs of dressier shoes. She also added a few jerkins in different colors. Paisley walked around the dresses. They were amazing. The detail of the stitching blew her mind. She let her fingers slip through the silk and shivered. She didn't wear dresses often, but she could see herself wearing a few of these.

"I have someone who makes the dresses for me. This one"—she pointed to a long, flowing black and white dress with a hood and floral lace detail—"would be for more of a formal dinner, while these"—she pointed out the dresses at the front of the store—"would be more everyday wear."

In the end, Paisley settled on three dresses and picked out several belts and other accessories for her journey. She had a blast and tried not to faint when the total was rung up, but she sucked it up and slid her credit card. It took two trips, but she and Addison hauled everything to the car.

After such a stressful shopping trip, they decided to drown their sorrows in every kind of festival food they wanted. Paisley took a bite of her French fries smothered in chili and cheese, and moaned as the flavors danced on her tongue. She smiled at Addison as she bit into her deep-fried cheesecake.

"Oh, wow," Addison said. "We need to take this recipe back with us."

"I'll see what I can do." That was another of her worries. What kind of food would she have to eat? She loved to eat and couldn't stomach not being able to have her favorites. She would have to add a couple of cookbooks to one of her suitcases. She let her gaze wander and stopped when she spotted a vendor off in the distance. "Come on." It didn't take them long to reach the booth where they were selling several different sizes of vintage trunks. She immediately took a liking to the two that sat at the front of the table.

"Those are at least a hundred years old, and as you can see they are in fantastic shape."

"May I open them?"

"Be my guest."

She opened them both and knew that she had to have them. The only backpack she owned was a Wonder woman one, and even though it was awesome, she couldn't see herself carrying the bag into Dangor. After a bit of haggling, they agreed on a price and the vendor even offered to take them to her car for her.

They spent the rest of the day enjoying several more treats, every ride at the festival, and face painting. Paisley left the festivities with a lion on her cheek and Addison with a butterfly on hers. It was an amazing day and one that she sorely needed. On the way back home, she stopped at a twenty-four-hour vet hospital and asked about different vaccines that Jynx would need for traveling to other countries. Doctor Wildon told her to bring her in the next day and she would fix her up. Her hope was that whatever the vet gave her would work to guard against anything they might encounter. She would leave her behind, if she had to, but she didn't want to. So much had already been taken away from her. She blew out a breath when she pulled into her parents' driveway. After shutting the car off, Addison handed her the bag of pork rinds.

"I really enjoyed today. Thank you," Addison said, taking a bite of her donut.

"Me, too. I believe it was certainly warranted after the week we've had."

"I agree, but your dad is right about the training. You can't always rely on your magic. Tomorrow we will get back to it."

She had to agree with her. The day had been wonderful and fun, but this wasn't a joke and it was time to get serious about what was happening. She hated to admit it, but before K.G. died, she was only going through the motions. Now she needed to invest a hundred percent, if only to honor her memory. The future held many unknowns, but it was time to embrace it and stop shying away. The Paisley of a few weeks ago would have crawled into a ball and cried herself to sleep, but that woman was gone. "Grab the rest of the snacks. It's still early. Let's gorge ourselves on all this food, watch a movie, then get a good night's sleep. I believe we're going to need it."

❧❧❧❧

"Paisley, wake up. Paisley!"

Paisley swatted at the hand that touched her face and rolled over in bed, covering her head with her pillow. Ignoring her mom's voice, she burrowed deeper under the covers, then shrieked a second later when the covers were ripped off her body and the pillow was pulled away from her head.

"Get up. Now."

Paisley narrowed her eyes. Her mom's voice held an edge she wasn't used to hearing from her, one that was laced with fear. Her eyes searched out the clock and she groaned when she saw what time it was. "It's only seven. Give me a few more hours and I'm all yours."

"We don't have a few hours. We must be at the Council house at eight thirty. Paisley, this is serious.

The Council has summoned you. It is unexpected, and your grandmother and I need to go over a few things with you before the meeting. So, get up, shower, and meet us in the living room in fifteen minutes."

"Whatever." She sat up and watched her mom walk out of the room. Everybody was getting good at telling her what to do. After her shower and pulling on a pair of well-worn Levi's and a light blue, long-sleeved sweater that depicted a cat floating in space, she headed to the living room in her bare feet. Grams and her mom were seated on the couch and Addison was standing by the window. "Good morning, everyone." She sat down in the recliner across from the couch. She thanked her dad when he handed her a cup of tea, then he went down to the basement. "I guess it's just us girls, then." Neither one of them smiled.

"Paisley."

"Grams." Paisley smirked.

"The Council's request to see you is a surprise. We were hoping you would be gone before a summons arrived." Her mom wrung her hands together.

"What's the worst thing that could happen? They already said they wouldn't punish me for Gloria's death." She squinted when her mom fidgeted on the couch.

"Actually, that's not what we're worried about. We're more concerned with the people you will meet who make up the Council."

"Oh." She eyed them over the rim of her cup.

"Yes," Grams said. "One member to be exact. Alexia."

"Who is she?" She sipped her tea and regarded them both. After the pleasant day at the Potato Festival she was feeling quite relaxed, despite her rude awakening.

Her mom stood up and started pacing. "She's a powerful witch. Even though she is on the Council, she has never pledged her allegiance to any one section. It's a bit unusual. She is— "

"Evil," Grams finished.

"Evil?" That seemed a bit excessive, even for them.

"She is a despicable person. She will do whatever she deems acceptable to gain the upper hand. She is only out for one person: herself. She talks a good game, but don't let her fool you." Grams shook her finger at her.

"She is an old, bitter woman. Steer clear of her. She kills without cause."

"If she's so powerful and evil, why doesn't the rest of the Council do something about her?" They were starting to put a damper on her good mood.

"Her seat on the Council was passed down from her mother. Members are not voted in. Her seat is secure."

Paisley finished her tea and set the cup on the coffee table. "So, she doesn't have morals. She's evil, old, bitter, and a killer. Did I miss something?" Whoever this woman was, she had gotten under their skin. She'd never had a reason not to trust them before, but after everything that had recently happened to her, she would form her own opinion on the matter.

"She is a first-class bitch," her mom supplied. "She has done nothing but criticize anyone who doesn't share her values. And maybe the most important thing: it's never been documented, but there are rumors that she practices dark magic."

Paisley squinted. "You mean like Lord Voldemort?"

"This isn't fiction, Paisley," her mom snapped. "Please take this seriously."

"It was just a question. I am trying to understand everything. Don't bite my head off. When do we leave?" Her good mood vanished in a cloud of dust.

"P.J., you don't have any questions about dark magic?" Grams patted her on the knee.

She had dozens of questions but was afraid to ask them. They both were out of sorts over this Alexia woman, but her mother seemed especially irked. She couldn't wait to meet this bitter, old, evil witch. "Maybe later."

"Well then, let's go."

By the time they had made it to a warehouse in the downtown area, Paisley just wanted to crawl back into bed. Her mom and Grams hadn't said a word since they left the house. "This is it?"

"Come along." They walked in through a back door of the warehouse. Paisley fiddled with the sleeves of her sweater. She had wanted to change, but her mom convinced her to wear the long sleeves to hide her bracelet. Even though Addison protested, Paisley had ordered her to stay back at the house, at her mom's insistence. They let it be known that under no circumstance should the Council know she was bonded to Lana. Paisley didn't care, but she was tired of all this cloak and dagger shit. She was just tired. Once she was finally allowed to sleep she was confident she would do so for a week straight.

After a quick ride on an elevator that had seen better days, they passed by several closed doors until they reached the end of the hallway and turned left. Directly in front of them was a long wall of windows that led into a large conference room. Several people were already seated at the table that sat in the middle of the room.

Paisley took several deep breaths, then followed the others through the open door. She only just managed not to jump when the door shut behind her. They were directed to three seats on one side of the table. She wasn't crazy about the fact that her back would be to the door, but she didn't argue when a man held her chair out for her. "Thank you." He nodded and took his seat at the head of the table. There was a chair at each end of the table, and four on either side. All the seats were filled except for the one directly across from her.

There were three men and three women, not including herself, her mom, and grandma. Of the three women, only one of them was of advanced age. She wanted to ask her mom if this was the infamous Alexia, but she kept her mouth shut. Although, by the relaxed posture of her mom's body, she had a feeling this wasn't her. Everyone was looking at her with what she could only decipher as curiosity. She swung her head around when the door opened, and she sucked in a breath when Gloria's mother stepped into the room. The chair-holding man, who now looked slightly familiar, directed Catherine to a seat that was set up in one corner of the room. Paisley pushed down the nausea that churned and resisted the urge to jump up and run out of the room. She hadn't expected her to be here.

"Good morning," the man said. "Paisley, I'm not sure if you remember me, but my name is Jeffrey and I was there the night Gloria died." *That's where I know him from.* Paisley nodded. "Good. I will go around the table and introduce everyone. Across from you is

Larry, Brandon, and Anita. At the other end is Lucille, and sitting beside your grandmother is Stella."

So, no Alexia. That was interesting. Paisley nodded at everyone and gave what she hoped was an endearing smile, but she wasn't sure she pulled it off when her mom pinched her leg. "It's nice to meet you all."

"And," Jeffery said. "You know Gloria's mom, Catherine." He pointed to the corner and Paisley nodded. "We are expecting one more, so we will wait a few minutes to give her time to get here. Alexia was running late this morning."

Paisley bit her lip and closed her eyes. After a few minutes, the air around her changed, her eyes flew open, and she jerked her head around to the door just in time to see the sexiest woman she had ever laid eyes on walk into the room. Paisley gulped and ran her eyes down the woman's body. She wore a dark blue Chanel button top, slim legs were encased in a pair of black Carolina Herrera trousers, and a gold belt completed the look. No jewelry was noticeable. On her feet, she wore a pair of five-inch red Prada pumps. *Oh, holy fuck.*

Paisley swallowed and ran her eyes along the woman's torso and was met by a pair of the bluest eyes she had ever seen. A pair of amused blue eyes that sparkled and conveyed just a hint of laughter at Paisley's expense. Paisley's eyes shifted downward and she couldn't help but notice the first three buttons of her top were left unbuttoned and showed an impressive amount of cleavage. Paisley gripped the arms of her chair and fought the urge to fan herself.

When she lifted her gaze a moment later, a smile curled on the woman's lips and Paisley had to remind herself to breathe. Her blond—almost white—hair, sprinkled with just a touch of gray, was short and wavy, and a lock of it kept falling over the woman's forehead. Paisley had an overwhelming urge to reach out and brush it out of the woman's eye, but she caught herself at the last minute. Paisley's heart thudded in her chest and she took a deep breath as the woman walked toward the table, pulled out the seat across from her, and sat down, her hands clasped loosely on top of the table.

Paisley glanced down and swallowed when she noticed the woman's fingernails were manicured and painted a deep red. *Oh, my god.* It felt like all the air had been sucked out of the room. Lana was a beautiful woman, but she didn't hold a candle to the woman seated across from her right now. She chanced a glance up to find the woman smirking at her. Paisley didn't dare look away from her gaze.

"Paisley."

Paisley couldn't take her eyes off the woman.

"Paisley!"

"Ow." She tore her eyes away to glare at her mother, who had pinched her. "What?"

"Jeffery called your name three times."

"Oh." She could feel the heat rise in her cheeks and decided that not looking in the stunning woman's direction would be the smartest move. She turned her head and zeroed in on Jeffery. "I'm sorry. Did you have a question?"

"Since Alexia is here we are going to get started. Let me start by telling you that you are not going to be punished for the death of Gloria, but we did have a few questions."

"Okay." She could feel Alexia's eyes on her but

she kept her own on Jeffery. *Play it cool, Paisley. Play it cool.* It was hard to keep calm when her heart felt like it was going to jump out of her chest. She didn't know what the hell her mom and grandmother were talking about. Alexia was not an old woman. From her looks, Paisley placed her in her late forties or early fifties. Maybe twenty years her senior, but she certainly wouldn't have a problem being bent over a table by the older woman. She shivered deliciously at the images in her mind's eye.

"Good. It has come to our attention that you just came into your powers, and by the way you acted on the night of Gloria's death, I would have to agree that certainly seems consistent."

She wasn't sure that was a question, but the last thing she wanted to do was piss these people off. "Yes."

"Your family has explained things to you?"

"Yes."

"How are you faring so far?"

"Okay." She debated elaborating, but decided against it.

"I know some of the other members have questions for you."

"All right." Paisley fought with herself not to turn in Alexia's direction.

"Paisley," Lucille said from the end of the table. Paisley turned toward her and kept her gaze averted from Alexia. If she would have been alone she would have patted herself on the back. "You must be feeling overwhelmed by everything that has happened, but you must realize that everyone in this room, including your family, has seen and done much worse, but not over a single person's death. Why did you lose your temper over such an insignificant one?"

Paisley bit her lip, closed her eyes, and counted to ten. When she opened her eyes, Alexia was staring at her and she couldn't decipher the look on her face. It was slightly out of focus. Paisley blinked a few times, shook her head, then turned back to Lucille. She stretched her fingers on top of the table, then shook them out before she reached up and adjusted her glasses. "I am not sure how you would like me to answer that. On the one hand, I can be straightforward and tell you to go to hell, but I've been there the past few days, and besides the drab décor, it wasn't such a bad place. Or I could tell you that she was my best friend and seeing her die in front of me has irreversibly changed me. I am not the same woman as I was a week ago, and I'm not sure that is a good or bad thing. Or I could say that seeing my best friend murdered right in front of me was the worst thing I have ever witnessed."

She glanced past Lucille to Catherine. "And it *was* murder. But I don't think any of those answers would be sufficient for you. Everyone is important to somebody. Contrary to popular belief, someone who considers themselves unworthy or unloved will always have someone missing them. To you, she was a nobody. To me, she was my first kiss and so much more. I have been through a lot in the past week, but I can honestly say I hope I never get to the point where I think anyone's death is insignificant. I don't even think that way about Gloria's." Lucille blinked, then nodded.

Jeffrey coughed and the man directly to Alexia's right nodded at her. "You seem to be having trouble controlling your powers."

She fought back the urge to roll her eyes, but grinned when Alexia did it for her. "Yes."

"Why is that?"

"Well." She ran her hand through her hair. "I just found out I had powers a few days ago. You don't expect a baby to walk straight out of the womb, do you? Give me some credit. It's not like a destroyed the town or anything." Paisley jerked her head to the corner when Catherine's chair toppled to the floor.

"No, but you did kill my daughter." Alexia raised her hand without looking away from Paisley. Catherine's mouth was moving but no sounds were coming out.

Jeffrey sighed. "Catherine, we agreed you could be here, but you need to sit back down."

"I have a question."

Paisley felt goosebumps pop out all over her skin with the sound of Alexia's voice. It was soft, but held an edge that seemed to float in the air before it swirled around Paisley and disappeared into the depths of her core. *Holy hell.* She had to get her shit together. It was just a voice. What was wrong with her? She ran her hands through her hair and squirmed in her seat.

"Alexia, go on." Paisley looked up into the eyes that she knew would haunt her dreams for the foreseeable future, and she almost lost her shit when Alexia lifted a pair of black-framed glasses and slipped them on, scanning a piece of paper in front of her. They took her sexiness to another level altogether. If she wasn't already flustered, this would have pushed her over the edge.

Alexia tilted her glasses and looked at her over the frames. "If given the chance, would you do things the same way again?"

Paisley sighed, took off her glasses, pinched the bridge of her nose, then slipped them back on. She knew it wasn't a simple answer. She had a feeling that her response would determine what type of woman she was in Alexia's eyes, and she knew beyond a shadow of a doubt that she wanted her approval. "I…" She tapped her finger on the tabletop.

"It's a simple question."

Paisley shook her head. "It's a trick question."

Alexia cocked her head, slipped her glasses off, and leaned forward on the table. Paisley had to force herself not to look down at the cleavage she knew was amazing. "Is it?"

Before the silence rose to unbearable limits, Paisley spoke. "Yes. To both questions."

Alexia nodded and leaned back in her chair. "I'm satisfied." Everyone at the table nodded and looked at Jeffrey.

"Good, now to one other matter. Your training. It is this Council's opinion that you need a mentor, and we have chosen one from among us to teach you."

"What?" Grams spoke up. "Paisley should be the one to choose." Paisley had a feeling Grams wouldn't be saying that if she knew who her choice would be.

Jeffrey shook his head. "It has been settled. Alexia will teach Paisley everything she needs to know."

Paisley knew exactly what she wanted Alexia to teach her.

"No," her mom said, jumping up from her seat.

"What?" What just happened? She needed to pay more attention.

"P.J., don't worry, I will handle this. You will not be taught by her." She pointed at Alexia, who was still seated and relaxed.

"No." Paisley stood up and looked at her mother.

"Paisley, I've got this." She touched her arm, but Paisley threw it off. "P.J.?"

"All anyone has been doing this past week is make all of my decisions for me. I am a grown woman. I can make my decisions myself."

"Paisley."

"Stop! God." She ran her hands through her hair. "Just stop. I love you both, but it is partly your fault I'm in this mess to begin with. Don't look at me like that. You said so yourself the other day. My powers are obviously more than I can handle. I need help."

"I agree, but not from her."

Paisley growled and turned toward Alexia. "When do we start?" Alexia smirked and stood up, pointing to the only empty corner of the room. Paisley stepped away from the table when her mom stopped her with a hand on her arm.

"Paisley, we are just looking out for you."

"I love you, but this time you're looking out for yourself. I am sure this will only take a few minutes, then we get to go home. I'm hungry."

Her mother looked resigned. "All right."

Paisley steeled her nerves and walked toward Alexia, who stood in the corner of the room with her feet crossed and her hands tucked loosely in her pants pockets. The thought of so much sexiness thrown into such a small package tilted Paisley's world on its axis. She shook out her hands and held her head high, but almost fell to her knees at the words that came out of Alexia's mouth when she was only a couple of feet from her.

"My, my. You're a wicked, wicked girl."

Oh, sweet hell. Paisley sucked in a breath and rubbed the back of her neck. What was she supposed to say to that? "I…"

Alexia wagged her finger in the air. "That wasn't

a question."

"Oh...okay." The look on Alexia's face was a mix of desire, curiosity, and an emotion she couldn't decipher but she sure as hell wanted to. It took all her control not to lick the pulse point that throbbed on Alexia's neck. She eyed her lips before looking up and meeting her gaze.

After a beat, Alexia nodded and pulled a piece of paper out of her pocket and held it out. When their fingers touched, Paisley jerked her hand back at the electricity that raced up her arm. "What the shit?"

Alexia chuckled, and Paisley would do anything she could to hear that again. "Be at that address Monday morning at seven thirty." She didn't wait for an answer, but turned and headed toward the door. Paisley didn't even try to stop herself from watching her walk away. The sway of her hips and the way those pants hugged her ass should be considered a crime. She wouldn't have denied herself the pleasure of watching her walking away for anything. She snapped herself out of her fantasy when Grams waved to her. She didn't know what she had just gotten herself into, but she couldn't wait until Monday to find out. After the crap week she'd had, things seemed to be looking up.

✿✿✿✿✿

Everything was quiet on their way home, and Paisley breathed a sigh of relief when they walked in the front door and her mom and grandma went down to the basement. Addison was waiting in the living room, and Paisley motioned for her to join her on the couch. She closed her eyes and leaned her head back, jerking upright when someone touched her cheek.

Lana stood in front of her, smiling. Panic threatened to overwhelm her, but she pushed it down and looked at the clock. She had been asleep for three hours. Lana wasn't supposed to be back for another five days. This couldn't be good. Not good at all. She figured she should say something. "What are you doing here?" It came out a bit sharper than she intended.

"Paisley," her mom snapped. "You know why she's here. To take you back."

"Not for another five days." This couldn't be happening. Not now.

"No, Paisley," Lana said, and ran her hands through her hair. "Things have changed. We need to leave now. I received word that our enemies know that I will be bringing you back with me. To throw them off, we need to leave now."

Paisley adjusted her glasses and frowned. If she left now she would never see Alexia again, and she knew that wasn't an option. For some reason, she was drawn to the her. She couldn't not see her. "We'll leave Monday afternoon."

Lana grabbed her hand and squeezed. "No, we need to leave in a couple of hours. Today."

Paisley threw her hand off. "No. I need more time."

"P.J., you have to leave now. This is your life we're talking about."

She threw her hands in the air. "Is it my life? Because around here lately everyone has taken the opportunity to tell me how to live it. I…" She ran her hand through her hair. "I was supposed to have more time. This is not what I want." She glared at her mother.

"And sometimes we have to do what we don't want to. It's time to grow up, Paisley." Her mom patted her arm, but Paisley shrugged it off.

"This isn't about me growing up." Her chest heaved and she fought down the urge to do something drastic. "If you can't already tell, I am grown up. No one here seems to realize that." She pointed her finger at Lana. "You weren't supposed to come for me yet." She thought she would have more time. Why did there never seem to be enough time? First K.G., then Alexia, now this.

"The choice was taken out of my hands."

Why was it always someone else's choice and not hers? She chanced a glance at each face, and at the simple nod from her dad, she had to force herself not to lose it. This isn't what she wanted, but she also knew she wouldn't be getting out of it. Not if anyone in the room had anything to say about it, and going by recent events, they would be the only ones who had a say.

"I…" Why was everything moving so fast? Now that she had a reason to stay, she had to leave. It might not have been the outcome her mom and Grams wanted, but this way they would get Alexia out of her life for good. She had a feeling that when she left this world, she wouldn't be coming back. She bit back a sob, and waved everyone away from approaching her. "Grams, will you help me put a protective spell around Jynx's carrier since it seems I won't be able to take her to the vet? And before anyone says anything, she is coming with me. I will be leaving my life and everyone I love. I will not leave my cat behind."

"Of course, sweetheart."

Paisley nodded and pointed at Addison. "Help me get my stuff together."

"Of course."

They walked out of the living room and down

the hallway. When they entered the bedroom and shut the door, Paisley slid down to the floor. Addison sat down beside her as Paisley buried her head in her hands and cried. Cried long and hard for what she was leaving behind, for what would never be, and for the unknowns she was getting ready to walk into.

After what seemed like an entirety, but was only a few minutes, Addison stood up and offered Paisley her hand. Without speaking they gathered Paisley's belongings, and one by one Addison carried them into the living room. When she came back for the last trunk, Paisley gathered Jynx in her arms, looked around the room for the last time, and walked into the living room. Everyone grew quiet when they entered. She handed Jynx off to Lana and grabbed her dad's arm, dragging him into the kitchen. "What if I can't do this?"

Her pulled her into his arms, and she laid her head against his shoulder and held him tight. "I believe in you. Please, Paisley, believe in yourself. Be sure to look up my family when you get there. They will help you."

"I don't love Lana."

"No, you don't."

"I'm not even sure I like her. What do I do?" She sniffled and griped him tighter.

He pushed her to arm's length and looked in her eyes. "What do you do? Do not settle. Do not live a life that everyone else has dictated for you. This is your life. We only get one." He ran his hand down her cheek, pulled her back into a tight embrace, and whispered in her ear. "I don't care who you end up with as long as you know that she is the one. I will support you in any decision you make. If she loves you, I don't care who she is."

She pulled back and kissed him on the cheek. "Thank you, Dad. You don't know how much that means to me. I will make you proud."

"I'm already proud of you. Don't ever doubt that."

She sniffled and accepted the tissue he handed her. "Okay."

"Okay. This is your chance to shine, sweetheart. Grab onto it and never let go, and if you find the one that makes your heart sing, don't let go of her either."

"I'm going to miss you."

"This isn't good-bye, just…see you later."

"Well." The smile didn't quite reach her eyes. They both knew this was good-bye. She turned away from him and headed back into the living room.

Lana pointed outside. "Addison and I took your things out. Whenever you're ready."

Paisley nodded and took Jynx from her mom, kissed the top of her black, fuzzy head, and slipped her inside her carrier. "Grams?"

"Stand back and I will put a protection spell around it." While her grandmother worked, she turned to her mom and sank into her embrace.

"Oh, P.J., I am going to miss you. Be strong. Be brave. But above all, be yourself. I think you're remarkable as yourself. Listen to your teachers and you will be untouchable. I am so proud of you." She ran her fingers down Paisley's cheek.

"I'll do my best."

"I know."

"Paisley, I'm finished."

Paisley accepted the carrier and handed it to Addison. "Would everyone please give me a few minutes alone with Grams?" She bit her lip and kept her back to her when everyone walked out of the living room. As soon as Grams slipped her arms around her from behind, Paisley started sobbing and gripped the hands that were wrapped around her waist. "I don't know if I can do this. I don't know if I can leave you." Grams slid around to her front and put her hands on Paisley's shoulders.

"Look at me." She cupped her cheeks.

Paisley didn't bother to wipe the tears away that fell. "How am I supposed to leave you? Why me? Why now?" She gulped in deep breaths but her tears continued to fall. "I'll never see you again."

"Paisley—"

Paisley cut her off. "I won't. I can feel it. How am I supposed to say good-bye? I love my parents, don't get me wrong. But you, you're my everything." She pulled her glasses off and swiped at her eyes. "This isn't fair."

Grams gripped her hand and led her to the couch. "Sit down. This is your time. You can do this. I have faith in you. I always have. We will all die, sweetheart. That is a given. Nothing lasts forever. I will always be here." She patted Paisley's heart, then her head. "Memories are amazing things. Promise me something."

She wouldn't deny her anything. "Okay."

She tapped Paisley's chin. "Promise me that when you get there you will not dwell on my life and how many years I have left. Do not put your life on hold for what might be happening here. Promise me you will live, and not just live, but thrive."

Paisley sobbed and pulled her into a hug. It was the hardest thing she'd ever had to do. "I promise."

She patted Paisley's cheek, then handed her a

tissue. "I love you, P.J."

"I love you, too, Grams. I always will." They both stood up and headed to the front door. Paisley reached for and gripped Grams's hand.

"Paisley, stand up straight and take a few moments to get yourself together. You've said your good-byes, and I am sure you will have a good cry when you lay your head down tonight, but right now, I don't want to see any more tears. This is your destiny, and sweetheart, you're going to be extraordinary."

Paisley watched her walk through the front door, then she turned and glanced around her childhood home. She straightened her shoulders, walked across the room, and lifted a framed photograph down from the wall. It was taken a couple of years ago at Christmas. Grams and Gramps stood on one side of the tree, and she and her parents stood on the other. Everyone was smiling. She sniffled, slipped the picture under her arm, took one final look around, then walked out the front door.

❧ ❧ ❧ ❧

When they reached the town limits and Lana accelerated, Paisley allowed herself to relax back into the seat. No one had said anything since they pulled out of her parents' driveway, and for that she was grateful. She turned her head when something touched her shoulder, and she accepted the chocolate bar Addison handed her. After a couple of hours, they turned onto a dirt road and entered a wooded area. She wasn't sure where they were; she should have been paying more attention. She sat up straighter when she spied a large barn off in the distance.

"That's our destination," Lana said.

Paisley's heart thudded faster in her chest the closer they came to the barn. This was it. Lana slowed, then drove around to the back of the barn and pulled inside, stopping twenty or so feet in front of the far wall. As soon as Paisley opened the door and stepped out, she fell to her knees and sucked in a deep breath. Energy raced through her veins and she flexed her fingers where they were already starting to glow silver. She ignored Lana's hand and reached for Addison, who pulled her to her feet.

She turned and rested her head against the car to get her bearings. If she'd questioned this was some type of portal before, her doubts were squashed now. The energy inside the barn was tangible. The air around them literally shimmered. Addison pointed to the far wall, and Paisley turned just in time to see a large horse-drawn carriage walk through the wall. "Amazing."

Lana settled the horses and pointed to the bags in the trunk. Four guards picked up the bags and settled them atop the carriage. "Are you ready, Paisley?"

Paisley opened the car door, grabbed her Wonder Woman backpack—which held the book her mother gave her, the family photograph, the binder her dad gave her, and numerous other personal items she couldn't part with—and slipped it on. She paid no attention to the guards who were staring at her. "Ready, Jynx?" She pulled the carrier out of the car and nodded at Addison. "This is it, huh?"

Addison smiled. "It is. It will take some getting used to, but..." She winked. "I think you're up for the challenge."

Lana rubbed her hands together. "Ready?"

"As I will ever be."

"Good. I won't be riding in the carriage with you and Addison, but I will be riding beside you. We don't anticipate any problems, but if they arise, have no fear, our guards will take care of it."

"Your Highness." A tall, thin, soldier walked up to Lana and bowed. "We are ready when you are."

"Paisley." Lana held her hand out and wiggled her fingers.

Paisley clasped their hands and held on tight when Lana interlaced their fingers. Lana may not be her favorite person right now, but seeing her in her element helped to put her at ease a bit. She gripped the handle of the carrier, took one last look around, and nodded. She thanked the guard that held the carriage door open for her, then slid Jynx's carrier in and hoisted herself up. Lana smiled and shut the door after Addison climbed in. "Addison, what can I expect crossing the barrier?"

"Honestly, I don't know. I don't carry any magic abilities. I don't know if it's different for those who do."

She reached up and adjusted her glasses. "Lana's never said?"

"Lana doesn't have magic abilities."

"What about at my house?"

"When she crosses the barrier, for some reason, she receives limited abilities, but when we go home, they disappear."

"Oh. I didn't know." Paisley hugged the carrier to her side when the carriage was set into motion. She leaned her head back and closed her eyes.

"Paisley, wake up."

Paisley shook her head and slowly opened her

eyes. Lana sat across from her in the carriage seat. She raised up and stretched, then noticed the carriage had stopped. "Where's Addison?"

"She's waiting outside."

"Why are we stopped?"

Lana smiled and squeezed her hand. "We're here."

Paisley's head whipped around to look out the carriage window, but all she saw were trees. She raised a shaky hand to her glasses and pushed them up the bridge of her nose. This was it. At least that answered one question. She didn't feel anything when they crossed over the barrier. Jynx grabbed at her arm through the slits of the carrier, and she lifted it up and smiled at her. "I guess it's time, sweetie." After such an exhausting week, she was ready to relax. At least for a day or two. "I'm ready." Lana nodded and opened the door. Paisley accepted her hand and carefully climbed out of the carriage. Before taking in her surroundings, she grabbed Jynx's carrier and pulled it out. After several heartbeats, she turned around and her breath caught in her chest.

A moderately sized, two-story stone house sat in front of a huge lake. Soldiers were stationed around the lake at different vantage points. The house itself wasn't as big as she had expected, and for that she was thankful. Bright green vines hung down one side of the house and draped themselves out and onto the ground. At the other corner of the house a dozen rose bushes, all in different shades of red, were scattered around.

At the far end of the property, a large stable stood. Behind the house and past the forest, the Matek Mountains stood tall and proud. Dozens of peaks rose high into the clouds and even from where she stood, she could see that most of the mountaintops were covered in snow. It was, in a word, breathtaking. She didn't want to admit it, but the house and the entire area put her at ease. "It's beautiful."

The smile that lit up Lana's face almost took her breath away as well. That is, until she remembered another smile that certainly did take her breath away. Alexia's. Shaking her head to rid herself of the foolish memory of a woman she would never—and could never—have, she grasped Lana's arm and let her lead her into the house.

❧❧❧❧

Paisley rolled over and her eyes flew open, taking in the unfamiliar surroundings as a deep ache formed in her chest. Out of habit, she swiped at her eyes, but no tears were forthcoming. Considering she had cried more in the last week than in her entire life, she supposed it was a good thing that her tears had all but dried up. The only comfort was Jynx, who lay curled up beside her.

Light streamed in from the window above her bed and she could hear someone moving about downstairs. After arriving the previous day, Lana had been gracious enough not to overwhelm her with too much information. The last thing she needed was sensory overload.

After a pleasant but simple dinner, Lana had showed her to the guest room, telling her it was too soon to be sharing a bedroom, and bid her a good night. Now in the harsh light of the morning, an unexpected feeling enveloped her: excitement. Since she was here, she might as well get to know her new home.

With each step down the staircase, she clenched her hand around the railing. At the bottom of the stairs, Addison nodded at her and pointed down the hallway. When she entered the kitchen, Lana stood with her back to her, looking out the window. When Paisley reached her, Lana smiled, then handed her a cup of tea and a bowl of some type of stew. A bowl of bread already sat on the table. Paisley sat at the table and motioned for Lana to join her. After a tentative bite, she deemed it acceptable, then took a sip of tea before she spoke. "What exactly is it that you do?" Paisley blew on her spoon before taking another bite.

"Thank goodness I was the second born, because I never wanted to be queen. My passion lies elsewhere. After you eat, I will take you on a tour of the estate. I love to garden. There are four separate orchards on my land. Two different types of apples and two different types of peaches. I also grow raspberries, blackberries, blueberries, and strawberries. People come from all over to buy produce from me, but most of my product is already taken by the royal estate and quite a few regulars." Lana's eyes lit up as she described the different varieties of fruits.

That wasn't what Paisley had expected at all. "Wow. That's amazing. I would love to see everything."

"On top of that, I also help the royal historians archive our histories when I have free time. It's fascinating."

Now that was something she could get behind. She loved reading about history. "Will you take me to the library sometime?"

"Of course." Lana fidgeted.

What now? "Yes?"

"I didn't want to throw everything at you at once,

but you should know that we will be having dinner with my parents and brother tonight."

Paisley's spoon clunked into the bowl. "I just arrived. I was hoping for a couple days of rest. At the least." She adjusted her glasses and bit her lip. "I don't have a choice, do I?"

"We always have choices, but when the king requests your presence—especially his daughter's new bride—then no, you don't have a choice."

"I kind of figured that. I know we're going to the castle, but is this a formal affair or causal?"

"If you consider what you have on casual, then you will definitely need to change into something more formal."

"All right. I can do that."

"Good. Are you finished eating?"

Paisley pushed her bowl away. "Yes, and it was delicious."

"I am happy to hear that."

Paisley picked up her cup and took another sip of tea. "What happens now?"

"I guess that depends on you, but our top priority will be to find you a teacher. I have someone in mind, but we will discuss that later."

"I know your father is king, but what kind of government does Dangor have? Is it anything like what I know?"

"Similar. Dangor is the name of the country we are in. There are four countries that make up the continent, Belnor. Dangor is the largest, followed by Arbordor, Manchester, then Canon. For now, we are only going to discuss Dangor. Brinkenshire is one of the ten provinces that make up Dangor. Each province is made up of three districts. I won't get into all the provinces, but for our sake I will say that Brinkenshire's districts are Grayville, in which the royal estates are located including this house, Galena, and Lake County. Each province has a governor and each district has a mayor. Each mayor answers to the governor, who in turn answers to the king. Are you still with me?"

"Yes."

"To be honest, I am not sure you will ever have a reason to visit Manchester, Arbordor, or Canon. I have never visited them. They can be a bit hostile toward my father and his views. And truthfully, they're aggressive toward each other, but since Dangor is the largest of the four, we've never really had a problem with them."

"I see. I don't plan on being cooped up here for the rest of my life."

Lana held her hands up. "I am not saying that at all. I love to travel. Trust me. There is plenty of country to see."

Paisley stood and stretched. Jynx walked in from the living room, and Paisley scooped her up and into her arms. After one last kiss to her stomach, she put her back on the floor. "So, what can I expect from dinner with your family?" She turned toward the window and watched as the water rippled in the morning sun.

Lana stood up and stepped next to her. "They can be a bit much upon first meeting. Especially my mother. I know she means well, but sometimes she goes a bit overboard. Don't worry. I'll be there and I won't let them do anything."

"What do you mean, 'do anything'? What can they do?" She was sure they could do plenty, but she wanted to hear it from Lana's lips.

"They can do a lot. My mother tends to threaten and coerce when she is put into any new situation. And you are a new situation. They know what you mean to me, and I have already warned them."

"What do I mean to you?" Paisley kept her gaze averted, afraid of what she would see in Lana's eyes.

"Paisley, I know this isn't the most ideal situation, but you are my wife and I don't take that lightly. I know what it means to be bonded to someone. I will not disrespect this pairing. It is my destiny and I will fulfill it." She reached for and caressed Paisley's hand. "And I hope you will fulfill it with me."

There were a million thoughts and images running through Paisley's mind, but one kept taking precedence: Alexia smirking at her after the end of their meeting. It was a dream and she was so out of reach. She shook her head and had to remind herself again that even if something had happened between her and Alexia, Alexia wasn't here and Lana was. She had promised Grams that she would live and thrive, and that's exactly what she would strive to do. "I'll try."

❧ ❧ ❧ ❧

Paisley breathed in the fresh air and smiled as the cool breeze rushed through her hair. Being near or on the open water always brought a calmness to Paisley, and that's exactly where Addison found her an hour after Lana's tour of the property had been completed. Paisley leaned back on her elbows on the grass and kicked her legs out in front of her. The brightness of her surroundings was like out of fairy tale, especially the wildflowers that grew in bunches all over the estate grounds.

Addison sat down beside her. "Settling in?"

"Trying. It's all so surreal. I mean, come on, this

is so far-fetched that if I wasn't living it myself I would have whoever spoke such nonsense committed. What a ride."

"You're just getting started."

"Thank you. So…" She sat up and pulled her knees into her chest. "What can I expect tonight?"

Addison was quiet for several minutes. "The king is a man of supreme power and he isn't afraid to show it, if warranted. Don't patronize him and don't ask him a direct question. But he is a man of his word. Lana's brother is a sweetheart and will make an excellent king. Feel free to talk to him and ask questions. He and Lana have a great relationship."

"Okay. That leaves the queen."

Addison sighed and ran her hands through her hair. "Yes." She nodded. "The queen. You could probably get away with asking the king maybe one or two questions since you're new, but do not under any circumstances ask the queen one. She is ruthless. Some say she wields more power than the king. She is not easy to impress, and she holds a grudge. Every time I am in her presence I avoid looking at her altogether just to be on the safe side."

Paisley looked at her to see if she was joking, but one look at her face told her all she needed to know. "So I shouldn't try and impress her?"

"You won't, so don't even try. She is a hard woman to please. She is just a hard woman, period. Beautiful, but hard. Don't get me wrong. I don't see her ever doing anything that would jeopardize the country, but she wouldn't hesitate to take out a few to save the many. And she loves her husband and her kids fiercely."

"Thanks, Addison. After our talk, I feel loads

better about tonight." She rolled her eyes. What in the hell had she gotten herself into? She stood up and offered Addison her hand, who readily took it. "I best be getting back."

"You'll be fine. Don't worry so much."

Paisley cut her eyes at her, and Addison laughed and patted her shoulder. "I'll try and remember that."

The walk back to the house was quiet and short. Lana was waiting for her when she got back, and Addison took up position outside the front door. "What should I wear?"

"One of those dresses with the hood will be appropriate. I like the black and white one." She shrugged and bit her lip.

Paisley leaned forward and placed a quick kiss on Lana's cheek, and smiled when Lana flushed. She would, for the moment, at least try to be cordial to Lana. "How long before we have to leave?"

Lana coughed. "You should probably be getting ready. It takes around an hour in the carriage."

"What are you going to wear?"

"The first outfit you saw me in."

Paisley winked. "Good choice." Once in her bedroom, she opened the trunk that housed her more formal dresses and pulled out the one Lana was talking about. It was warm today, but the fabric was a thinner material and she didn't anticipate wearing it would be uncomfortable. After slipping the dress on, she adjusted the sleeves and walked to the mirror that sat in the corner of the room. She smoothed her hands down the white bodice and inhaled as she took all of it in. The cut was perfect and she felt amazing.

Deciding to put her hair up, she picked up a barrette from the vanity that sat next to the mirror, gathered her hair up, and clipped it in place. Heels wouldn't do, so she grabbed a pair of flats from inside the trunk and slipped them on. After touching up her makeup she petted Jynx, who lay on the bed, and headed out the bedroom door. Lana was waiting in the living room for her and stood up when she walked in.

Lana smiled. "You look amazing."

"Thank you. So do you. Red is a good color for you." She ignored the blush racing up Lana's neck and cheeks. "So, are we ready?"

Lana bowed. "After you, my Lady."

Paisley winked at Addison, who held the door open for her. "Wish me luck." Addison grinned and winked back. Outside a carriage was waiting for them. She thanked the soldier who held the door open for her, and relaxed back into the seat when Lana climbed in next to her. Lana knocked on the carriage door twice to set it into motion.

"You have nothing to worry about, Paisley. My family only wants the best for me." She picked up Paisley's hand and placed a kiss in her palm. "And you are what's best for me."

Paisley didn't pull her hand back when Lana clasped it with hers and laid it in her lap. She would try, for the sake of this situation, but she still couldn't help the doubt that surfaced every time she was alone with Lana. Her nerves pulsated, but there was an underlying current that left her feeling off-balance. But before she could figure out what that meant, first she had to get through tonight.

⁂

Even though neither one spoke, the ride to the

royal estate was pleasant and comfortable. Lana had been right; it took under an hour for the carriage to stop in front of the castle. And what a castle it was. As soon as her feet were on solid ground, Paisley assessed the structure in front of her. At least ten stories of brick rose high into the sky. Surprisingly, there wasn't any type of fence surrounding the castle, but she was sure there were plenty of guards stationed around it. Before she could take in the grounds, Lana touched her arm and pointed to the open door in front of them. Paisley took her arm and ascended the two steps, nodded at the butler who held the door open, and walked inside. She wasn't sure what she had expected, but the reality wasn't at all what she could have imagined. They entered a large room. A large plain room. In front of them were four separate doors, spaced fifteen feet apart.

Lana pointed to the farthest door. "Each door leads to a different part of the castle. We'll go through the one on the far left. It leads to our private residence. We won't worry about the other ones right now." She squeezed Paisley's hand, nodded at the guard by the door, and smiled when he held it open for them.

"Have a pleasant evening, your Highness."

"You do the same."

As soon as the door shut behind them, they walked farther into the castle, then rounded the corner. Paisley breathed a sigh of relief. The room they stopped in was large, but unlike the previous room, this one looked lived in. A large fireplace was positioned on the far wall and two large couches sat in front of it. Chairs were scattered throughout the room along with several plush rugs. Dozens of paintings hung on the walls, and one wall was made up entirely of shelves that were packed with books. The room, unlike the castle, put her completely at ease. She adjusted her glasses and took several deep breaths. Now was not the time to let her guard down. She didn't know these people, and time would tell if she would ever be able to trust them.

"This way." After a short walk down yet another hallway that was lined with more pictures, they entered a room similar to the one they just left behind. The only difference between this room and the last were the three people seated on the couches.

The knots in Paisley's stomach twisted and she held back a grimace when an older gentleman, dressed in black pants and a white long-sleeved tunic and black vest, stood up. The gray at his temples set off his good looks. Paisley bit her lip. Lana had his eyes.

"Lana, my dear." He walked up to her with arms wide open and she fell into them and kissed him on the cheek.

"Father, I want you to meet someone." She motioned Paisley over and grabbed her hand. "Paisley, this is my father, King Perry. Dad, this is my wife, Paisley."

Paisley wished Lana would have told her what the protocol was in these situations, but decided to go with the standard greeting. She offered him her hand and he laughed, pushed her hand aside, and pulled her into a hug. "Paisley, it is so nice to meet you."

His smile was discerning, but she would give him the benefit of the doubt. "You as well, Sir."

"Sir?" a feminine voice sneered. Paisley looked past him when an elegant woman stood up from the couch and approached them. Her blue and gold sleeveless dress hugged her body and fit her slim frame to perfection. Lana's eyes were the same as her father's, but the rest of her features came from her mom. They both had the same black hair and chiseled jawline. She remembered what Addison had said and kept her mouth shut, waiting for the queen to speak again. "Sir will never do, young lady. He is a king and as such you will address him that way. Your Highness, my King, or your Majesty will do. You may address me as my Queen."

Paisley bit her jaw to keep her temper in check. She may have been a nobody to these people, but she was Lana's wife. With the force of a hurricane it became quite apparent that this night and her future would be anything but pleasant if the woman standing in front of her had anything to say about it. She would have to make sure that she didn't give her that kind of power. "Of course, my Queen." She smiled and took in the last occupant in the room. He was taller than Lana, but there would be no denying that they were siblings.

"Well," he said. "I don't stand on such formality. You may call me J.J."

"J.J.?"

"John Michael Roberts the second. I figured it was the same as John Jr."

"J.J. it is, then." He laughed and led Paisley to one of the couches, motioning for her to join him. The king and queen sat down on the couch opposite them, and Lana sat down to her right and took her hand.

"So, Paisley," J.J. said. "How are you settling in?"

"It's been an adjustment, and to be fair it's only been one day. Overwhelming doesn't quite cover what I've been feeling, but with time I'll adjust and make the most of my situation."

"Oh, yes," he said and leaned closer to her. "I do have to say, being married to my sister is quite the situation. She can be a handful. Make sure you have plenty of maple syrup and pecans on hand. Trust me." He winked. "She is a sucker for those two, especially if the pecans are dipped in the syrup. You'll have her eating out of your hand in no time."

"I'll remember that." They both laughed before a cough opposite them shut them both up.

The king sipped from the glass in his hand. "We will do our best to help you adjust. Lana will make sure you have everything you need. Don't hesitate to ask her for anything. If it is within our power, we will get it for you."

"I will. Thank you." She allowed her body to slip closer to Lana's and didn't miss the glare that the queen threw her way. Paisley tensed when she opened her mouth to speak, but at that moment a servant walked in and informed them that dinner was ready. The king stood up and instructed everyone to follow him into the dining room.

The dining room must have only been for family, because the table only seated six. The queen sat on one end, the king the other, and Lana and J.J. sat opposite each other in the middle of the table. Paisley sat down beside Lana and closer to the king, so she wouldn't have to feel the queen's gaze on her at all times. To her surprise, there were five different courses that were all delicious, and no one spoke during the meal. Once the last plates had been cleared, the queen stood up and walked around the table to sit beside her husband.

"Paisley," the queen said. "What did your parents think of your decision?"

"What decision would that be?"

She cocked her head. "The decision to come here, of course?"

Paisley held her tongue for a few seconds, to get her thoughts in order. In the end, she decided to go with the truth. "It wasn't my decision."

"Really? You didn't have a choice? I find that hard to believe."

"No. I didn't have a choice. Lana never asked me before she put the cuff on my wrist, and I didn't have a choice but to come with her. Lana and my family decided that for me." She picked up her glass and took a sip of the apple cider she had requested.

"Lana, is that true?" J.J. asked. Disbelief fluttered across his features.

Lana nodded and sighed beside her. "Yes. Things happened so fast that I had to act fast. I couldn't risk anything happening to Paisley before I had a chance to put the cuff on her."

"I see," the queen said, then looked directly at Paisley. "You made it sound like you didn't have any say in it."

"I didn't. Think what you will, but the last week has been the worst of my life, and the people *in* my life have taken the choices about my future out of my hands for now. I can assure you that will not always be the case."

The queen flicked her hand in the air and the gold bracelets on her wrist jingled. "Yes, Lana said you had powers. Tell me, what is the extent of your powers?"

Before she could answer, Lana spoke up. "Mother, that's one of the questions I had for you tonight. I was going to ask you about teachers for Paisley. Her powers are new to her and she will need someone to teach her. If you could help me, we can pick one out for her."

"We?" the queen questioned.

Lana nodded. "Yes. You and me." The queen

glanced at Paisley as she arched her eyebrow and took another sip of her drink.

"See? All decisions have been taken out of my hands."

Lana jerked toward her. "No, Paisley. That's not what I meant. She knows people."

"I understand that, Lana, but the least you could have done was invite me into the discussion. You may have put this cuff on my wrist, but you are not my keeper and I will not be kept. I have lived a long life so far without your counsel, and I am confident I can live another thirty-two years without it." Paisley downed the rest of her cider and ignored the quiet in the rest of the room.

"You're right, Paisley. I'm sorry." Paisley nodded and looked everywhere but at the occupants of the room.

"Beatrice Markers would be your best bet for a teacher. She's competent and capable. She is an accomplished witch and will be able to guide you to sort your powers out," the queen said with exaggerated disinterest.

Paisley nodded and turned to Lana. "I'm sure you know where she can be located?"

"Of course."

The king clapped his hands together and five servants walked in carrying small plates, with what looked to be pieces of cake on them. "Now that that's finished, let's enjoy dessert."

Paisley accepted the plate and took a small bite, but could feel the queen's gaze on her. Reluctantly she chanced a glance up and met her eyes. The nerves just below the surface vibrated, but she kept them in check and never broke the queen's gaze. When the queen quirked her lips and took a bite of her cake, Paisley looked away and took another taste of hers. Even the burst of raspberry covered in chocolate couldn't stop the churning in her stomach. J.J. and the king weren't so bad, but the moment she laid eyes on the queen, she knew they would never get along. Her dad told her to trust her gut, and right now it was telling her to steer clear of the queen. She would have to watch her back and do whatever possible to make sure they didn't become enemies.

❦❦❦❦

The next morning dawned bright and early, and despite their dinner the previous night, Paisley woke up refreshed and ready to face the day. Each new day was a new beginning, and she would do her best to make sure she never forgot that. Out in the hall, she nodded at Addison and Jynx, and followed them both downstairs and into the kitchen. Lana sat at the table and stood when they entered.

"Good morning."

Paisley sat down beside her. "Good morning." She filled her plate with some fruit salad, a piece of raisin bread smothered in butter and honey, and a few spoonfuls of fresh yogurt. She accepted the glass of apple juice Lana handed her. Even after two days, her concerns about the food she would be eating was somewhat put at ease. So far, so good. "Do you make the apple juice from your apples?"

Lana lit up. "We do. Apple juice, apple cider, and a nice apple wine. We also make a really nice peach wine."

"I would love to try them."

"Of course. I will bring up a bottle of last year's apple wine from the cellar for after dinner."

Paisley kept quiet as she finished the rest of her breakfast, then reached for another piece of raisin bread. "I would like to meet my dad's family. Do you think you can find out where they live?"

"I would be honored to help you." She sighed. "But first, I think it would be prudent to start with your teaching. After breakfast, I will accompany you to meet Beatrice. When you return home for dinner tonight, we can discuss your family."

Another choice taken out of her hands. She finished off the bread, drank the rest of her juice, and stood. "I'm going to get dressed, then we can go." Once inside the sanctuary of her room, she threw herself down on the bed. So much for relaxing today. She groaned and stood up. Not sure what to expect from the meeting, she pulled on a pair of well-worn jeans and a plain white T-shirt. Next were her sneakers, then she pulled her hair back into a ponytail and slipped a ball cap on.

To hell with what anyone thought of her. If she was going to do this, she was going to do it in comfort. Lana checked her out, but didn't question her outfit when she walked back into the kitchen. Her eyes scanned the room and stopped when the spied a pile of bags stacked in the corner of the room.

Lana followed her gaze. "I took the opportunity to stock up on a few more bags of Jynx's favorite food. I won't be able to go back every month, but I will try to go back to your world in the future. I bought the biggest bags they had and I will have the guards secure them in the cellar."

Stacked in the corner of the room were five

eighteen-pound bags of Meow Mix. A shudder passed through her at the thoughtfulness of Lana when it came to Jynx. She sniffled and filled up Jynx's bowl. If not a year, the bags would last her quite a while. "Thank you. That means more to me than you will ever know."

"I also took the liberty of picking up some treats and a few other things I thought she might like or need. Flea medicine, toys, stuff like that."

"When?"

"I bought everything before we left your world, and I had somebody go back to the barn, load everything, and bring it back." She shrugged and finished her tea. "It's the least I could do."

Paisley walked up to her and kissed her on the cheek. "It was thoughtful and not something I will soon forget." She was touched beyond belief and figured she could concede the choice of a teacher taken out of her hands. "I'm ready."

"Good." Lana pointed to Addison. "Addison, you will be staying with Paisley while she is with Beatrice." At Paisley's raised eyebrow, Lana explained. "It's not that I don't trust her, but it's just that I don't trust her. She is an accomplished teacher, and that's what you need, but it is not going to hurt to have Addison accompany you."

"I'm not arguing," Paisley said, filling two water bottles and slipping them into her backpack along with a few pieces of the raisin bread, two apples, and an assortment of beef jerky. "I like Addison." She slung her backpack on. "The more the merrier."

She slipped her arm through Addison's and allowed her to steer them out the back door and into the carriage. Lana took up the seat across from them. "So," Paisley asked once they were on their way. "What can I expect from Beatrice?"

Lana smirked. "She knows her stuff and you will be able to trust her teaching. Now trusting her as a human being is another matter. Don't be deceived. Everyone, or at least a part of everyone, is only out for themselves. But I wouldn't be sending you to her if I didn't feel confident that she's the right choice for you. Listen to her. She knows what she's talking about."

Paisley looked out the window and watched the trees pass by. After twenty minutes, they pulled onto a long dirt road. Paisley's breath hitched in her chest when she caught her first glimpse of the house. It was small, but it was well kept, covered in vines and pink and purple flowers. A huge garden sat to the right of the house and a small fenced-in area sat to the left.

Behind the house was an open meadow. It looked like a painting out of a Thomas Kinkade calendar. She accepted Addison's hand when they climbed out of the carriage and followed Lana up to the door. Before she could knock, the door was opened by an old woman. Even from where she stood, she could trace the wrinkles on her face. To anyone else the smile would have been considered inviting, but Paisley could see the fakeness of it.

"Beatrice," Lana said as she guided Paisley closer, "this is Paisley and—"

Beatrice cut her off and grabbed Paisley's wrist, drawing her near. Paisley fought the urge to recoil and jerk her hand back, and was rewarded with a genuine smile. Beatrice dismissed Lana without taking her eyes off Paisley.

Lana touched Paisley arm. "I will send the carriage back for you in a few hours."

"All right." Paisley turned back to the woman

and didn't feel a bit of dread when the carriage turned and left. "So. What happens now?"

Beatrice let go of her hand, walked to the corner of the house, beckoned them to her, picked up a hoe, and thrust it into Paisley's hand. "Now, I am going back in the house and you are going to weed the garden."

"What? You can't be serious." Paisley eyed the hoe, then the garden. It was so overgrown she wasn't sure where to even start.

"I am quite serious, and I would advise you not to question me again."

Paisley stepped back when a spark of red flashed in the woman's eyes. She couldn't be sure if it was a real threat, but she wasn't going to take her chances, at least not yet. "Fine." Beatrice nodded and walked back into the house, shutting the door behind her. Paisley walked toward the garden. "Addison, the least you can do is keep me company."

"Of course."

Paisley didn't have to look to see the smile in Addison's eyes. "I guess my first lesson is how to weed the garden?"

"It would seem so."

"Guess I should get started then?"

"I guess you should."

"No chance you will help me?"

"Nope. It is my duty to protect your life from certain death." She pointed to the weeds. "This is not certain death."

"I figured you would say something like that." Paisley indicated a stump Addison could sit on and handed off her Wonder Woman backpack. The garden wasn't as big as she first suspected, but it looked past its prime. She scratched her neck, pulled the bill down on her cap, and got started.

It wasn't the first lesson she had expected, but the physical labor would at least help to keep her in shape. If she was honest with herself, she was glad to have a reprieve from an actual magic lesson. She knew the time would come, but for now she was happy being normal. Even if normal meant weeding a garden in less than ideal conditions.

⚘ ⚘ ⚘ ⚘

The next day and the day after went the same as the first. She spent all morning weeding the garden, then went home, took a bath, and fell into bed, waking only when Lana informed her dinner was ready. After she ate, she went back to bed and didn't wake until the next morning. They still hadn't had a chance to discuss finding her dad's family. Today had started out no differently than the others.

"You know," Addison said after taking a bit of her apple. "You're over halfway done. Only a few more days left." She shrugged and threw the core into the nearby forest. "No telling what she will have you do next."

Paisley took a drink of water. "I know, right? To be honest, it hasn't been all that bad, and I'm not sure I'm looking forward to what happens next. It's strange in this world, but at the same time, it doesn't seem so foreign. If that makes sense."

"It does." The next words of her mouth were cut off and Paisley turned toward her when something caught Addison's eye. Off in the distance, standing atop a hill, she could make out the silhouette of a woman. She narrowed her eyes, but couldn't make out any specific details. She couldn't shake the feeling that she knew her or at least had seen her before. As they watched, the woman turned and walked back down the opposite side of the hill.

"I see her once or twice a month. Nothing to be afraid of, I assure you." Paisley and Addison both jumped when Beatrice started to talk. Paisley grabbed her chest. Where had she come from? *Good grief.* They would both have to start paying more attention. "Come along you two. I made enough soup for everyone."

Paisley eyed Addison, who just shrugged and followed along behind the woman. Paisley breathed a sigh of relief when they walked inside and the interior was just as cozy as the outside of the house. The soup smelled amazing. It was the first time either one of them had been invited in.

"Sit down." She indicated the small table that sat adjacent the front window. She set three bowls of soup on the table along with a loaf of crusty bread, and poured them each a glass of water. "Eat up. We'll talk after you both finish your lunch."

Even though the soup turned out to be bland and she had no idea what was in it, she ate it anyway. From the look on Beatrice's face, she wouldn't have dared not to eat it. She smiled, picked up her bowl, and drank the rest of the broth. Beatrice nodded at her and offered her more, but Paisley waved her off. Addison grimaced and finished her soup off as well.

Beatrice cleared the table, then retook her seat. Paisley shrunk back in her chair at the glare Beatrice threw her way. Beatrice picked up an empty coffee cup and set it on the edge of the table. "Paisley, I want you to float the cup in the air a few inches."

Paisley adjusted her glasses and shook her fingers

out. It didn't look like a trick coffee cup, but one couldn't be sure. She leaned across the table, picked the cup up, and turned it over in her hands. When she was satisfied, even though she didn't know what she was doing, she set the cup back down and closed her eyes. How hard could it be? She could wing it.

It was just a matter of projecting the confidence she knew was buried deep within her. She opened her eyes, turned her hand palm up, and raised it a few inches in the air. The cup rocked back and forth on the table, and Paisley bit her lip when it settled back down. She shook her fingers out, then raised her hand again and jerked her fingers up. She jumped in her chair when the cup flew up and embedded in the ceiling. Addison laughed beside her, but she didn't dare look at Beatrice. She could feel the heat radiating from her.

Beatrice waved her hand and the cup appeared back on the table. The ceiling had repaired itself. Without looking away from Paisley, she spoke. "Addison, come around the table and pick the cup up."

Paisley narrowed her eyes as Addison reached for the cup, but couldn't pick it up. She frowned, grabbed the cup, and tried again. Her face was turning red and sweat had already beaded on her forehead. Paisley touched her hand. "Stop." She turned and looked at Beatrice. "I don't understand."

Beatrice took a sip of her tea before she answered. "The cup is enchanted."

"But I picked it up."

"Indeed, you did." She took another sip of her tea.

Paisley stood and started pacing, then marched across the room and reached for the cup, once again picking it up. Without rhyme or reason, she reared her arm back and threw it at the wall, but before it collided with the wall it stopped abruptly. Addison put herself between Paisley and Beatrice.

Beatrice held up her hand. "I didn't stop the cup."

Paisley spun around. "How?"

"If you had wanted the cup to shatter, it would have. Your intent behind it wasn't pure. If your intention was for it to hit the wall, nothing would have stopped it." She stood up, pushed her chair in, and fixed another cup of tea. "And honestly, I don't even believe you have to use your hands for most of your magic. Some, of course, requires a vessel through which to flow. But other magic only has to be thought of to execute it." She quirked her eyebrow, blew on her tea, then took a sip.

Paisley stared at her hands. "So…"

"That's enough for now," Beatrice said. "You need to get back to weeding."

"Just like that."

She shrugged. "You've been doing a good job. Don't tell me you've already forgotten how to."

"What about that woman?" Addison asked.

Beatrice waved off her concerns. "Don't worry about her. She is not my enemy and she will not bring any harm your way."

"Stupid cloak and dagger shit," Paisley mumbled. She marched out the front door, picked up the hoe, and headed to the garden. Something compelled her to look back and her eyes latched on to the figure in the distance. She couldn't shake the feeling that she knew her from somewhere. But how could that be, when she didn't know anybody here? She knew for a fact it wasn't Lana. The shape of the woman was all wrong. Addison walked up beside her and eyed the woman as well.

"Nothing we can do about her now. Best get back to weeding."

"Addison is right, Paisley. Don't fret on the woman."

Paisley turned and faced Beatrice. "I'm taking tomorrow off." She ran a hand through her hair. "I am tired. The day after tomorrow I'll be raring to go." She didn't wait for Beatrice's approval. She didn't need it because she was taking tomorrow off whether the woman agreed to it or not.

"Paisley, take your day of rest. But be ready to finish the job when you get back."

Paisley smiled sweetly at her. "Of course."

Addison sat down on her stump, dug some jerky out of Paisley's bag, and took a bite. After she swallowed, she spoke. "You should have Lana take you to the marketplace tomorrow. You'll like it, and who knows? You might get lucky and see your mystery woman again."

Paisley doubted it, but it couldn't hurt. "I will ask her. Thanks." Walking to the far corner of the garden, she lifted her hoe and plunged it into the earth. She couldn't wait to go home and take a bath.

⚜ ⚜ ⚜ ⚜

Paisley slipped her sneakers on and pulled her hair back in a tie before putting her ball cap on and walking into the kitchen where Lana looked her up and down, then handed her a cup of tea. Paisley adjusted her glasses. "What?"

Lana shook her head, but she had a smile playing on her lips. "You do realize, sooner rather than later, you will need to start wearing clothing that is more relevant to this world, right?"

"I know, but for now, my own clothes are keeping me grounded."

"I understand."

Paisley finished her tea, fed Jynx, then rocked back on her heels. "So?"

Lana laughed. "Bit excited?"

"Of course. I get to leave this house and it isn't to go to Beatrice. I can't wait to see everything." To see and be seen by total strangers, especially these people who unnerved her, was a thrilling thought, but she was looking forward to just getting out and about. It was just what she needed. "So?"

"Let's go." Lana held the door open for her and they both climbed into the carriage, followed quickly by Addison. The second day she was here, Paisley had informed Lana that if she was going to have a personal guard, the only person she would fully accept was Addison. In the end, Lana had given in to her demands, although a bit reluctantly.

"How long will it take to get there?"

"About fifteen minutes," Addison answered. "It's a bit like the festival we went to. I think you're going to like it."

"I am sure I will." She turned to Lana. She didn't want to ask, but Lana said anything she needed all she had to do was ask for it. She wasn't used to relying on someone else to take care of or pay for something she wanted. "What if I find something I want?"

Lana dug in her bag, pulled out a small pouch, and handed it to Paisley. "That should be plenty for you, but if you need more, all you have to do is let me know."

Paisley accepted the pouch and slipped it into

her bag. A few days ago, Lana had explained the value of each of the coins of their currency. It wasn't a hard system, and after a couple of hours she had their value down. Her hand instinctively grabbed the door when the carriage came to a stop. Lana stepped out first and offered Paisley her hand, who grasped it and allowed Lana to help her down. She was still waiting for the fireworks every time she and Lana touched, but so far they weren't anywhere to be found.

"Turn around, Paisley."

Paisley stood still while she closed her eyes and took in the sounds surrounding her. People laughed, shouted, and in the distance, she could hear a baby crying. She inhaled as a mixture of sweet and spicy wafted her way. At a tap on her arm, she turned around and opened her eyes. The marketplace stretched as far as she could see. Stalls lined both sides of a stone pathway five feet wide, allowing plenty of foot traffic to flow easily. Guards were stationed throughout the market, and people were everywhere.

In the distance, the stalls leveled off to make way for a large fountain and what looked to be a seating area. The vibrant fabric colors that draped the stalls put a smile on her face. It was amazing. Her face lit up when Lana pointed out a sign off to their left. Her eyes scanned the map of the marketplace: food, fabric, toys, household goods, etc. She bounced on her feet and ignored the looks strangers were throwing her way. "I'm ready."

Lana smiled and offered her hand. Paisley hesitated, but figured that because she looked so different, if the people were to see her with Lana they would understand faster who she was. After all, she was royalty now. Lana was beautiful, nice, and a fantastic catch; she just wasn't the catch Paisley wanted.

An hour and a few pastries later, she and Addison made their way to the center of the square. Lana said she had a bit of business to take care of and left them to their wanderings. The fountain was ten feet wide and the water shot at least ten feet in the air. Paisley walked around it a few times, but couldn't quite figure out how the fountain worked. She raised her head and looked through the water, until a figure in the distance drew her attention. She blinked a few times, then walked around the fountain, but the woman was gone. *No, it couldn't be.*

Addison walked up beside her. "What is it?"

"I…" Paisley ran her hands through her hair. "I thought I recognized someone." She shook her head. "It doesn't make sense. Probably my eyes playing tricks on me." It couldn't be her. It wasn't possible. But she would recognize that white hair anywhere. Alexia couldn't be here. She walked a few feet, stopped, looked around, then turned, only to come face-to-face with the woman who had occupied her thoughts since their first meeting. "Oh…" She grabbed her chest and took a step back. "You. How?" The look on Alexia's face froze her on the spot.

"You." Alexia's face was hard.

How was Alexia standing in front of her? She cursed her heart when it sped up. "What? How can you be here? I don't understand."

"Me? How are you here?" She rolled her eyes, then grabbed Paisley's wrist. She dropped it like it had burned her when she saw her cuff. Paisley sucked in a breath and tried to stop her racing heart, but one touch from Alexia sent her nerves into overdrive. *Oh, mercy.* "You came here that Monday. Unbelievable. Is that what you and your family had planned all along?" She shook her head and stared off into the distance. A mixture of hurt, sadness, and disbelief marred her beautiful face.

What was happening here? All she wanted to do was put that smile back on her face. Alexia had it all wrong. "No. I left on Sunday. A few hours after meeting you." Paisley had to get her to see reason. "I didn't want to come, I wanted to wait until after our meeting on Monday, but I didn't have a choice. Is that what you're so upset about? I wanted to wait." She reached for her arm but dropped her hand back by her side at the last second.

Alexia laughed. "You think I'm upset because you missed our meeting?"

"What else could you be upset about? We'd only just meet."

Alexia shook her head, then looked up and studied Paisley's face. "You don't know, do you?"

"Know what?" By this time, people had started to look their way. Paisley couldn't care less, but this was a private conversation and she didn't care for them to be privy to it. Without even asking, Addison walked toward the crowd and told them to back up.

"I—"

"Mommy." Paisley's eyes shot to the ground, where two little girls stood behind Alexia. How had she not noticed them before? Their arms were tightly wound around the older woman's legs. They couldn't be any older than three or four years old. She knelt on the ground so she was eye level with them. They shrunk behind Alexia's legs.

"Hi." Paisley waved at them. The last thing she wanted to do was spook them. They were so cute.

Alexia crouched down and pulled both girls around her. "We'll leave in a minute." They both nodded.

"Oh my goodness, Alexia. They are adorable. They're yours?" She folded her hands in front of her so she wouldn't reach out and touch them. Black curls cascaded down to their shoulders. The smallest one had on a yellow dress, and the other wore a pair of brown pants and a blue top.

"Yes," Alexia bit out. "They're mine, and because of your mother and grandmother, I almost lost them forever."

Wait. What? She shook her head. No, that couldn't be right, but deep in her gut she knew it was. "I don't understand." The thought of these little ones without their mother was unimaginable.

"When you didn't show up, your mother and grandmother went to the Council and told them that I must have done something to you because they had dropped you off at my loft, then left. When you didn't return home, they became suspicious. The Council acted swiftly and attacked me. I almost didn't make it back here to my girls." She squeezed them closer to her body.

"No. They…wouldn't do that. No…" Why would they do that? She knew they hated Alexia, but to have the Council go after her, when they knew where she was? It didn't make any sense, but she couldn't discern any deception in Alexia's words. On the other hand, with the way they were behaving about Alexia…it would make sense. "They knew where I was." Her eyes locked with Alexia's. "They hate you, but I didn't think them capable of this." She reached out and touched Alexia's hand, and felt content for the first time since arriving in Dangor. With unshakable certainty, she knew this was what she wanted. Who she wanted. They had a chance now, however slight, and she wouldn't fight it. She just had to find a way for Alexia to want the same things. After only meeting her twice, she knew she didn't want to live without her.

After a moment, Alexia seemed to make up her mind. She pointed to the smallest child. "This is Amelia, and this is Zoey."

Paisley beamed at them. "It's nice to meet you both." She looked up to Alexia. "This probably isn't the best time, but how can you be here? I didn't think I would ever see you again. I'd hoped, but..." She shrugged. "Hope isn't something that I can believe in."

"You hoped?" She cocked her head, then let a small smile grace her lips. "I had hoped to, but I also didn't think it would be possible. When you didn't show up, I figured your mother and grandmother had talked you out of it."

"No." She caressed Alexia's hand, amazed at how soft the skin was. She wondered if the rest of her body was just as soft. She grinned and caught Alexia arching an eyebrow in question.

"Paisley." They both jerked their heads around, and Alexia held tightly to her girls when footsteps pounded their way.

Paisley stood up and stepped in front of Alexia. "Lana?" A handful of guards had accompanied her.

Lana grabbed her arm and tried to move her away, but Paisley threw her hand off and eyed the guards that kept inching closer to them. Out of the corner of her eye, she watched Alexia stand up. "Care to explain what you're doing?"

Lana pointed to Alexia. "She's evil. Get away from her and I will take care of this."

Alexia made to move around Paisley, but Paisley held her arm out to stop her, never taking her eyes off Lana. "I don't know what this is about, but you will not lay one finger on her or her girls. I won't stand for it."

"You will move away from her now. She is dangerous." Lana glared at her, and for a split second, Paisley doubted her actions, but one look at the little ones behind her solidified her resolve.

Oh, Paisley knew Alexia was dangerous, just not the danger Lana was talking about. "If she's so dangerous, why is she allowed in the marketplace to begin with?" She patted a curly head when small arms wrapped around her leg and love flooded her body at the girl's act of trust.

Lana glared at her. "Get away from her. She is a wielder of dark magic. Paisley, you have no idea what she is capable of. Trust me. I am only looking out for your best interests." Lana stopped short when Paisley's loyal soldier arrived on the scene. "Addison," Lana warned. "Don't."

Paisley raised her hand and tightened her fingers around the pendants hanging from her necklace. "We both agreed that Addison was *my* guard. So, she is looking out for my best interests, not yours, Lana. Now, I'll leave with you, but Alexia and her daughters will be allowed to leave safely. Unharmed. If it looks like that won't be the case, I will wipe out as many people as necessary in order for them to leave safely. Lana, I like you, but don't test me. The last woman that did… Well, you know what happened to her. Don't you?"

Lana groaned and motioned for the guards to back off. "You'll come home with me?"

"Yes. I do believe we have quite a bit to talk about. Namely why you think you can dictate who I can and can't talk to." The crowd around them backed away when the guards shooed them off. Paisley could see fear in some of their eyes, respect in others, but sadly the majority looked at her like she was a disgrace. She addressed the crowd. "If any of you feel the need to harass the three ladies behind me, don't. My powers are unpredictable at the best of times. So, it would be in your best interests not to test me. But, feel free to try. Just don't be surprised by the outcome." She let the words linger in the air and turned toward Alexia. "Go."

"Paisley." Alexia spoke low enough that only Paisley could hear. "You shouldn't have done that. Do you realize how many enemies you've made?" She shook her head. "Silly girl."

"Maybe, but…maybe. Go." As Alexia and her daughters walked off, the crowd parted for them to walk through. Paisley kept her hand around the pendants, ready at any second to rip them from her neck and unleash whatever power necessary to ensure their safety. When she lost sight of them, she turned back to Lana, who was fuming.

Lana stalked up to her. "What were you thinking?"

"Well, Lana." A voice from behind them spoke. A petite woman with long red hair moved to stand beside Lana. "Never a dull moment. I am so glad I picked today to visit the marketplace." She held her hand out to Paisley. "I'm Clara, best friend extraordinaire to Lana here."

Paisley accepted her hand. "I'm sure it's a pleasure."

Clara laughed. "Oh, Lana. You're going to have your hands full with this one."

"Clara, now isn't the time."

"Really? I think it is."

Paisley looked between them. "What I would like to know is, as I asked before, if Alexia is such a bad, evil person, why is she allowed to be around people at all?" She wiped her brow. The temperature had been steadily rising all morning. When Addison handed her a small, wrapped pastry, she readily accepted it and took a generous bite. *Apple. Yum.*

Clara huffed. "I'll let Lana explain it, because I don't agree with it."

"Clara, we all know your feelings on the matter. Look, Paisley, we have plenty of protection around here, but sometimes the threat is more than we can handle, so on the off chance that we need her, we call on her. For her help, she isn't banished or killed. It works out for everyone," Lana said, as if that explained everything.

Paisley swallowed the lump that suddenly formed in her throat. "What happens if she doesn't help you? Will she just be banished?"

Lana scratched her cheek. "Well, no. She would be killed."

Paisley had a bad feeling about this. "What about her kids?" She looked between Lana and Clara. Clara averted her eyes.

"They would also be killed. Look, Paisley, you're not from here. We can't allow the likes of her to run free. You're royalty now, and as royalty we have to think of all the people, not just one person."

Alexia didn't have a choice, and now she couldn't even go back to their world. Her family had made sure of that. She handed her unfinished pastry to Addison. "I see." Any respect she had for Lana just flew out the window, and any feelings she might have nurtured for her were vanquished. "You're just a bunch of hypocrites. Her magic is evil and vile until you have use of it. Nice. Some example you're setting for everyone. Am I going to be allowed to leave safely, or do I have to be on alert going home?"

Lana reached for her hand but Paisley took a step back. "No one will harm you. If they do, they will never live to see another day."

"I guess that's something." She turned to Addison. "Walking, how long will it take us to get home?"

"If we leave now, an hour. Plenty of daylight left."

"Good. Lana, we're leaving and I don't want any guards following us. I won't be held responsible for my actions if they are."

"Of course."

"Addison, let's go." It wasn't until they were free of the marketplace that Paisley spoke again. "Do you know where Alexia lives?"

Addison didn't miss a step. "I do."

"I wish to visit her tomorrow after my lesson."

"All right." Addison touched her arm. "She's the woman we saw on the hilltop, isn't she?"

Paisley swallowed. "I believe she is."

"I've never had a problem with her. I have your back; you don't have to worry about that." She bit her lip. "She means a lot to you, doesn't she?"

Paisley cut her eyes to her, but her steps didn't falter. "I can't explain it. I only met her once, back in my world, but I can't get her out of my head. Do you know how she could travel between worlds?"

"No. I don't question those things. And for the record, when you can't get someone out of your head, that's the best kind of distraction."

"Oh, I don't know. I think I've made a mess of things with Lana."

"I wouldn't count on it. She likes you. She's smart, but she will probably chalk this up to you being new here. Since you defended Alexia, the guards will be on alert for her presence anywhere you go. Just a heads-up."

When Paisley stopped walking, so did Addison. "Do you think they will try and harm them?"

"Maybe." She sighed. "I...they won't stand for what you have done today. Especially the queen. You've made more enemies than you could possibly realize, but you have also made plenty of allies. Not everyone feels the same way about the magic Alexia practices."

"Okay." They continued walking as Paisley contemplated her actions. If given the choice again, she would do it all the same way. The only problem was that not only was Alexia invading her thoughts, now two little girls also fought their way in. She couldn't explain it, but she wasn't going to fight those feelings either. No matter what she had to do to ensure their safety, she would.

Alexia might be a powerful witch, but she also clearly had to rein in her powers because of the rules they had in place for her. Paisley also knew that Alexia would do whatever was necessary to protect her kids, even sacrificing her life in the process. Paisley would make sure Alexia wasn't put in that position because she didn't have any such rules to follow. Maybe it was time to heed her father's words. As long as she drew breath, Alexia would always have someone on her side.

❧❧❧❧

Lana confronted Paisley in the living room when she arrived an hour later. She held a hand up to stop

Paisley from speaking. "Let me talk first. I don't know how you and Alexia know each other or what you were to each other in your world, but this isn't your world. Your place isn't with her or to defend her. Your place is here with me. You have responsibilities now. You are my wife and a royal. You cannot behave like that! What were you thinking? No, that's right. You weren't thinking. Were you?"

Paisley held her tongue until Lana seemed to run out of gas. "Are you done?" She had some nerve speaking to her in that manner.

Lana glared at her. "For now."

Paisley settled on the couch and picked up Jynx. "Will you let me talk and not interrupt me?"

"I'll try." Lana sat in the chair across from her.

"No." She shook her head. "Don't try. Do."

"Fine," she grumbled.

"You have no idea what I'm going through. No one can. This is singlehandedly the most overwhelming experience of my life. Contrary to what you believe, this bracelet doesn't necessarily make me yours. Maybe to you, but to me it's nothing. I am not your possession. Not now, not ever. I have been trying. Granted, probably not hard enough, but I've been giving you what I can. No one asked me if this is what I wanted. I wasn't given a choice. You chose for me. You will not tell me who I can befriend and who I can't. To threaten to kill kids is despicable, and if that's what the life of a royal is about, I don't want any part of it. Good grief. You cannot expect me to be okay with all of this. If you are, you're delusional."

"You don't understand what she's capable of." Lana huffed and threw her hands up.

"Do you honestly have any idea what *I'm* capable

of? Because I don't."

"That's different." She relaxed back into the chair.

"How?"

"You're my wife. I don't care what happens to Alexia."

Paisley laughed and continued to run her fingers through Jynx's fur. "Yes, you do. She's your get-out-of-jail-free card. 'Don't worry, if something bad happens we can call on Alexia. She'll fix it.' That's bullshit. Then you threaten her life and her kids."

Lana waved her hand in the air. "We won't be needing her in the future anyway."

Paisley frowned and a feeling of unease settled within her. "What do you mean?" Her stomach dropped when Lana grinned.

"Like you said. We don't know what you're capable of. Your powers could far exceed hers."

Play it cool, Paisley. Play it cool. She stood up and held Jynx securely in her arms. "If you think I'm going to roll over for you, you're dead wrong. What do you think is going to happen? When I come fully into my powers, you'll be able to kill her? Like you said, she is powerful. I can't see her just letting you kill her or her kids."

Lana shrugged and leaned back in her chair, crossing her arms. "We have our ways. She isn't invincible."

Paisley turned away from her and looked out the window. She'd underestimated Lana. That wouldn't happen in the future. These people weren't her friends. They had an agenda in place long before she was brought here. She wouldn't forget that. Tomorrow she would warn Alexia. "You have to realize this won't endear me to you."

She heard Lana stand up. "Paisley, you have to understand we have our policies in place. They are for the betterment of everyone. Alexia, in the end, will only have been a means to an end. Even the Council knew that."

Paisley stiffened and turned toward her. "What did you say?"

"She's a means to an end."

"No." She shook her head. "You said, even the Council knew that. You knew what the Council was planning. Did you plan this with my mom and grandma? Answer me!"

Lana took a step back. "We all had your best interests at heart. I won't apologize for that."

She sat Jynx on the floor. This was a nightmare. "I see." She wouldn't win this argument, but as Lana mentioned, there were far bigger things at play, and she would find out what they were. Somehow Alexia played an integral part in that. "I'm glad everyone knows what path I should take. It's quite a relief knowing I don't even have to think for myself. Everyone else will do that for me."

Lana reached for her, but Paisley kept out of her grasp. Lana threw her hands in the air. "Paisley, look. We all love you and want what's best for you."

She couldn't be serious. "We don't even know each other. You don't love me. I certainly don't love you."

"If you would just give us a chance…"

That would never happen, but she wouldn't tell her that. For Alexia and her kids, she would try to hold her tongue and put up a front. "You're right, I haven't given us a chance." She adjusted her glasses and sighed. "This is all new for me. Everything is a bit much. It's all hard to take in. Can you understand that? It's stressful." When Lana nodded, Paisley relaxed.

"I know, but you can't do what you did at the marketplace again. We need our people to look up to us. I won't tell you who to become friends with, but please reconsider seeing Alexia again. If you steer clear of her, the guards will, too."

So that's how she was going to play this. "All right. I think I'm going to lie down. It's been a long day."

Lana kissed her on the cheek and Paisley let her. "I'll wake you up before dinner."

"Sounds good." Without waiting for her reply, she headed upstairs to her room. Once inside, she leaned against the door and slid down it until her butt hit the floor. She pulled her knees to her chest and rested her head on top of them. What a mess she had gotten herself into.

Now she knew no one could be trusted. Except, maybe Addison and Alexia. Tomorrow she would ask Beatrice about her dad's family. Maybe she would be able to lead her in the right direction and they would be a few more people to have in her corner. Right now it was looking a bit sparse.

❧❧❧❧

The next morning, after a quick breakfast, they headed off to Beatrice's. It was a fast trip and Paisley quickly began her task of weeding the garden. It was nice to have a dull routine to follow. A couple more days and she would be finished. She let her thoughts wander with the mindless labor. What was Alexia in the grand scheme of things? How could she travel between worlds, and why did everyone hate her so much? She didn't think it could only be because they thought her magic was dark. She bit her lip and studied Addison, who had been quiet all morning. Deep down she knew she could trust her. "Who exactly is Alexia?"

"I don't really know. I remember hearing her name for the first time about ten years ago." She crossed her arms and shrugged. "To tell you the truth, I'm not sure anybody really knows a lot about her. She comes and goes as she pleases, and now that I know she can travel between worlds, that would explain her longs absences."

"And her kids. Are they hers? I mean, biologically?" She would place Alexia in her early fifties.

"No, they aren't, but per the law they're hers. She befriended a young woman a few years ago and when the woman died—mysteriously, I might add—she took the little girls in. She loves them. That's obvious. She wouldn't let anything happen to them, and before you ask, no, I don't think she had a hand in their mother's death."

"No, I don't imagine she would." For the next hour, they were both silent. The only sound was the hoe digging into the earth and the occasional grunt Paisley let out when she pulled a stubborn root out of the ground. She accepted the rag Addison handed her and wiped her brow and the back of her neck. She grimaced when more sweat dripped down her chest. Paisley continued her task with laser focus, until her guard companion cleared her throat, causing her to miss her stroke and send a clump of dirt flying into her leg. She glared at Addison, who pointed to the house.

"Beatrice said lunch is ready."

"All right." Today's fare was a thick stew. It

smelled like home, but she again had no idea what was in it and she didn't feel like asking. After the first couple of bites, she was confident she wouldn't die from eating it, so she finished it in record time but waved off seconds. She downed the rest of her water, then refilled her glass and everyone else's.

Beatrice leaned back in her chair. "How was the marketplace?"

Paisley sighed. "Like you don't know."

"I know what other people have told me. I was asking you what happened. Everyone has a story, I just figured I would ask you yours."

Paisley tapped her fingers on the tabletop. "She didn't deserve the way they were talking to her and about her. For god's sake, she had her kids with her." She pushed back from the table and stood up.

"No, she didn't."

Paisley spun around but didn't hear any malice in Beatrice's words or see it on her face. "I don't really know her, but I met her once before…" She shrugged. "I just couldn't allow them to speak to her in that manner."

"You do understand that she practices dark magic."

"What exactly is dark magic? Does it have a different meaning for different people, or is it a universal definition?" Her heart raced when Beatrice stood up, pointed at her, and smiled.

"They will underestimate you. Let them. Everyone has their own ideals. In my book, she is not evil and doesn't practice dark magic, but there are those that don't like her and have categorized what she performs as dark. I believe that you will give them pause. It is my opinion that you should limit how many people know the depths of your powers."

"What is the depth of my powers?"

"Who really knows? I don't, but it is something we will figure out together."

Paisley ran her hands through her sweat-soaked hair. "I don't mind finishing your garden, but for my sake and for those I care about, I really need to learn more. I won't have those I care about hurt because I couldn't protect them."

She nodded. "I understand, and we will get into the thick of it after you finish weeding my garden." She held her hand up. "Trust me, after you are finished I believe we will both understand why I have started this way. There are surprises around every corner, and Paisley, once you're finished with the garden, we will just think of it as your unexpected beginning."

"That's awfully cryptic."

"You have no idea, my dear."

"May I ask you something?"

"Go on."

"I want to visit my dad's family, but I don't know where they live. Lana, I believe, has been avoiding telling me." She pulled a folded piece of paper from her back pocket and handed it to Beatrice, who took it, eyed the paper, then refolded it and handed it back to her.

"I do know where they live." She smirked over the top of her cup.

"Well?" She waved her hand in the air.

Beatrice didn't answer her but turned to Addison. "Do you know where the old Henshaw place is?"

"Yes."

"Go a few miles past that and take a left at the first fork in the road, go another mile, then take another left. They have a small homestead on a few dozen acres." She turned back to Paisley and smiled. "Dear, you're in for a treat. If you can trust anyone, you can trust them."

"I don't know them and they don't know me."

"No matter. They are loyal to a fault, but only to family and a few close friends. They will not turn their back on you."

"Even after what happened?"

"Even after what happened."

"Okay." She finished her water and tapped Addison on the arm. "Guess I should get back to it."

Beatrice shook her head and handed her a small pack. "There are a few snacks in there. You're finished for today. Go visit your family."

"Really?"

"Yes. If you leave now, you will have time to visit with them before nightfall. Paisley, even after meeting them, I still expect you tomorrow morning."

She couldn't decipher the look on the older woman's face. "I'll be good to go."

"Have a safe trip."

"Will do."

It only took them an hour, walking, to reach the first turn, and another thirty minutes to turn on the second road. Paisley's steps faltered for a second when a large two-story house came into view. Directly behind the main house were two smaller buildings. A large open field sat to the right of the house, and a huge garden was laid out on the left. A man was standing by the fence watching their approach. *You can do this. Play it cool.*

Her fingers tightened around her necklace, and Addison stiffened beside her when she caught sight of what she had done. Paisley waved off her question and dropped her hand back down to her side. The man kept his arms slung over the fence, and his face didn't give anything away the closer they got to him.

As they stepped up to the fence and the man raised his face, Paisley gasped and ran her hand through her hair. He wasn't her dad, but she couldn't deny this was more than likely one of his brothers. This man was family. She adjusted her glasses, then gave him her full attention. Before she could say anything, he swung the gate open and motioned them through.

Paisley laid a comforting hand on Addison's arm, then walked through the open gate. When the gate was secured behind them and before Paisley could react, the man grabbed her in his arms and squeezed. She was stunned, and by the time she got her bearings he had pushed her to arm's length and wiped his eyes with the back of his hand.

"You're the spitting image of your father."

Wow. He knew who she was. "I…Yes, I guess I am."

He patted her arm. "Come. I am your uncle Malcom. Everyone will want to meet you. You've only been here for a short time, and it seems you've inherited your dad's knack for trouble."

Paisley laughed the first real laugh since she left home. She doubled over, her laugh quickly turning into sobs. Before Malcom could know what hit him, Paisley stood up, wrapped her arms around him, and cried into his shoulder. All her pent-up emotions poured out and he held her while her tears subsided. Without a trace of embarrassment, she pulled back, took off her glasses, wiped her eyes, then replaced them. "Thank you."

"You're among family now, and we stick

together." He slipped her hand through his arm and led her to the house. Faces peeked out behind the curtain, and she took a deep calming breath when he reached for and opened the door, motioning them in. The house was a bit deceiving. The inside was a wide-open space and quite a bit larger than the outside would lead someone to believe. Off to the left was the kitchen and beyond that was two hallways. Her eyes lingered on the far wall, until she allowed her eyes to scan the room.

Besides herself, Addison, and Malcom, there were five other people in the room. An older woman sat in a rocking chair situated by the window, and a middle-aged woman with graying, long brown hair stood beside her chair. Two men sat on a long sofa that was pushed against the wall, and by the looks of it, they were around the same age as Malcom. A woman around her own age stood beside the couch.

In every face and the way they held themselves, she could see her dad. For the first time since coming here, there seemed to be a light at the end of the tunnel. She turned to Addison and smiled, but jerked her head around when the door to the kitchen opened and another woman walked in. Their shocked gazes locked, and Paisley took a step in her direction. "Alexia?"

Alexia stepped farther into the room, followed by her two little ones. "Paisley." Her voice didn't hold the warmth Paisley had hoped it would. She tried to mask her disappointment, but she knew she had failed when Addison stepped up next to her.

"What are you doing here? In this house?" Paisley stuffed her hands in her pockets and rocked back on her heels.

Alexia crossed her arms. "On the off chance I need someone to watch my girls, they are allowed to stay here."

"You trust these people?"

She arched an eyebrow. "You don't?"

"That's not the question I asked."

Alexia patted her daughters' heads. "Yes, I trust them."

Paisley held her gaze for a few moments, neither one of them breaking eye contact, until Paisley nodded. "Okay." She turned back to Malcom. "Please introduce me to everybody."

"Of course." If he was bothered by her and Alexia's interaction he didn't show it, and neither did anyone else in the house. He walked her over to the woman in the rocking chair and knelt next to it. He placed his hand over hers that lay in her lap. "Mama, this is Paisley, Daniel's daughter." The woman's eyes widened and she chocked back a sob and stood up.

Even though she looked fragile, she walked with purpose to Paisley and placed both her hands on Paisley's cheeks. Then she smiled. "You look just like him." She pulled her into a hug and Paisley readily accepted the comfort from her grandma. She felt a bit self-conscious hugging since her clothes were soaked with sweat, but if her grandma didn't mind, she wouldn't make a big deal of it. The old woman trembled in her arms, but when she pulled back her blinding smile lit up the room. "It is so nice to meet you, my dear. You can call me Nana."

"Okay." Paisley bit her lip and pulled her backpack off her shoulders. After unzipping it, she pulled a large binder out and handed it to her. "I brought pictures. Dad insisted. He wanted you to see what he's been up to." The woman who was standing beside the rocking chair stepped forward.

"I'm Olivia." Her eyes held a mischief the same as her father's.

"Dad said I would probably get along with you best. He was always saying I was just like you. Of course, it wasn't until recently that I knew where he came from, but…just another day, right?"

"Just another day," Olivia agreed. She took the opportunity and introduced everyone else in the room before sitting down beside her mother. The binder still lay closed in her lap.

"I know we just met, and I don't want to be rude, but I need to speak to Alexia alone for a moment. While we talk, it will give everyone the opportunity to look through the binder. Dad also included letters for all of you." When everyone was engrossed with the binder, she turned back to Alexia and pointed to the door she had walked through. Alexia hesitated, then nodded, directed her kids to the couch, and walked out the door.

Paisley patted them on the head when they walked by her, then stopped Addison with a hand on her arm. "Stay here." She held her hand up. "Don't fight me one this one, Addison. I'm perfectly safe. Besides, you know some about my dad and my family. If they have questions, answer them."

She opened the door and walked outside. Alexia stood beside the fence with her hip leaned against it and her head down. Today she wore form-fitting gray trousers and a pale blue sweater. It looked like cashmere, and Paisley knew for a fact the clothes were brought over from her world. Paisley had more pressing concerns than what Alexia was wearing. "How do you know my family?"

"Your father and I went to school together."

⁂

Paisley kept her face neutral but inside she cringed. Her dad was fifty-four; that would place Alexia around the same age. Oh, god, was this the reason her mother hated her so much? Surely, Alexia and her father weren't *together*, together. Alexia looked as calm as ever, and as smoking hot as ever. Paisley felt anything but calm or hot. She could only guess at how dirty she was. She shook her head to rid it of images of Alexia and her dad.

"Paisley, stop. I can see what you're thinking." Paisley gasped and stepped back. "Not literally." She rolled her eyes. "Nothing happened between your dad and me. We're friends."

"Okay." It felt like a load had been lifted off her shoulders and she visibly relaxed. Alexia smirked. Then it dawned on her what she said. *Are* friends, not *were* friends. "How can you skip between worlds? What's the purpose? In order to be on the Council, you had to have been born in our world. Who are you? Really." She screamed and smacked the fence post. "Why does all this crazy shit happen to me? First Lana, then my mom, then Gloria, then you, now them." She pointed to the house. "Let's not forget the queen, who hates me, by the way. Oh, and Beatrice." She slumped against the fence. "To be fair, Beatrice is okay and I do have Addison. I like Addison," she mumbled. She couldn't decipher the look on Alexia's face. "Why do my mom and grandma hate you? Why did they accuse you of making me disappear? What the fuck is going on?" She stomped her feet and waved her hands in the air.

Alexia slipped her hands in her pants pockets.

"Are you quite finished?"

"I believe so." How could one woman look so sexy just standing there? Her body quivered and she sucked in a breath when Alexia grinned at her. "I am done."

"Why did you defend me in the marketplace? Don't give me a bullshit story either. Do you have any idea what you've done?"

"Lana made it quite clear what I'd done." Alexia's eyes flashed a deep red, but it only gave Paisley pause for a second. She knew deep down Alexia would never hurt her. She waved her hand in the air. "Not physically. It was implied that should I visit your house, she would know, because there are guards stationed around it. She also let it be known that once I fully come into my powers they are going to use me to protect this area and not you." She sighed. "I was ready to give her a chance. Ready to try..." She took two steps closer to Alexia. "Until the marketplace happened. I've learned in the last couple of weeks that life is short and my life is fucked up. When I knew I wasn't going to be able to meet you...it hurt. I can't explain it. It's just...you felt right. It's not a secret, and I'm sure you know, but you are an incredibly attractive woman. You're sexiness personified and I am quite affected by that. When I thought I would never see you again, I was ready to embrace my new life. My grandma asked me to give it my best try. I was, until..."

Alexia looked taken aback. "The marketplace," she whispered.

"Yes. I don't believe in fate or some notion that my life has already been written and I must follow a certain set of predetermined rules. I am not of this world." She tapped the cuff on her wrist. "This wasn't my choice. My choice was taken away from me. But I do have a choice now. I'm just not sure how to go about getting what I want." She cocked her head.

"And what do you want?"

"You." Paisley smiled when Alexia gasped. She felt a deep satisfaction when Alexia's cheeks colored. So, she could be rattled.

"Me?"

"You have to know how you affect me."

"I do." She tapped her chin. "I'm old enough to be your mother."

"Not with the things I think about doing to you."

Alexia laughed, then drew her eyes from Paisley's boots all the way to her eyes. "I'm not, not affected by you either." They stood side by side against the fence.

She grimaced. "I know I don't look my best right now."

"Paisley, you look fine. Beatrice must be working you awfully hard?"

"You have no idea." They stayed side by side and basked in each other's presence.

Alexia turned to her. "You're playing a dangerous game."

"I've always been good at games."

"Oh, Paisley."

She laid her hand atop Alexia's and squeezed. "I'm not sure I know what I'm doing. My life is messed up right now, but the one thing I know for sure and the one thing I am not fighting is the pull I feel toward you. Before I left, I told my dad I didn't love Lana and I wasn't sure I would ever be able to. He told me to find someone I could trust and hold on to her, no matter what happened and no matter who was against it. I don't want to fight this." She lifted their clasped hands and brought them to her chest. "Do you?"

"Paisley." She shook her head. "No, I don't, but I don't really know what *this* is. I'm an old woman."

"Me either, but won't it be fun to find out? Your age is the least of my worries. Good grief, I almost fainted in the Council meeting when you put your glasses on."

Alexia chuckled. "Indeed, it will be fun." Paisley kissed Alexia's palm then pulled her hand back. "What is it? Already changed your mind?"

"No." She stuck her hands in her pants pockets and held Alexia's gaze. "Beatrice hasn't even started teaching me anything yet. She wanted me to move a cup. I need help. I need someone to show me what to do. I have no clue what I'm doing. Right now, she has me weeding her garden. I need to be prepared for anything that might happen. I need to be ready to protect you and your girls at a moment's notice. How can I do that if I haven't been taught?"

"Paisley." She traced Paisley's jawline. "First, give Beatrice a chance. She will teach you, but it will be on her own timeline. I wouldn't go so far as to say trust her, but I don't think you cannot trust her. Second, I am hated by a lot of people, including Lana and her family. If she were to find out I was teaching you, I don't know what she would do or what the consequences would be. Do you really want to risk your life because of me and my girls?" She shook her head. "It's not worth it."

"You are worth it. I trust you. Don't ask me why or how, but I do. I feel it in the pit of my stomach. It's a fire burning me from the inside out. I know you could protect your girls. you would die for them. But who's going to protect you?" She bit her lip. "Look, I like you. Let's see where this goes. Nice and slow. I'm in no rush to get to the finish line, but rest assured, I do want to get there." She ran a shaky hand through her hair. "You intimidate the hell out of me."

"If you want to go nice and slow, which I agree with, you're going to have to stop looking at me like that."

"Like what?"

"Like you want to lick me from head to toe."

Good god. Paisley groaned. *Play it cool. Play it cool.* She coughed. "Good…good…okay. Yes, I agree. No devouring. Check." She diverted her eyes to the ground, counted to ten, then took a step away from her. Alexia liked her. This was good. She could work with this. In the Council room she was so unattainable, but now, if she wanted to, she could reach out and touch her. Where once there was no hope, now she was filled with it. Life just got a whole lot sweeter. "When can we start my lessons, and where are we going to go? You can't teach me at your house."

"I'll teach you here. You can ask their permission, but they won't mind."

"I have to be at Beatrice's the rest of the week, then on Saturday, another family dinner. Which I am over the moon about." She rolled her eyes. Pushing her nerves and anxiety as far back as she could, she stepped into Alexia's personal space, kissed her quickly on the cheek, and stepped back. "I think we need to go back in the house, explain everything to my family, and figure out when my first lesson will be. I can assure you, I won't be missing the first one for anything. But answer me a question. You said my dad and you *are* friends not *were* friends. What does that mean?" She turned away from Alexia's penetrating gaze, then spun back around when it dawned on her who Alexia was. "You.

It's you. You're the one that visits my dad once a year, on the fishing trip, to tell him about Dangor. Why?"

Alexia relaxed against the fence. "It was as much of a shock to me as it was to him when we ran into each other again. As it was to Cliff. It was like those two years had never happened. He was quite excited to receive news of his family, and I was happy to provide it."

"You visited my world more than once a year, though."

"I did, but your father and I only visited once a year. We felt it would be better that way. He was homesick at the time, but he also realized he had a family that needed him. He needed to keep his mind focused on his family."

"He said he never told you about me, but you don't seem all that surprised that I'm his daughter."

Alexia sighed. "I am a member of the Council, therefore I know about your mom's family line and I know about you. We, meaning the Council, thought that after a certain age, you wouldn't develop abilities. Of course, we kept tabs on you, but when nothing came to be we concluded that you were barren."

"You kept tabs on me?"

"Not me specifically, but someone did." She held her hand up. "But from all of the reports, their interest in you died when you turned thirty. They felt that if nothing had happened up to that point, then nothing would."

"And what did you think?"

"What I thought at the time didn't matter. I only have a seat because it was passed down from my mother."

"So you knew what I looked like before our first

meeting?"

"Yes, but nothing prepared me for you in the flesh. You are a beautiful woman, Paisley, and don't let anybody tell you any differently. I was especially surprised when you went against your mother in front of the entire Council."

"I was fed up with everyone making my decisions for me. I was at a breaking point when I walked in there, then you happened, then my mother...I'd just had enough."

"We all reach those points."

Paisley sucked in a breath when the wind blew a lock of Alexia's hair down her forehead, and without thinking Paisley reached up and pushed it out of her eyes. She bit her lip when Alexia captured her hand and placed a kiss on her palm. "I hate to break this moment, but I have to know."

Alexia's eyes sparkled. "Ask your question."

"Why do my mother and grandma hate you so much?"

Alexia let her arm drop, but didn't let go of Paisley's hand. "That I don't know. I don't have anything concrete. I know she believes I practice dark magic and that could be the cause. I don't believe she ever knew about me and your dad meeting. So, I don't think it's that. She has never liked me, even from our first introduction. At this point, your guess is as good as mine."

"Fair enough. I still don't know what possessed them to pull the stunt that they did." She shook her head. "Anyway, we should head back in." Alexia nodded and led the way toward the house. Paisley had a sinking feeling that her mother did know about their meetings and drew her own conclusions. If that wasn't the case, she had no clue, but she had a funny feeling that her mother's hatred for Alexia was far deeper than either one of them realized, and she hoped it didn't play another part in what was happening around her or cause her any more trouble.

❧❧❧❧

As soon as they entered through the back door, all eyes were on them. Paisley waved off the question in Addison's eyes and focused on the people around her. No, not people. Family. It still felt surreal to be here with them, while the rest of her family were in a completely different world. Her aunt stepped forward.

"I take it you two worked out your differences?"

"What differences?" Paisley grinned and Alexia snickered.

"Good." She pointed to the couch. Paisley sat down first, and even though there wasn't much room, Alexia sat down beside her. Alexia angled her body so her back was to the person beside her and she slipped her arm on the back of the couch behind Paisley's head. Paisley wouldn't pass up the opportunity, so she shifted her body so she was leaning back against Alexia.

As Alexia relaxed, everyone else in the room did, too. Amelia was sitting on Nana's lap and Zoey was standing in front of her, staring at her. Her little hands were balled into fists. She had a feeling she was the more vocal of the two.

"Would you like to sit on my lap?" Paisley held her breath, but didn't break eye contact with Zoey. She feared that would be a complete disaster. As her heart dropped and her resolve stared to waver, Alexia squeezed her shoulder and she patted Paisley's lap.

Zoey inched herself forward, and when she was close enough to touch her, Amelia jumped down from Nana's lap and climbed into Paisley's without a second thought and snuggled into her. Paisley held her tight, but was at a loss of what to do when Zoey's' bottom lip started to tremble. "Alexia?" she said quietly.

"Zoey," Alexia said softly.

"Mommy."

"Come here." Alexia picked her up and cradled her to her chest, all without moving her arm from behind Paisley.

"Addison, come here." Paisley handed Addison the compact camera she kept in her pocket and told her to take a picture. She wasn't sure how long the battery would last on the camera, but at least she would always have the picture of them. Their first family photo. She could almost believe they were in their own house, sitting on their own couch, until her aunt spoke.

"How is your dad, really? Pictures can only tell us so much."

"He's good, actually. It hurt to leave them, but I hope one day to be able to see them again. If not, I hope in time I can find a way to deal with everything that has happened." She didn't voice it, but she knew the three that surrounded her would go a long way in making that happen.

She relaxed back into the couch when Amelia started playing with her necklaces. "He's happy. He and my mom have an amazing relationship. He misses everyone here, of course, but like me now, you have to find a way to push those pieces back, and he's found a way to do that. If it helps, he told me he doesn't regret anything that has happened. If given the chance, he would make the same decisions. He's a good man."

"Did he teach you to fight?" her uncle asked, leaning forward in his chair with his elbows resting on his legs. He looked so much like her father in that moment she had to take a deep breath to compose herself before answering.

"Yes, although everything happened so quickly, I didn't get much training in."

"I would love to teach you," he said.

"I don't know how much free time I am going to have, but I would love you to. Even though I fought his lessons, I did enjoy them and I do need to get more training with my dagger."

Her uncle stiffened. "What does the dagger look like?" Every eye in the room was on her.

"Addison, slip my dagger out of the side pocket of my backpack." Addison unzipped it, then handed the dagger to her uncle. Several different emotions crossed his features when he unsheathed it. The mix of feelings were clearly shared by everyone else in the room. Hannah, her cousin and Malcom's daughter, looked over her dad's shoulder.

"Is that Grandpa's dagger?"

"Yes. Dad gave it to Daniel when he left. It's been in the family for at least a hundred years. I didn't think I would ever see it again."

Paisley sniffed, holding her tears at bay. Alexia squeezed her shoulder. "Do you want it back? I can carry something else."

"No." He shook his head. "Dad gave it to Daniel, and Daniel gave it to you. You're family, Paisley, and it will be up to you to pass it on when the time comes." He sheathed it, then handed it back to Addison, who slipped it back into the backpack.

"When your dad was younger he always wanted

a big family. I'm surprised you're an only child." Nana broke the silence.

"They did want a big family, but Mom had complications delivering me and the doctor advised her that she wouldn't be able to have any more. I know they wished they would have, but they never felt like they were settling. Dad said he would never risk Mom's life for another baby. He loved her too much."

"That sounds like Daniel. Loyal to a fault," Olivia said.

She snuggled back against Alexia, and over the next two hours Paisley answered any questions they had the best she could. It was hard to concentrate on them with Alexia running her fingers through her hair. Amelia and Zoey had fallen asleep over an hour ago, and she knew by the way Alexia kept shifting her body that they would have to leave soon.

In the coming weeks, she hoped Zoey would come around. Maybe on her next visit to the marketplace she would pick up a couple of chocolate bars for the girls. Bribing them couldn't hurt. It had always worked on her when she was younger, so she didn't see any reason why it wouldn't work on them.

"Paisley?"

She tilted her head back. "Yes."

Alexia kissed the tip of her nose and Paisley almost turned to mush right on the couch. "Your nana is talking to you."

Paisley jerked her head around and couldn't contain the blush that crawled up her neck when Nana gave her a knowing smirk. "Go home, Paisley. You're about to fall asleep on the couch."

"As much as I would like to stay here all night, she's right, Paisley. The girls get awfully cranky when they don't sleep in their own beds at night."

"You're both right. It has been a long day." She untangled herself from the couch and had to tear herself away from Alexia and her family. She laid Amelia down beside Alexia. Today had been a good day, and maybe her lucky streak wouldn't end anytime soon. She kissed Alexia on the cheek, grabbed her backpack, and followed Addison out of the house. She couldn't wait until the time came that she didn't have to leave them, but today wasn't that day.

❧❧❧❧

Despite her strong assertions to the contrary, she missed her first lesson with Alexia, and it tore her up inside. Addison knew a young boy she trusted, so Paisley sent a note to her aunt to give to Alexia, explaining why she was missing her lesson.

After she completed her weeding of the garden that morning, Beatrice had assigned her the task of digging up a few small trees that had sprouted up in the garden. Of course, since this was Paisley, nothing ever went according to plan. The first few trees came up easy. By the fourth tree she was on her hands and knees, scraping the dirt away from the roots with her fingers. She slumped down as sweat tricked down her nose, and stared unfocused until the sun reflected off something in the hole. "Give me the water."

Addison tossed the bottle, and Paisley caught it and poured water over the object. *What the...?* She grabbed the small shovel, and as carefully as possible, dug underneath the item. When there was enough space for her fingers to get around it, she pulled until it began to loosen. With a final tug the object came loose, and Paisley fell backward with a thud. She stared at the object in her hand, not believing what she was seeing. "Addison, is this what I think it is?"

"Yes, it is."

Paisley jumped at the sound of Beatrice's voice. "So, it *is* an egg?"

"Yes."

Paisley stood and tried to hand it over, but Beatrice took a step back. "I cannot take it. Only you will be able to care for it."

Paisley scrunched up her nose. "Care for it?" It was roughly the size of a football, in multiple shades of blue and purple. She kept a firm hold of it, but kept it at arm's length and eyed it warily. It looked old and weathered. Several small fractures could be seen running along every available surface. "There can't possibly still be something alive inside."

Beatrice didn't bat an eye. "It's a dragon egg."

Paisley eyed the egg, then Beatrice, then Addison. "A dragon egg? Really? Isn't it a bit, I don't know, small to be a dragon?"

"Come inside and I will explain. Bring the egg. Do not let it out of your sight."

Paisley instructed Addison to grab her backpack while she followed behind Beatrice, holding the egg to her chest. For some reason she couldn't explain, she already felt she had to protect it.

Beatrice waved to the table. "Sit." Once everybody was seated and she had served them each a cup of tea, she started talking. "Dragons come in all shapes and sizes. It is true the larger varieties are nothing more than stories told, but dragons did and still exist in some form." She pointed to the egg Paisley had set on the table. "What you hold in your hands is a rare egg.

I can't recall the last time a Palm Dragon hatched in this area of the country. There are still Dragon Masters in existence, and to fully understand your dragon you must be taught by one."

Paisley stuttered. "My dragon?"

"Yes. You would have never been allowed to pick the egg up out of the ground if it hadn't called to you. That's why I had you weeding. It has long been rumored that a dragon egg was buried in the ground on this property. In all my years, no one has been able to locate it. Don't you find it funny it only took you less than a week?" She arched her eyebrow.

Paisley ran her fingers over the hard surface of the egg and sighed. Did she need this complication in her life right now, with everything else going on? She adjusted her glasses and chanced a look at Beatrice. The answer was written plainly on the old woman's face. Whether she liked it or not, she had just become the sole owner of one dragon egg. "What exactly is a Palm Dragon?"

Beatrice pushed back from the table, stood, and walked to the bookcase in the corner of the room. She pulled down a small hardbound book and set it down in front of Paisley before retaking her seat. "That is the complete history of Palm Dragons thus far. Palm Dragons are just that—when they are born they can sit in the palm of your hand and they don't get much bigger." She bit her lip. "Don't let their size fool you. They are one of the rarest, but also one of the most magically based dragons ever to live. To tell you the truth, not much is known about them. No one, to this day, can fully say what powers they hold. There are varieties within: fire, ice, and lightening, just to name a few. Do not let anyone know that you have the egg or the book. I am only telling you this in the presence of your guard because you trust her. Addison, do not tell anyone what you have seen here today."

"I won't."

"I still don't understand. How does this affect me? Why did the egg choose me?"

"The dragon that lays dormant inside the egg chose you and it did so for a reason that is known only to it, and when it hatches, to you. You should be proud of that fact. The dragon chooses its master."

"So, I'm a Dragon Master then?" That sounded cool, to be able to train a dragon and have it do her bidding. Maybe her day was looking up. "What do I have to do to care for it?" She nudged the egg. "It's an old egg. Do I do anything special?"

"No. Just keep the egg out of sight and with you at all times. It should fit in your backpack. Keep it there."

"Okay."

Beatrice stood. "I believe that will be all for today. You should take the rest of your day and look over that book. It will give you some insight into the type of dragon you have been granted."

Paisley also stood, along with Addison, and she slipped the egg into her backpack while Addison held it open for her. After securing the pack on her back, she turned to Beatrice and finished her tea. "Thank you." A dragon egg in her Wonder Woman backpack. If that didn't make her a superhero she didn't know what would.

She rocked back on her heels and crossed her arms across her chest. "I have to say being a Dragon Master is pretty cool." Paisley started to fidget under Beatrice's gaze. After a few tense moments, Beatrice seemed to make up her mind.

"No, my dear," she said, a smile slowly splitting her face. "You are not a Dragon Master. You, Paisley, are a DragonWitch." She held up her hand. "And before you ask, I will not get into that right now. Just suffice it to say that all will be revealed in time. Do not mention that to anyone either." She pointed to the door. "You both have a wonderful day."

Paisley turned on her feet and walked out the door. First she finds out she is the sole owner of a dragon egg, then she is told she is a DragonWitch. The title seemed self-explanatory, but she wondered if it was that simple. She was a witch, and she apparently now owned a dragon. She still couldn't wrap her head around it, and until she saw the thing hatch she would reserve all judgment on the matter. She probably should have gotten used to the unexpected.

❧❧❧❧

After leaving Beatrice's, they'd only been walking for twenty minutes or so toward her family's farm when Addison grabbed Paisley's arm and stopped walking. She held up her hand to ward off any questions, and Paisley scanned the area but didn't see anything out of the ordinary.

She closed her eyes but didn't hear anything weird either. Granted, she wasn't an expert in such matters, so she cracked open one eye and looked toward Addison, who tensed beside her, then pulled Paisley behind her when three men walked out of the shadows of the trees to their left. Paisley had never seen anyone wearing the types of robes these men had on. But by the look on Addison's face, it was clear she knew exactly who the men were.

The three men were roughly the same height as her, and even though the robes concealed the men's clothes, it wasn't hard to tell they each held a slim build. The two men in the back were clean-shaven, but the man in the front had a beard that went down to the middle of his chest. When he took a step forward and held out his hand, Addison drew her sword.

He moved his hand in a circle. "We mean you no harm. This is the first opportunity we've had to meet the new princess, and wanted to offer her our sincere congratulations."

"Your kind isn't welcome here. You step out of the shadows like ghosts before us. The Brotherhood dare confront a member of the royal family." Addison took a step forward and was attempting another when Paisley walked up next to her.

So, these three men were members of the Brotherhood. The insignia stitched onto their robes must have been an indication of their rank, since all three symbols were different. They looked friendly enough, but from her experience, looks could be deceiving. She shrugged. "So, you've met me. Now what do you want?" She had to fight the urge not to fidget or bring attention to her backpack. Now that she knew it was there, she would have a hard time not looking at the egg ten times a day. The last thing she wanted was these men finding that she had one. Her dad had told her she didn't have anything to fear from them, but she wasn't about to let her guard down.

Paisley opened her mouth to speak, but clamped it shut when out of the corner of her eye she spotted five soldiers step up behind them. They were not soldiers for the royal family. Her first ambush. How quaint. She crossed her arms. "Really? What do you hope to accomplish by doing this? I am no threat to you."

He spread his arms wide. "We'll be the judge of that. You haven't been around long enough for anyone to miss you, now have you?"

"Lana would miss me."

He cocked his head to the side. "Maybe, or maybe she would miss what you could offer her. Your power is immense. I can tell that by looking at you. The pendants that hang around your neck can only do so much. You need someone to teach you."

"I have a teacher."

He snickered. "Beatrice is an old fool. You need someone that would be willing to go to bat for you. Someone willing to stand beside you in battle. Someone who would gladly die for you."

She had that with Alexia. She bit her lip and fought the urge to fiddle with her glasses. It almost sounded like he wanted to be the one to teach her. The ruby felt warm against her skin. "What do you really want?" She watched their facial expressions, but all three remained neutral. "And why the extra protection?" She pointed to the soldiers.

"I really only wanted to meet with you, and the added protection is just a precaution. One can never be too careful."

"I hear that." She bit her lip. "So you will let us pass freely?"

"In time. First though, let me give you a word of warning since you're new here. These people"—he waved his hand in the air—"are not your friends. To them, you are a royal. They will not treat you like you should be treated. They will treat you how they think you should be treated. Do not trust them. Everyone has their own agenda. Remember that."

"Even you?"

"Even me." Paisley kept her feet planted on the rocky ground as the members of the Brotherhood, along with their soldiers, walked back into the trees. As she lost sight of them, she released a breath she didn't even realize she was holding. Without looking at Addison, she spoke. "What do you think?"

"I think we need to be getting you home and not to your family's. Please don't argue. They will understand, and tomorrow after Beatrice's you will go to them, explain your absence, then you will train with Alexia. For now, I believe to keep up appearances, you need to go home and spend time with Lana. She does not need to feel isolated right now. You don't have to love her—or even like her—but with everything still up in the air and your powers still untapped, you need to make the effort."

Addison was right. Things were still up in the air. She would miss seeing Alexia, but she would spend the rest of the day with Lana and Jynx, just relaxing and enjoying the evening. "You're right. Onward bound."

❧❧❧❧

After a week of training with Beatrice and Alexia, her grasp of her magic was starting to reveal itself, but she was still a long way away from having a firm grip on it. She came home exhausted and hungry every night. Lana never complained or questioned her, and she always had dinner waiting for her when she arrived home.

Paisley still didn't feel any type of spark when she was around her, but she had finally admitted to herself, if a bit reluctantly, that Lana could become a friend.

Maybe. She would never fully confide in or trust her, but she wasn't against spending time with her. What she didn't enjoy was dinner with the royal family she was forced to attend once a week.

They had arrived at the castle right on time for dinner, and Paisley still felt like she was going to a firing squad every time she entered through the doors. This was their third dinner together, and thankfully the queen hadn't been present for the second, but such wasn't the luck tonight. Paisley avoided her stare, but she could feel her eyes boring into her. Paisley knew it was only a matter of time until the queen addressed her.

"Paisley," the queen said. "What have you been doing with your time?"

It seemed like an innocent question, but Paisley knew better, and she fought the urge not to squirm under her gaze. "I have been learning quite a bit from Beatrice. I only wish that I could learn more. She is a good teacher. I didn't think I would ever get her garden weeded for her." She chuckled, then took another drink of her wine.

The queen threaded her hands on top of the table when their dinner plates were taken away. "She is a fine teacher and will bring out the best you have to offer. A little bird told me that you have also been spending time with your family."

To keep her hands from shaking, Paisley clasped them in her lap. When she looked up, the queen's eyes bore into hers, and at that moment she knew the queen knew that she had been training with Alexia. She also knew that she would never come out and say it. "I have enjoyed getting to know my dad's family. I miss my grams back home, and even though it isn't the same thing, my dad's mom has been a godsend to me."

"Family is important," she said, moving her hands away from the table when a bowl of fresh fruit was set in front of her. "I, for one, would never do anything to jeopardize the safety of my family. Nothing and no one will ever harm a hair on their heads if I have anything to do about it. Don't you agree, Paisley?"

"I agree." She finished her fruit in record time, because there wasn't anything else left to say. When Lana had finished hers she informed everyone she and Paisley would be going home. After arriving, they sat on the couch, each lost in their own thoughts. The silence was bordering on uncomfortable when Lana spoke up.

"Do you have something you need to tell me?"

Paisley turned to face her. "What's this about?"

"My mother can be a bit forceful at times, but she is never without reason. Can you think of anything that you've done or said that would cause her to doubt you or your ties to this family?"

Paisley tried to remain calm, but on the inside she was freaking out. Did Lana know, too? She wasn't about to tell her and risk not seeing Alexia or her kids again. That wasn't an option. "No, I've done nothing to risk your family. I have enjoyed getting to know my family. It's the next best thing to having my dad with me. They give me a reason to carry on." It wasn't a total lie—they did help her regain a sense of family and she did enjoy spending time with them, but seeing Alexia every day was what kept her going.

Over the past week, after her lessons were completed, they had started to open up to each other more. Paisley told her about her childhood and Alexia shared stories about her girls. Physically, they had kept their distance, but every evening Paisley would place a kiss on Alexia's cheek, and every evening Alexia would draw her into a hug before they departed. It was getting harder and harder to leave her each time. Never in her life had she ever grown so close to someone in such a short amount of time. K.G. would have been proud of her.

The overwhelming need to be around Alexia scared her, but there was no way she could fight her attraction. She dared not speak the word love aloud, but she felt it and she believed Alexia did, too. Looking at Lana now, Paisley felt a twinge of guilt, but it wasn't enough to make her back off or change the course she had set for herself. No, she would continue her path, and be damned if anyone or anything stood in her way.

Lana stood up and started pacing, then abruptly turned toward Paisley. "There is something else I wanted to discuss with you."

She looked nervous. That couldn't be a good thing. "Okay." Paisley tried to remain calm, but when Lana sat down next to her and picked up her hand, she started freaking out.

"You've been here for almost a month and you still sleep in the guest room. I don't want to rush you, but do you think maybe you could try sleeping with me, just for a few nights? We're married, Paisley. I understand your need to train and see your family, but we hardly spend any time together." She bit her lip. "What I'm trying to say is, can you maybe devote a bit of time to working on us? If we don't even give us a try, we're doomed before we start, and I want to see if this can work."

Paisley fought down the nausea, slipped her hand out of Lana's, and stood up. She knew she should be spending more time with her, at least to keep up appearances, but the fact was she didn't want to. It already felt like a betrayal to Alexia that she even lived in the same house as Lana. Now this. She would have to concede something larger for Lana not to become suspicious.

"You're right. I have been awfully busy. Everything is so new and exciting, it's hard to prioritize everything. Lana, I'm trying my best here." She tensed when Lana stepped up behind her and wrapped her arms around her waist. This is not where she wanted to be and this was not whose arms she wanted around her. She stepped out of Lana's embrace and ignored the hurt that flashed across her face. "I'm sorry, but I'm not ready yet." She straightened Lana's collar. "Please, give me time."

"Time." Lana ran her hands through her hair. "All right. I don't believe I have a choice."

"No, you don't." As she and Jynx's lay in bed that night, she knew she had more than likely hammered another nail in her coffin after talking with Lana, but she didn't care. Now that she had found Alexia, she wasn't about to do anything to jeopardize their growing relationship.

❧❧❧❧

"Paisley, focus." Alexia stood a good twenty feet away and held one of her hands in the air. "You have to focus."

Sweat dripped down the back of her neck as she attempted to execute Alexia's instructions. She shook her head of any inappropriate thoughts. They seemed to come unbidden when Alexia was anywhere nearby and they had been working closely together on her magic for hours. It wasn't her fault Alexia looked especially yummy today in her tight-fitting black and gray dress, with an inappropriate amount of cleavage showing. It was getting harder and harder to concentrate on the tasks at hand because her eyes tended to stray downward. To distract herself, she chanced a glance at the back porch. Amelia and Zoey sat in rapt attention along with Olivia.

Turning back to Alexia, she shook her hands out, rounded her neck, and focused. She closed off her mind to everything but what she wanted to accomplish. They had been focusing her energy on throwing up a force shield around different objects. Today she was supposed to throw one up around herself, but she decided to try something different. On the count of three, she threw one hand out toward Alexia, and a moment later she threw the other one in the same direction.

After a few seconds, a fireball the size of a basketball flew toward Alexia, only to hit a barrier at the last moment, then disappear. Paisley grinned, but one look at Alexia's face had her rethinking her strategy. To hell with fear. She took a few steps forward until she was standing directly in front of Alexia, who arched an eyebrow. "Please don't be mad at me. I know I didn't exactly follow your instructions, but it worked." She took another step forward only for her body to be propelled backward and she fell on the ground. *What the hell?* "Really, Alexia? You did that on purpose." She stood up and dusted her pants off.

"Paisley." She pointed around her. "This isn't my doing. This is still your barrier." She planted one hand on her hip and played with the necklace that hung around her neck with the other one. "You have to bring the barrier down. I couldn't."

Paisley walked in a circle, touching the air around her to determine how big the barrier was when someone on the porch screamed. She jerked her head around. Olivia looked terrified. She ran to the porch. "What?" Everybody looked fine.

"I can't touch them," her aunt said.

Paisley walked around the girls, and sure enough they had barriers around them too, but unlike her aunt, they seemed fine. "You girls okay?" They both nodded and she turned and walked back to Alexia.

"You put barriers around them also?" Alexia looked troubled.

Paisley blinked. That wasn't the reaction she was hoping for. "I guess."

"Take them down. Now."

Paisley closed her eyes and thought about everything she had done. A moment later she felt a hand on her shoulder and she opened her eyes. Alexia's eyes were shining. "Paisley, what were you thinking about when you threw the barrier up? It's important that you remember what it was." She squeezed her shoulders.

"Why?" She grimaced as Alexia's grip tightened.

"Because it shouldn't have gone around them, too, if you only intended it for me."

"I was thinking about how I wanted to impress you. So, I came up with the idea to protect you from my blast. I can't explain it, but I felt it the moment the barrier went up. The fireball, although cool, wasn't my intention. I only wanted to test the barrier. I didn't imagine a fireball, per se."

"You wanted to protect me?" She looked thoughtful.

"Yes."

"From what?" She loosened her grip on Paisley's shoulders.

"You're kidding right? From everything. People want you and your girls dead. Why do you think I'm doing all this? Not for me. Who's going to protect you? Do you really think I can stand here while people threaten your life and the lives of your girls?" She ran her fingers through her hair. "Don't ask me to do that. Please. I don't know what I would do if something happened to any of you…if I could have protected you, but didn't know how." Her tirade was cut short when Alexia grabbed her by the collar and pulled into a blistering kiss. Paisley tensed for a moment, then melted into Alexia's body and kissed her back. She slid her arms up Alexia's back and pulled her closer. It was everything a first kiss should be and she never wanted it to end. The kiss deepened and Paisley lost all thought of time, until a small hand pulled at her pants leg.

She reluctantly pulled away and looked down. Two sets of eyes looked up at her. "We want kisses, too," the girls squealed.

Paisley knelt, pulled them into her arms, and showered their faces with kisses. Amid squeals, tickles, and laughter, Paisley felt like she had finally come home. All the pieces fell into place when Alexia pulled all of them into her arms. Paisley kissed her neck and inhaled the scent that was all Alexia. "Why now?" she whispered in Alexia's ear.

"Because without thinking about it you chose us over everything. There shouldn't have been any way for you to put a barrier around all three of us so effortlessly. I couldn't break the barrier. You created them out of love. You love us enough to use all your power to protect us. It's a dangerous proposition, because it will leave you vulnerable."

"I will do it again, if I have to. Nothing will happen to you or them if I have anything to do about it."

"That's why now. It was time. We've been dancing around this for weeks." She caressed Paisley's neck.

"Let's quit dancing then."

"Yes, let's, and we need to get back to work." All three of them groaned and Alexia chastised them. "Girls, it's important for Paisley to learn everything she can. There are bad people in the world. She must learn how to defend herself. All right?" Two heads nodded. "Give me and Paisley a kiss then go back to the porch."

Paisley held both girls a second longer than necessary. Now more than ever, she knew what she was fighting for. She stood up and Alexia ran her fingers down Paisley's arm to capture her hand. With Alexia putting her trust in her she had to put hers in Alexia. She picked up her backpack and walked them to one of the outbuildings in the backyard. "Come along." Once they were both settled at a small table, Paisley set her bag on the table, unzipped it, and pushed it in Alexia's direction.

Alexia didn't touch the bag. "Where did you get this?" Her eyes were wide.

"I found it when I was digging in Beatrice 's garden. She told me not to show it to anyone and that it was a Palm Dragon." Alexia stood up and started pacing. "She also told me I was a DragonWitch."

Alexia sat back down and peeked back into the bag. "I've only seen a dragon egg once, and that was in passing. This is beyond anything I would have believed for you. No wonder you could encase us in a barrier with no problem."

"I don't understand?"

"Dragons carry magic. They are magic. Whatever type of magic your Palm Dragon carries has already bonded to yours. You can channel the dragon's magic through you and allow it to mix with yours. This is amazing. You're amazing. I bet the Council had no idea about this."

"Beatrice didn't tell me much. She gave me a book and told me to read it, but I haven't had much time. All I've been able to do is skim it." She pushed her glasses up the bridge of her nose. "I take it this isn't that common?"

"No, it's not common at all. I've only heard of a DragonWitch in very vague terms. You need to ask Beatrice more about it, make her tell you the answers. I will see what I can find out through my channels." She reached across the table and picked up Paisley's hand, holding it between hers. "Are you okay with everything that's happened?"

She sighed. "With you and the girls, yes. With everything else, I'm not sure. I don't know what to do about Lana or my entire situation with her family. My magic is getting easier to control. On top of that, I have a dragon egg and I had a run-in with the Brotherhood." Paisley explained the incident in detail, because Alexia insisted.

Alexia waved off her concerns. "The Brotherhood preach a good game, but in most insistences they're harmless. I wouldn't see too much into it." She pulled her hand back and bit her lip. It was the first time Paisley had ever seen her nervous. "There's something I wanted to ask you."

She would answer her anything. "Go on."

"The situation with Lana…what exactly is it?"

Paisley frowned then it dawned on her what Alexia was asking. "Come here." Reluctantly, Alexia stood up and Paisley scooted her chair back and pulled her down onto her lap, forcing Alexia to wrap her arms around her neck. Paisley held her tight around the waist and nuzzled her neck. She would give anything to live openly with her and her girls.

"We live together, in separate bedrooms. At this point, I guess, we would be considered more like roommates than friends. We have kissed a few times, but only once since I arrived here and that was before us. I don't love her, nor do I have any feelings for her. The longer I am with her, the more I keep finding fault with her. I don't know if that's my doing or hers. When I come downstairs in the morning I hope to see you, but when I see her it tears me up inside. That's not fair to her or to me. Or you."

She caressed Alexia's cheek. "I didn't choose any of this. Not my powers, or coming here, or Lana. Everyone chose for me. The only thing I've chosen for myself is you and the girls. I don't want there to be any doubt in your mind. Lana is nothing to me, but you are everything." She curled her fingers around Alexia's neck and pulled her close, only to be interrupted by a knock on the door. She groaned when Addison spoke.

"Paisley, I don't mean to bother you, but it's getting late. We should be heading back. It will be dark soon."

"I'll be out in a minute." Alexia's grip loosened and she stood up. Paisley zipped her bag and slipped it onto her shoulders. At the door, she pecked Alexia's lips and led them out. Addison was already back at the house. She slipped her hand through Alexia's arm. "Do you believe me?"

Alexia stopped them both and looked into Paisley's eyes. "Yes, and I don't say that lightly. You have somehow gotten under my skin. I won't say the age difference doesn't bother me, because it does." She placed a finger over Paisley's lips to forestall her talking. "But, you don't seem to be bothered in the least by it and I will play off that. I am honored that you have chosen me and I will search through every book or notebook I have to see if we can undo this." She tapped Paisley's bracelet.

"Even if we can't, I will be with you. Make no doubt about that. No one and nothing will stop us from being together."

"Please don't promise something you can't deliver on. Even if we do get separated—Paisley, it could happen. Even if we do get separated, I will always wait for you and always try to find you."

"I couldn't have said it better myself." She captured the tempting lips in front of her and melted into the kiss until someone coughed behind them. She broke the kiss and rested her forehead against Alexia's. "I can't wait until tomorrow."

Alexia squeezed her close, then pushed her away and took a step back. "Addison is right. You need to go."

"Right." As she passed by her, she kissed her cheek, then proceeded to the porch where she kissed her aunt and the two little girls before joining Addison at the gate and heading toward home. Halfway there, Paisley couldn't keep quiet any longer. "Will you tell Lana about Alexia and me?" She held her breath for the answer.

"No. I know what you've been through since the start of this. My loyalty lies with you now, not the royal family. I find no fault with Alexia or her girls. I pledged my life to yours the moment I took the assignment. That being said, I will gladly lay my life down for yours, but I can't do the same for your Alexia or her girls." She stopped walking and grasped Paisley's hand. "You protect them and I will protect you." Addison dropped her hand and continued walking. Paisley hoped it didn't come to that.

⁂

The next day found her once again alone with Alexia. After an intense training session, they were seated beside each other on the back porch with their legs dangling over the side. Paisley enjoyed training with her, but she enjoyed their quiet time even more. Just being in the older woman's presence calmed her. "I can feel my powers getting stronger."

"They are. You're doing remarkably well, Paisley." Alexia slipped her arm around Paisley's waist and pulled her snug against her side. "It's so peaceful here."

Paisley melted into her embrace and kissed her on the cheek before resting her head on her shoulder. The sun was starting to set and she knew she would have to go back to Lana soon, but not for another hour or so. "Which do you prefer, here or there?"

It took a moment for her to answer. "They both have their advantages and disadvantages. If you're talking about overall, there, but if you're talking about the present, here. I wouldn't have you three if I was still in our world."

"True, but at least we had air conditioners."

Alexia chuckled. "That's not what I miss the most."

"What do you miss?"

"The convenience of the other world. It was so much easier to get things done."

"Oh my god, I know. I miss the food. The food here is fine, but nothing like what I was used to. I would kill for a bag of Doritos and a two liter of Sprite Zero." They both laughed then lapsed into a comfortable silence. "If given the choice between the other world, or you and the girls, there would be no competition. You all would win hands down."

Alexia sighed and slipped her hand under Paisley's shirt where it rested against warm skin. "Realizing I was attracted to you was one thing, but realizing that attraction is growing into feelings is quite another. You are special to me, Paisley, please don't ever doubt that. I may not be able to say the words, but they're there on the tip of my tongue."

Paisley raised her head and smiled. "You don't have to say them. I know." She leaned forward and nipped at Alexia's lips before pulling her forward and kissing her. The kiss deepened and Paisley slid her hand under Alexia's shirt and ran her fingers along her ribcage, but groaned when Alexia hissed and pulled away from her, reaching under her shirt and stilling Paisley's fingers.

"As much as I would love to move forward..." she pecked Paisley's lips, "we can't. Now isn't the right time."

"I know." She slipped her arms around Alexia's waist and snuggled into her embrace. She would never get tired of the arms wrapped around her, and she would never take the woman in her arms for granted. After everything that had happened to her and all the revelations, finding Alexia had been a godsend.

At this point, she didn't know what she would do

without her. She pulled back and pushed Alexia's hair out of her eyes. Alexia probably wasn't aware, but her eyes told such an amazing story and held such depth that Paisley had to remind herself to breathe every time she lost herself in their depths. She might not have been able to speak the words, but they were there shining in her eyes.

Alexia kissed the tip of her nose, bringing Paisley out of her mental meanderings. "Penny for your thoughts?"

"You. I was thinking about you." She draped her hands around Alexia's neck. "You are simply breathtaking. I can't believe you have taken a chance on me, on us. I will fight for the three of you until my dying breath. I know it sounds crazy and I can't explain it, but this, between us, feels so right. It blows my mind." She rested her forehead against Alexia's. "I never thought I would have these types of feelings for anyone. The only person who came close was K.G., but in the end we were much better off as just friends. Just to be clear, I don't see that happening for us."

"And what do you see for us?"

"I think that if I told you that, it would scare you. For now, all I'll say is, I'm not going anywhere."

Alexia sighed. "I am sorry about K.G. I don't think anyone thought Gloria was that reckless. I certainly didn't. If I had known, I would have done something to stop it. I can't vouch for the Council now, but before I was chased out of town..." She rolled her eyes. "They were supposed to take steps to regulate the witches better."

Paisley pulled away from her, slipped her arms under her legs, and lifted her onto her lap. Alexia sighed and reached her arms around Paisley's neck. "I hope they have, for everyone's sake." She bit her lip.

"What?"

"I can feel the dragon's magic more and more. Sometimes it's scary, other times, it's a welcome relief to know I'm not alone even when I'm the only person in the room."

"Your dragon has already claimed you, and by the sound of it, wants to bond with you before it hatches. As it gets closer to time for it to hatch, the magic and the bond will only intensify. Let it. If it is within your power, don't fight it. Your dragon won't hurt you. At times, it will feel overwhelming, but once it hatches, most of the hard work will already be done."

"I am a bit excited to meet it and I can't wait for the girls to meet it also. How cool is that going to be?" She tightened her hold around Alexia's waist. "I love them already, you know."

"I know."

"I love you, too." She turned to face her and was surprised when Alexia leaned forward and captured her lips.

"I know you do. I can feel it every time you look at me. In every touch and every kiss. I hoped I would find someone to spend my life with, but I never dared dream it would be someone who wanted me for me. A lot of people would consider you a brave woman, Paisley, for trying to tame me."

"Oh, I'm not trying to tame you." She peppered her jaw with kisses. "I love you just the way you are." She leaned forward and groaned into Alexia's neck when the back door opened and someone walked out. "Addison, I guess it's time to go?"

Addison stepped off the porch steps. "It is."

"Okay." With one last kiss, Alexia stood up and

pulled Paisley with her. "Tomorrow then."

"Of course. Nothing would stop me from seeing you. Addison, I'll be right back." Paisley followed Alexia inside and kissed both sleeping girls on the cheek. "I wish I didn't have to go."

Alexia drew her into a hug. "We'll see you tomorrow afternoon. Go. You know I hate it when you travel at night."

Paisley snickered. "I love you, too."

⁂

With a hop in her step, the next morning she bounded down the stairs and came to a halt when she entered the kitchen. Clara and Lana were leaned across the counter with their backs to her, talking extremely close. Maybe she wouldn't have to worry about hurting Lana after all. She didn't want to interrupt but she needed to get going. "Good morning." They jumped apart. "Hello, Clara."

"Paisley, it's good to see you. That's actually why I'm here."

"Oh?" Paisley bit into the peach and moaned as the juices ran down her throat. She would have to grab a few extras. The girls would love them. Maybe some apples, too.

Lana pecked her on the cheek and Paisley had to fight the urge to pull away from her. Best not to play her cards just yet. "You've been working awfully hard with Beatrice, so I thought you could use a day off. Clara is here to take you around. I know you haven't had time to explore and I've been so busy."

Paisley threw her uneaten peach away, the sweetness turning sour in her stomach. She adjusted her glasses and counted to ten. "You took it upon yourself to give me a day off? I don't have a say in this?" It would mess up her time with Alexia, and she needed to confront Beatrice today about being a DragonWitch.

"Look, it will be good for you to get out of the city. See the sights." Lana smiled.

That didn't sound good. Not good at all. It sounded rehearsed. "How far out of the city?" She rocked back on her heels. Addison stiffened bedside her.

Clara finally spoke up, but Paisley noticed a slight twitch in her hand. "A few hours."

"So an overnight trip?"

Lana took a step in her direction. "Yes."

Now she knew something was up. Lana had never suggested she travel before, and to do so during the peak of her training was suspicious. There was no way she would miss two days of training. "No."

Lana spun around to face her. "What?"

"I said no. I have plans today. I am at a place in my teaching that I don't want to put off."

"I talked to Beatrice and she said you could have the two days off."

"Lana, as much as you like to think you run my life, you don't. I make my own decisions, and if Beatrice already has plans I will spend the day with my family." She tried to shake off the dread filling the pit of her stomach, but something was wrong.

She frowned when Lana smirked at her, and as coldness seeped into her pores she heard a familiar voice screaming in her head. She grabbed her backpack off the table and ran out the back door toward the marketplace. The rhythm of her footsteps were in sync with Addison's, and she could hear other sets of feet running behind her. As the screams and cries grew louder in her mind, she threw her hand out in front of her. She didn't know why she was headed to the marketplace, but wouldn't second-guess herself. The only thought crossing her mind was that her girls were in trouble. As she pushed past the vendor stalls, bypassing shoppers, she skidded to a halt beside the fountain.

Ahead of her, Alexia was surrounded by guards and two soldiers had a hand on each of the girls' shoulders. Tears were running down their faces. The queen and her personal guard stood a few feet from them and turned when Paisley, Addison, Lana, and Clara entered. Paisley chanced a glance at Alexia, and she put her hand up in front of her and smiled. The barrier had worked. Her eyes narrowed when she realized she had encased the guards inside the girls' barrier.

She heard a slow clapping and turned toward the queen. "Bravo, Paisley, but there seems to be a bit of a problem." She pointed to the girls, and the guards squeezed down on their shoulders making them cry out and Paisley's blood run cold. She took a step closer, threw off Lana's hand, and tugged on her necklaces. They came off cleanly and she handed them to Addison, who tucked them into her pocket.

"I think I still have a few tricks up my sleeve." The queen's smile faltered for a second but was quickly put back in place. When she nodded at the guards, Paisley raised both of her hands and twisted them in the air before flicking her fingers in an outward motion.

The guards' bodies flew out of the barriers and landed on the ground in front of the queen, their heads hanging at unnatural angles. It took her a moment to ground the magic pulsating just below the surface, but instinct quickly took over and she swept her arm in an arc around her. Every guard surrounding them fell into a heap on the ground.

"They're not dead, but if you push me they will be." She would not back down to this woman. She was relishing the feeling of power when all at once she knew she had been played. The smile that overtook the queen's face made her insides quiver. It was at that moment that she realized that to keep Alexia and the girls safe, she would have to let them go. The queen would always use her love for them against her, to control her. Her heart screamed in agony as she chose her next words. "I want it written that Alexia and the girls are never to be touched again, and they will be able to roam freely without the threat of attack or death." Alexia closed her eyes and Paisley turned away from her as a tear ran down her cheek.

The queen chuckled. "Done. You will continue training with Beatrice, and then you will do our bidding. Yes?"

"I won't sign anything to that effect."

"I won't ask you to. You are my daughter-in-law; it's time you started acting like it. You are mine now, Paisley. I don't care what happens to the woman or the brats, but I don't want them setting foot in this town again. They will be banished."

"Fine." Silver sparks flew from her fingertips, and for the first time she didn't snuff it out. The power coursing through her veins made her shudder and she knew, no matter what, these people would one day feel the full extent of her powers. From out of nowhere, she felt an added pressure to her magic and realized it was the dragon making its presence known. The queen might have thought she had won, but the truth was far from it. Paisley had complete control of the situation. "I want papers guaranteeing their safety delivered to my family's home in two hours. I will have that time with Alexia and her children. I'm not asking."

"Lana, you do realize your bond mate is in love with another, don't you? It's quite a disappointment." The queen sighed. "But, you made a wise decision not to heed the almanac's words. Paisley was a much better choice. Good day."

Paisley filed the queen's words in the back of her mind, but she had more important things to worry about. She knelt on the ground and lowered all three barriers. The girls ran into her arms, and she scoped them up and stood. She felt Alexia and someone else touch her shoulder, then was engulfed in a puff of smoke. She opened her eyes to find they were in her family's yard. Paisley buried her head in Alexia's neck. When the tears finally dried, she raised her head. "You know this is the only way to keep you safe. I will find you again. Don't doubt me."

Alexia smiled but it didn't reach her eyes. "Doubt you? Never. We'll wait for you. Always." The kiss left her breathless, but she had things to discuss before she said good-bye to them. She would see them again and no one would stop her.

"I love you all, and as much as I would love to stay in your embrace, there are a few things I need to know."

Alexia stiffened at her tone. "What?"

"As much as you can teach me. We have under two hours. If possible, can you leave your journals here, for me to read? I would love to stay cuddled, but there is so much I need to know. Things have escalated and..."

Alexia wiped Paisley's tears. "Let's get started."

Saying good-bye to Alexia and the girls two hours later was the hardest thing she'd ever had to do. After the messenger had dropped off the papers, Alexia read over them three times, deeming them fine and complete before she signed them. After a quick hug, Paisley and Addison left. The one time she dared to look back, Addison forced her head back around and shook her head no. It would only hurt her in the long run, so she heeded her thoughts and kept walking.

She wasn't sure what she would find when she reached the house, or who would be there. The only one she wanted to see was Jynx, but when she walked through the door, her anger skyrocketed when she spotted Clara and Lana lounging on the couch like nothing had happened, like her entire world hadn't been upended yet again and it was partly their fault. "I told your mother I would do her bidding, but it won't be from this house." Lana jumped up. "I'm packing my things and moving in with my grandmother. She's already agreed."

Lana sighed. "Paisley, think about this."

"You lost any right to me the moment you smirked at me in the kitchen this morning. The girls had bruises on their shoulders and I had no doubt that your mother would kill all of them. You thought it was funny. I am taking my cat and my things and leaving."

"You can take your things, but not your cat."

Paisley stopped with her foot on the first step and slowly turned around. Addison handed her back her necklaces and she slipped them in her pocket. If Lana had done something to her cat… "And why is that?"

Lana ran her hands through her hair. "She's gone."

"Gone?" This was not happening. This could not be happening.

"I can't find her anywhere. She must have gotten out the open door."

Paisley turned on her heel and marched up the stairs. She threw her bedroom door open and slumped onto the bed with her head in her hands. She would not allow herself to cry in this house. She would wait until she was in the safety of her family's home. Jynx couldn't be gone. No. She would ask her aunt about a locator spell.

An hour later, all her trunks were packed and her uncle and cousin had pulled up outside the house and loaded everything for her into the carriage. She did a quick check of the surrounding area and called for Jynx, but she never came.

"Paisley, you didn't even give us a chance. You do realize we are bonded. You can't ignore that. You will always belong to me." Lana reached for her, but Paisley stepped back.

"That may be the case, but you've never had my heart, nor will you ever. I will find a way to break this bond, and god help the people that stand in my way. You made your choice, now I am making mine."

⚜ ⚜ ⚜ ⚜

After Paisley's uncle and cousin unloaded the carriage, she was left alone in the house with her aunt, grandmother, and Addison. She wasn't up to chatting with them, so she excused herself to her room to settle her nerves until she felt like talking. First Alexia and the girls, and now Jynx. As soon as she shut the bedroom door her eyes landed on a stack of journals on the desk and a folded piece of paper that lay atop them. Her feet moved of their own accord and she picked up the letter, tracing her name written on the paper in Alexia's elegant script. The people that did this to her would pay. No matter what she had to do, or how long she had to wait, they would pay.

With trembling fingers, she unfolded the letter and gasped when she saw two small pictures drawn below the written words. She traced the pictures as a tear fell down her cheek and splashed onto the paper. Forcing her eyes away from the drawings the girls had left for her, she read what Alexia had written.

Paisley,

I can honestly say this isn't the way I intended for my life to go, but I embrace it wholeheartedly. You are our future. Don't forget that. We love you and will wait for you. Let them underestimate you. Prove them wrong. You are far more powerful than I am, and you haven't even fully embraced your magic. Embrace it now. Nourish it and let it grow. I have waited for you my entire life, and I refuse to give you up now that I've found you. I don't regret what you've done for us, but you idiot, we're not complete without you. Stay strong and don't trust anyone, unless they've earned that trust. Your family will always stand by you, as will Addison, I believe. Hurry back to us, but don't rush the process. I'm not sure how or when we'll see each other again, but I have hope that we will. You've won me Paisley, but you've yet to claim me. Don't procrastinate, Darling.
With all our love: Alexia, Amelia, Zoey

Paisley folded the letter until it was small enough to fit into her pocket, and slipped it inside where it would always be with her until they were reunited. She wouldn't let them down. With new resolve, she pushed every emotion that filtered to the surface deep down. Now was not the time to curl up on the bed and cry. She wiped her nose, opened the door, and walked back into the living room where everyone was waiting for her.

She nodded at her nana and aunt, then took a seat beside Addison, who sat on the couch nursing a cup of tea. Out of habit, she reached up and adjusted her glasses before talking. "When we were in the marketplace the queen said something to Lana that has stuck with me. She told her that she had made the right decision about me. The way she phrased it made it seem like Lana had a choice in the matter and she chose me, but I thought every pairing like ours was already predetermined. If that's the case, how did Lana accomplish it and who is her true bond mate?" Her aunt and nana shared a look before Olivia sighed and stood up.

"It is unprecedented to change what has been written. For Lana to have pulled off something like that, she'd have to have had the help of several important people. Only a few individuals have access to those scrolls. They are locked away in a room inside the Royal Library. It would be extremely difficult to get your hands on them."

"Paisley, that is true," Nana said. "And take comfort in the fact that if it's true Lana had a hand in changing the records herself or convincing someone to change them, it also means that you two do not share a true bond. This bond can be broken." She held up her hand. "I don't know how, but I know it can."

Paisley stood up and started pacing. It was good

news wrapped in a grenade. "The official documents are in the Royal Library. You're sure?"

"Yes." Olivia crossed her arms and frowned. It reminded Paisley of her dad. Olivia sighed and retook her seat. "I know someone who works in the library who might be able to help you, but you have to have permission of the queen to even enter the library. You must talk with her, Paisley."

That was just great. She stared out the window, wishing she had Jynx in her arms. This was her family and Addison was her friend, but as much time as she had spent with them, they still weren't familiar. Not like Jynx. "All right." The last thing she wanted was to talk to her, but she had start somewhere. "Also, my cat is missing. I brought her with me and she's gone. I don't know if Lana did something to her or if she really did run away. If you could look into that, I would appreciate it. I don't want to think about her out there all alone and hungry."

"I'll do my best, Paisley," Olivia said. "How are you holding up?"

She turned away from the window. "I can't think about them right now. I have to figure a way out of this mess. If I let them invade my thoughts, it will only set me back and I can't afford that. I don't want to be anywhere near the queen, but if that's what I have to do, that's what I have to do." She shrugged. Nana patted the arm of her chair and Paisley knelt beside it, taking Nana's hand.

"You can accomplish anything you set our mind to. Have faith, dear heart. I am with you, as is Addison and the rest of the family. You can rest assured that wherever Alexia is, she is also on top of things. You are not alone. Please hold on to that. We are family, and nothing is more important to us than family."

Paisley stood up and kissed her on the cheek. "Thank you. I think that for now I'm going to call it a night and dive into the journals that were left for me." When she was finally settled into bed, she opened the first journal and started to read. She took great comfort in the fact that this was Alexia's personal journal. After a few hours and rereading the same page five times straight, she believed she was ready to practice a spell.

The spell outlined how to conjure a fireball. It seemed simple enough. Even though she had created one once before when she and Alexia were training, she hadn't meant to. She read the spell one last time, laid the journal on the bed, and stood up.

After a dozen failed attempts, she focused on a fixed point on the wall, shook her hands out as sparks flew from her fingertips, reached her hand out, and willed it into her palm. It started as a spark, then continued to grow as her anger festered for the people who had already turned on her. Her heart raced as the flames licked at her fingers but didn't burn her. She stared transfixed at the shadows dancing on the wall. The fireball was roughly the size of a soccer ball. She flicked her wrist, and it started bouncing on her palm.

Despite the multiple failures, it wasn't as hard as she had expected. Alexia's notes were simple and precise. If all her other notes were similar, she knew she could do this. At the end of the spell, Alexia had written that it was possible to change the fireball to whatever you wanted it to be. She added that she had created a ball of water once before.

Paisley eyed the fireball, pulled her hand back so the ball floated in the air, then blew on it, per the spell's instructions. As soon as her breath reached the fireball, it turned into an ice ball. Just like the fireball, when the ice ball rested in her hand she didn't feel the cold. She grinned before making the ball disappear.

She climbed back into bed, hugged the journal to her chest, and tried to sleep. She knew it wouldn't be easy, but any new trick in her arsenal would help. Tomorrow she would ask her uncle to start training with him. If it was within her power, she would make it happen, and training was something she was in control of.

⁂

For once, Paisley looked forward to her training and was grateful Beatrice stuck to her teaching and didn't ask any personal questions. She considered asking her what being a DragonWitch meant, but the timing seemed off, especially considering the queen probably had spies everywhere. After a grueling three hours of training and an hour spent in the garden, Paisley and Addison left and headed toward the castle. Her uncle had insisted on them taking the carriage that morning, and Paisley had readily agreed. Even with the carriage, it still took them an hour to reach the castle gates. One look at Paisley and the guards let them through. She guessed that was one advantage to royalty, although there wasn't a doubt in her mind that the queen would be advised immediately of her unplanned appearance.

Once inside and without asking, she was taken to the queen's office. The queen didn't look up from the papers on her desk when Paisley walked in and took a seat. The office was decorated in reds and creams with splashes of black, and with the floor to ceiling windows along one wall, the office, unlike the woman sitting behind the desk, put Paisley at ease.

Since the queen still hadn't acknowledged her, Paisley took the opportunity to study her. What she could see of the navy dress was well fitted and low cut. Unlike Alexia's cleavage, the queen's didn't do a thing for her. She had to admit she was a beautiful woman, but the fact that she was the devil incarnate overshadowed her outward beauty. She fought the urge to fidget or sigh, and kept her mouth shut until the queen looked up from the papers she was reading.

She slowly raised her head and steepled her fingers together on top of the desk. "What brings you here today, Paisley? What could I possibly help you with? Surely, your training is taking up most of your time?"

"Yes, my Queen." Paisley bit her tongue to not lash out at her.

The queen snickered. "I can see your hatred for me written all over your face. But, let's face it. It wasn't my choice to send them away." She pointed at Paisley and chuckled. "That was all your doing. One thing you must learn is to never doubt your choices and always stick by them. I don't like you, but I know you will be an asset to me. You're powerful and I intend to make sure you can master your abilities. Now, what can I do for you?"

"Beatrice mentioned that there are quite a few books on magic in the Royal Library that she doesn't have access to, and she told me I had to get your permission before exploring it."

After an uncomfortable silence, the queen stood and motioned for her to follow. They exited the room and turned left at the end of the hallway, then made another two lefts before coming to a closed door. "I don't normally let just anybody explore the library. There are certain parts, of course, that will be off limits and I will assign a worker to assist you, but for the most part feel free to look around. I wasn't happy about the fact that you moved out of Lana's house, but I can't worry myself over such trivial matters. What I care about is your abilities, and if this helps even in a small way, then I am willing to allow it. But, mark my words, Paisley. If you try anything to hurt my family or if you break the rules of the library, then you will never be allowed to set foot through these doors again. Do I make myself clear?"

"Yes, my Queen."

She nodded at two of her guards, who opened the doors allowing them to walk through. From the outside, it didn't look like much, but from the inside it was amazing. Rows and rows of shelves were loaded down with books of all sizes, as were the bookshelves that lined three of the four walls. The room was massive, with walls at least fifteen feet tall. There were ladders placed every ten or so feet along the bookshelves. The floor was a warm maple, and what she could see of the walls were painted cream. Three large stained glass windows were placed near the ceiling on the far wall, letting in tons of natural light. Paisley looked up when an older gentleman and a woman walked toward them. "Your Highness," the man said, and they both bowed.

"Sydney," The queen addressed the man. "This is Paisley, Lana's new bride. She is to have access to everything except the off-limits rooms."

"Yes, my Queen."

"Paisley, this is Caroline. Caroline, you will be assigned to Paisley every time she searches the library."

"Of course, my Queen."

Paisley held out her hand, first to Sydney, then Caroline. Caroline didn't strike her as the librarian type. She was almost six feet tall, with long, curly black hair. Paisley could tell that under her long skirt and baggy shirt was an athletic build. She looked more like a warrior than anything else, but Paisley held her own fair share of secrets, so she wasn't about to question Caroline about hers.

Sydney, on the other hand, reminded her of her ex-neighbor. His beady eyes and receding hairline, coupled with his short stature, would have been almost comical if it wasn't for the uneasiness she felt just by being in his presence. She would have to watch out for him. "I can't wait to delve into the books. There is so much I have to learn."

"I'll leave you two to it. Paisley, good luck." Without a backward glance, the queen walked out the door, her guards following and shutting it behind them.

"Caroline, I can't wait to get started tomorrow."

"I will be happy to assist you." Her soft and smooth voice sent shivers down Paisley's spine, and she was looking forward to working with her. "Do you want a tour before you go?"

"No, I do need to be going. But thank you." Paisley quickly retrieved Addison and the two left the castle, but it wasn't until Addison pulled the carriage onto her family's property that she allowed herself to relax. Tomorrow would be a big day, and she had a feeling she would need all the sleep she could get.

The next day dawned bright and early, and after a simple breakfast Paisley and Addison again made their way by carriage to the castle. She had informed Beatrice by courier the day before that she wouldn't be at her lessons today. No, today she needed to focus on finding proof that Lana had somehow overridden the bonding process and chose her, instead of bonding with her true mate. If that were true, she also hoped she would be able to find a way to break the bond. Her aunt was also still searching for a way to track Jynx; one could never have too many eyes looking for a solution.

As their footsteps echoed down the long corridor, Paisley hoped she didn't run into the queen this morning. That was the last thing she wanted to deal with. And considering they made it to the library without any unwanted run-ins, luck did seem to be on her side for once.

She nodded at Sydney when the guards opened the door for them, and Addison took up position beside the doors after they had closed them. It didn't take her long to find Caroline, who was scanning a stack of books that had yet to be catalogued. "Good morning, Caroline." Today she wore another long skirt and a shirt that looked two sizes too big, but her eyes were bright and Paisley couldn't see any malice hidden within their depths. Best to be on alert anyway, as there was no telling who she could and couldn't trust within the castle walls.

"Paisley." She eyed her outfit, then motioned for her to sit down at one of the tables. Caroline took out a pen and a piece of paper. "Tell me, what exactly are you looking for?"

She narrowed her eyes at her. She hated to be judged. "What's wrong with my outfit?"

"I beg your pardon."

"My outfit." Paisley gestured to her body. "Why did you give me that look?"

"Truthfully?"

"Yes."

She stood up and sat down right beside Paisley, and kept her voice low. "If you want to fit in with the people of this world, you need to start dressing like them. I know you're probably more comfortable in clothes you are used to, but you really should try."

Paisley tugged on her glasses and ran her fingers along the tabletop. She knew Caroline was right, but throwing away this tiny part of who she was felt wrong. In the long run, though, she did need to start changing her clothes. "You have a point. Tomorrow I will dress accordingly. I hope it doesn't matter whether I wear pants, a skirt, or a dress."

"No, as long as they are world-appropriate."

"All right, and to answer your question, I don't exactly know what I'm looking for." She tapped her bracelet. "I would like to know how this works, though. It's all so confusing. The entire process. I don't like having my choices made for me, and I would like to learn what I've gotten myself into."

Caroline looked at her thoughtfully, and just when Paisley thought her acting had been found out, Caroline nodded. "I think I can help you with that." She stood up and walked around the bookshelf. After a few minutes, she returned with a nicely sized, leather-bound book. "This will explain the process of bonding and what it will mean for your future and that of your mate. It also has every bond that has ever been chosen written within its pages. It updates accordingly, so yours and Lana's will also be included."

"Where?"

Caroline flipped through the pages, looking for the right section. She skimmed a page with her finger, but when she found what she was looking for, she frowned and bit her lip. Suddenly, she slammed the book closed, grabbed the nearest one, and laid it atop the first. The hair on the back of Paisley's neck stood on end, halting her from talking. Sydney came into view.

"Paisley." His nasally voice put her on edge. "I thought this book would be right for you." He placed a large book in front of her. *The Complete History of Magic as Taught Through the Ages.* Even though she had Alexia's journals and Beatrice, she had to admit such a book could come in handy. She was itching to delve into it, but something else told her that this book probably excluded a lot of what she needed to be taught. As if reading her thoughts, he continued. "The queen has made it clear she wants you to reach your full potential and beyond. This book has not been censored or pared down in any way. If you study it, it will teach you a tremendous amount."

"Thank you." She wasn't sure what else to say, but she felt a great weight left off her shoulders when he was out of her sight. "That was odd."

"I dare say it was." Caroline still frowned. "He's right, that particular volume hasn't been whitewashed in any way, but before you go off half-cocked and try the spells and incantations within, you might want to talk with someone who knows what they're doing."

"Noted." Paisley patted the book in front of her, then pointed at the one Caroline had covered up. Without answering her, Caroline slipped the book out from under the one on top, flipped back through the pages until she found the one she was looking for, and passed it to Paisley. She tapped the part she wanted her to read. The entire page was a list of names. At the bottom, her name was printed, but the spot beside her name was blank. Hers was the only name that didn't have a pairing. "I don't understand. What's the significance of this?"

Caroline closed the book and turned her face away. When she seemed to have made up her mind, she turned back toward Paisley. "When word spread that Lana had chosen, I took the liberty of searching the book for the pairing. Her name was written first, followed by your name. Now her name is missing and your name is first. I've never seen that happen before. I don't think I've even heard of it happening before."

Another first. How many more could there be? "What does that mean, though? Does it mean that we're not bonded anymore? How can that be if I still have the bracelet on?"

"I think it means that you are an extraordinary woman, Paisley. It seems that you have chosen your own path to walk. It also seems that no one knows yet that Lana is not your bond mate. It would be best if no one found that out. This is the official book for that. It is the only one in existence."

If that was true, what would that mean for her and Alexia? Then a thought struck her. "Isn't this book supposed to be in a part of the library that is off limits to everyone, including me?"

"Perhaps." She kept her eyes glued to the bookshelf in front of them.

"I don't trust you."

Caroline slowly looked at her. "It is best you don't trust anyone." She leaned in closer. "The walls have ears, Paisley. But in time, I believe you will come to find that you can trust me."

Paisley shook her head. "You serve the queen." Deep down she might not trust Caroline, but she also didn't feel like she was her enemy, either. "I don't not trust you."

"Well, that's a start." She reached for the book.

"Wait." Paisley didn't know why, but she had a good idea that they wouldn't be the only ones looking at this book in the future. She placed her hand over the page, murmured a few words, then blew on it. As she opened her eyes, she watched as Lana's name magically switched places with hers, and her name appeared next to it. With any luck, the enchantment would hold. She was glad that she had reread the chapter in Alexia's journal dealing with enchantments four times last night. Time would tell how long it would last.

Caroline cracked a smile. "Nice." She stood up and walked away.

Paisley bit her lip and looked around. Somehow, she had changed her own fate. That's the only thing it could mean. The only question was why she still had the bracelet on. Maybe her aunt had discovered something helpful to share when she returned home later. In the meantime, she pulled the book Sydney had given to her closer and opened it to the first page. She had a feeling it was going to be a long day.

❧ ❧ ❧

The day flew by as she jumped headfirst into the book. Most of it didn't interest her, but the chapter on transporting was fascinating, and she filled four pages of her notebook with notes. In her upcoming session with Beatrice she would ask her to explain things and maybe practice a few of the spells with her. There would be a good chance that Beatrice would dismiss her, but she would ask anyway.

Her good luck for the day faltered when, on their way home, they had no choice but to stop their carriage because Clara was standing in the middle of the road ahead of them. Paisley eyed her, but didn't make a move to step down from the carriage. "Clara, what brings you to this part of the town on this fine day?"

Clara rolled her eyes. "I just wanted to talk to you for a moment."

Addison shrugged at Paisley's look, then they both climbed down from their seats. She hoped this would be a quick talk. She hadn't had anything to eat for a couple of hours and Nana had promised to make beef stew and apple turnovers with fresh cream for dinner. "You have ten minutes."

"I know your life is upside down right now, but do you honestly think the best course of action is to push Lana completely out of it? She's a good woman, if you would just give her a chance. Let her prove it to you."

Was she honestly stating Lana's case right now? Paisley leaned back against the carriage. "You can save your words, I've made my decision. Lana will just have to live with it."

"You're bonded to her. Do you even realize what that means? Your lives are intertwined. She cannot move on from you. You're such an idiot."

If Paisley hadn't seen it before, she saw it now. "Clara, I am only going to say this once. If you want Lana, go after her. I will not stand in your way."

Clara laughed, but it was humorless and devoid of mirth. "Do you really think it's that easy? You. Are. Bonded. No matter what, Lana will always take that into consideration. Nothing can break the bond. Nothing. You can create a life with Alexia all you want, but if you think it's going to last, you're dead wrong. Once it's written it cannot be changed. That's why no one cares about how you're acting right now. In the long run, it won't matter. You will always come back to her. Always."

She sounded so sad it crossed Paisley's mind to wrap her into a giant hug, but the thought quickly passed when it dawned on her what Clara had said. If they were truly bonded, wouldn't she feel a pull toward Lana? She didn't feel anything. She had to admit, when she first laid eyes on Lana she did feel something toward her, probably lust, but that pull was shattered the minute Alexia walked into her life.

She knew without a shadow of a doubt that Alexia was her future, but considering what Clara had just said, she couldn't let anyone know that. She pushed off the carriage and looked into the distance. "I wasn't sure what I had been feeling, but now it makes sense. Even though I don't love Lana, there is something there." She caught Clara's eyes and felt an unease like she had never felt before. "I can't explain it, but there is something there."

Clara nodded and wiped at her eyes. "It won't go away. The longer and harder you fight it, the more you'll be pulled toward her."

"I will keep fighting it as long as possible. Right now, I need to focus on me and learning everything I can. Later I'll worry about Lana and what everything means."

"I'm sorry I stopped you in the middle of the road."

"That's all right." Paisley bit her lip and locked eyes with Clara one last time. Her tears where still running down her cheeks, but they didn't pull at her heartstrings anymore. It was clear to her now that Clara was faking it. Oh, she might be in love with Lana, but the show she had just put on was all for play. Paisley just didn't understand why. "We should be going."

"Of course. I'm sure we'll run into each other again."

"I'm sure we will." They both climbed onto the carriage and Addison set it in motion. Paisley didn't bother looking back at Clara. She could feel her hatred geared toward her even when the carriage turned onto the road leading to her family's estate.

"Do you really feel a pull toward Lana?" Addison asked.

"No, I was lying."

Addison cut her eyes toward her. "You were really convincing."

"Really?"

Addison laughed. "I believed you, and I am sure Clara did, too. I'm not sure what game she's trying to play."

"You noticed that too, huh?"

"Yes."

"You sure she believed me?" Paisley pushed the hair off her face.

"I do, and I will look into her affairs. See who she's been hanging out with."

"That's a good idea." Once inside the house, she wrapped Nana in a hug, kissed her on the cheek, and went to find her aunt. Since dinner wasn't ready, she figured they could get their talk over with. She found her sitting on the back porch. "Did you find anything out?" She sat beside her on the swing.

"I did."

"As did I." Paisley told her everything she had discovered.

"Considering what I found, that's unbelievable. Word has it that a bond cannot be broken, but if Lana's name truly was erased from the book, then you have done the impossible. Is there something you're not telling me, Paisley? Surely, you know you can trust me."

And Paisley did trust her, but three people besides her already knew about the dragon, and she was sure that the dragon was the reason the bond had been broken in the first place. She was on a slippery slope. "It's not that I don't trust you, it's just that the fewer people that know, the better."

Olivia eyed her, then turned her gaze back to the horizon. "I understand that. It also came to my attention that one's own powers can be enhanced with the help of a certain creature."

Paisley hid her smile. "You don't say."

"It's also came to my attention that while this creature might propel one's powers, it can also have longer-lasting effects."

Now she was intrigued. "Really?"

"It is said that a dragon not only amplifies a witch's powers but can also grant her heart's desire."

Wow. She hadn't read that in her dragon book yet. If that was true then the dragon was the one that could break the bond, but that didn't explain why she still had the bracelet on. Her aunt followed her gaze and ran her fingers along the band of the bracelet.

"It is probable that the reason you still have it on is because your true bond mate is out there and you haven't bonded yet. Whose name was written first on the page?"

"Mine."

Her aunt stood and leaned on the railing. Paisley joined her. "The first name written signifies the person who initiated the bond. For the bond between you and Lana to be true, her name should have been written first. This means that you will be the one to initiate the bond. It is most likely that you were bonded with Lana. That is what allowed you to cross over the barrier, but once you arrived something happened. Or should I say, someone."

"Alexia."

"Yes. From the very first time I saw you two interact, it was clear there was a bond there."

"I couldn't fight it. Her name was always on my lips and her face always in my dreams. I didn't even know her, but I know I can't live without her now. It doesn't make any sense."

"Oh, I don't know. I think it makes perfect sense." She turned Paisley toward her and grasped her shoulders. "You love her. It's that simple. You truly love her. All of her. I have no doubt that you two will be reunited. Keep on the path you are walking and you will see them again. She has always been a friend to this family and I trust her with your heart. You will see her again, trust me."

"It's my one hope."

"Even more than seeing your family in your other world?"

"Yes." Saying it didn't scare her as much as she thought it would. She did miss her family, but if she had to choose she would choose Alexia and the girls every time.

"Come." She patted her arm. "Dinner's ready. Don't fret too much. We are all here for you. You're family."

She said it like that explained everything. Family. Maybe it did. She did have a family here and it was time she spent more time getting to know them instead of always focusing on herself. She knew she would see Alexia again. Only time would tell when, but that didn't mean that she couldn't learn more about her family in the meantime. "Aunt Olivia, I would really love to know more about you. Maybe we could talk after dinner?"

Olivia slipped her arm around Paisley's waist. "I think that's a splendid idea."

⁂

After an unproductive meeting with Beatrice the next day, who refused to help her with the transportation spell, the library was another matter. Caroline was as helpful today as she had been the previous day. She kept her mouth shut when Caroline passed a small pamphlet in her direction even though neither one of them had seen Sydney yet that day. Caroline had mentioned to her that she hadn't even seen him when she arrived at seven that morning. Which, according to Caroline, was odd.

Paisley made note of Caroline's discomfort but decided not to worry about something that hadn't happened yet. It wasn't until she was nearing the end of the pamphlet that she found an article that she was looking for. *Bonding As It Pertains to the Royal Family.*

The article had been written over a hundred and fifty years ago, but Caroline said it was still relevant for today. When she reached the third paragraph, her heart started pounding.

As not to taint the Royal bloodline, a bond mate shall only be made with another Royal. Never shall a commoner be chosen to bond with the Royal bloodline. As it is written, so shall it be.

She jerked her head up when the library doors slammed open and quick, heavy footsteps, followed by a slower, softer *click-click*, headed their way. Caroline grabbed the pamphlet from her and slipped it inside one of the books on the table before jumping up from the table and making herself scarce. Paisley wanted to protest, but thought better of it when the queen came into view. Paisley tamped down her magic, which seemed to always flare up around her, and clasped her hands in her lap.

"Paisley, Paisley, Paisley. You haven't been honest with me." She paced in front of the table. Paisley kept her mouth shut but made sure her bag stayed on the floor beside her foot.

"I'm not sure what you're referring to, my Queen." Playing dumb had gotten her out of some tricky situations before.

She stopped pacing and cocked her head. "I believe we need to have another talk. You seem to be under the impression that you can act any way you want and keep things from me. I can assure you that is not the case. I find it quite disturbing, this new information, and quite extraordinary." She tapped her finger on her lip. "A dragon egg."

Paisley sucked in a breath. She didn't know what was worse: the fact that someone told her or the fact that she knew she wouldn't be able to deny it. There were only four people that knew besides her: Beatrice, Addison, Olivia, and Alexia. She knew Alexia and Addison would never have talked. She hated to think it, but she didn't know her aunt well enough to trust her, ever after their talk, and Beatrice, was…well… Beatrice. "How did you find out?"

"I can be extremely persuasive. I bet you're running the names over in your head wondering who told me. Tell me something, Paisley, which one of them can't you trust? The number of people you must have told is probably small. Can you count them on one hand? Does it make you feel better or worse that someone close to you betrayed you?" She laughed, then took a seat opposite Paisley. "I do have to say that this works out better than I ever could have imagined. You're a Dragon Master. No wonder your magic has been so powerful. To have a Dragon Master protecting me will be quite astonishing."

"Protecting you?" Her day just went from bad to worse.

"Yes, protecting me. That is what all this is about. You will be my personal guard, and when the dragon hatches you will bind it to me."

She wasn't sure she could trust the queen's answers but she needed to know. "I have a dragon book Beatrice gave me but it didn't say anything about binding the dragon to someone. What exactly does that mean?" She would need to get another book.

"I will inform Caroline to find you a book on the matter. Beatrice is good at training, but for this you will need someone quite different. I have put a few feelers out for someone who would be willing to train you and your dragon. You do know that the dragon will stay with you at all times, yes?" Paisley nodded. She had read that part. "A Dragon Master cannot be bound to their dragon, it's simply not done. But if they so choose they can give the binding to someone else. That doesn't mean that the dragon leaves its master, but what it does mean is that if the person the dragon is bound to is ever in trouble, the dragon will leave its master and protect its charge. Even if its master's life is also in peril."

"That doesn't seem wise." Not one bit.

"It's not. Only a few Dragon Masters choose to freely bind their dragons with anyone. If they choose not to, then the dragon will always protect its master."

"You're going to force me to bind my dragon to you?"

She snapped her fingers. "You catch on quick, Paisley. And don't think of it as me forcing you. Think of it as you helping me out for the greater good."

This wasn't good. Wasn't good at all. "Why do you want my protection? You don't even like me. I am sure there are far more powerful witches than me in this world that would gladly protect you."

"You are far more powerful than even you know, I believe. I was skeptical before but willing to give you a chance to prove yourself. But now, I won't let you go anywhere." Paisley knew there was no arguing with her so she kept her mouth shut. "I also talked to Clara. That woman is a lost cause. Pining over someone who will never want her. Pathetic."

Paisley frowned at the thought of seeing Clara and Lana standing in Lana's kitchen. It would make sense. "Is Clara of royal descent?" she blurted out.

The queen narrowed her eyes but answered the question. "Unfortunately, yes, she is and tries to play on that, but mark my words, her royal blood is whitewashed and she is no better than a commoner."

"I'm a commoner."

"Paisley, you stopped being a commoner the moment you bonded with my daughter." She pointed her finger at her. "You will be remembered in the history books. The Queen's Knight."

On paper that sounded like an excellent idea, but it was the worst thing that could ever happen to her. "That doesn't sound so bad," she lied.

"There are worse things one could be. Getting back to Clara. You shouldn't fight the pull toward Lana, but I know why you're doing it and it doesn't have anything to do with that dark witch and her brats. You just don't like the idea of someone making choices for you." She waved her hand in the air. "Get over it. My daughter is a fine catch. Take the time to find yourself if you must, but we both know that you will eventually find yourself back in her arms. Don't make her wait too long. It will only make you both suffer when there isn't a need. But for now, I will keep her away. You do need to study. Are you finding anything helpful?"

"Actually, yes. The book Sydney gave me has been quite informative, and if I could get that book on dragons, that would be a help also." She adjusted her glasses. "Also, I've noticed Beatrice mixes her own potions and different medicines. I feel that that would be good to learn, but I wouldn't even know where to begin looking. Is it okay if I ask Caroline or Sydney to find me a book on the matter?"

The queen smirked. "Of course. Now that I know what your potential could be, the library is open to you, except the Royal Archives. I will inform Sydney and Caroline that you will be allowed in the other rooms."

She stood up, smoothed her skirt, and patted Paisley on the cheek. "I am so glad we were able to have this talk. Aren't you?"

Paisley bit the inside of her cheek and stood. "Yes, my Queen."

"One more thing before I go. I would like to see your dragon egg."

Paisley knew it wasn't a request, so she leaned down and grasped the strap of her backpack, placed it gently on the table, and unzipped it. The queen looked down into the bag but she didn't attempt to touch it. She scrunched up her nose. "It doesn't look that impressive, does it?"

Paisley couldn't help it. She laughed. "I'm not laughing at you, my Queen, but that was the first thought I had upon first seeing it also."

The queen eyed her clothes, then nodded. "Better than what you've been wearing, but if you give it a bit more effort I'm sure you'll get there." She turned on her heels and walked back out. Paisley didn't relax until she heard the library doors shut.

"She's right you know," Caroline said, sitting back down beside her. "Your clothes are nicer today." She slipped a book in Paisley's direction.

Today she had worn a pair of fitted brown trousers, with a light blue sleeveless V-neck tunic. A pair of stylish but practical brown leather boots and a simple brown belt completed the look. After two training sessions with her uncle, he had made her a leather case for her dagger that hung off her belt. Even if she never used it, it brought her a sense of peace in an otherwise hectic situation. She did have to admit, no one stared at her like they would have if she'd been wearing her jeans and a tank top. It was nice. "Thank you." She lifted the book up, but there wasn't much to it. Probably no more than fifty pages that were bound with twine.

"I believe there is a story in there that will be helpful to you. I couldn't help but overhear that you have a dragon egg. One of the stories in the book is dedicated to The Goldenmare Triad. One of the Triad, Rosemary, is one of the last dragon trainers left in the country. I don't believe the queen will recommend her for you. One, because she is around your age, and two, because the Triad isn't well liked. They are traitors to their countries. I won't get into the story, but you can read it all there. You can have that copy." She paused, seeming to weigh her words. "You realize that the queen won't stop until she has everything she wants, don't you?"

Paisley absentmindedly flipped through the book. "I am aware, yes."

"Do you have any idea how uncommon it is in today's society for someone to possess a dragon egg?"

"Are dragon eggs really that rare?" She found that hard to believe.

"No, eggs aren't rare at all, but being able to pick one up is. Dragons are picky creatures. They choose their master. Has anybody besides you touched your egg?"

"No."

"That's because they can't."

"What would happen?"

"Essentially nothing on the outside, but the dragon inside the egg knows its master, and until the dragon feels completely safe it won't hatch. If the dragon feels that there is any sort of threat to it or to you, it won't hatch. If the wrong person fiddled with the egg too much, or tried to hatch the egg themselves, the dragon would die."

"So if I keep coming here, it won't hatch?"

"Correct. Dragons are also quite finicky. And contrary to what the queen believes, unless the dragon wants to be bound to her, it won't be. You can force the dragon to, of course, but no one would like the outcome. Dragons are loyal. The dragon that has chosen you would gladly lay down its life for you. But if a dragon is forced to become something it's not, then the outcome could be disastrous for everyone involved. Read the story of the Triad tonight and it will give you a feel of what being a Dragon Master or trainer, if you will, means. But keep in mind, the story isn't only about Rosemary. It's also about Kennedy and McKenzie, the other two women involved in the Triad. It's a riveting story, if I do say so myself."

"I'll look at it tonight, but I also want to try a transportation spell."

"On yourself?"

She looked skeptical, and Paisley didn't blame her. No matter how much power she had, she was still a novice. "Not on me. I thought I would start small. Maybe a teacup."

"Well good luck with that. I hope you're successful."

"We shall see."

On the ride back home, Paisley took the opportunity to skim the part of the Triad story that dealt with Rosemary specifically. She'd become a Dragon Master at the age of twenty-two. It seems the inception of the Triad was a result of some sort of joke between three neighboring countries. Every twenty-five years, all three kingdoms would gather to renegotiate their standing treaties, each kingdom offering something unique from their country in exchange for resources needed from the other two. On one such occasion, each king had a daughter of age to wager in the negotiation. Each king thought up ridiculous demands of the other two for ratification of the treaty, to flex their dominance, and to dispatch the conference quickly. In return, they each gave up one daughter for marriage as part of their ante, believing their daughters would never assent to the conditions of the agreement. The joke ended up on the kings when all three daughters banded together against their fathers' casual gambling with their lives, and agreed to the proposed treaty and all its ridiculous terms. The kings, thoroughly embarrassed and shown up by their children, banished their daughters from their home countries because of their "defiance and disloyalty." These daughters formed The Goldenmare Triad. The book didn't say where the Triad was located, though it did mention that Rosemary, on occasion, would agree to train new Dragon Masters. Paisley shut the book, then slipped it into her bag. She would read the rest of the story later.

"Addison, what do you know of The Goldenmare Triad?"

"Not much. I don't think there is much to know. They mostly keep to themselves. I'm not even sure anyone knows what the women look like. Some rumors are that the reason their fathers gave their hands in the treaty to begin with was because the women were unattractive and without any skill set whatsoever." She shrugged.

"But, is that what you believe?" She found it hard to believe that Addison would have been the one to alert the queen that she had a dragon egg, and until such time that she found out it was her, she would keep trusting her.

"The women must have had something to offer. I think the kings were outsmarted. Their daughters knew what they were doing. Some don't even think the story is true, but I don't see how it cannot be true given that the three countries started trade agreements and opened up certain parts of their lands to allow the other countries to set up outposts."

"So you believe Rosemary is real?"

"Yes. Why?"

"Well, it would be nice to train with someone of my own choosing."

"That may be the case, Paisley, but no one knows where the Triad reside. No one has been able to find it. I hate to say this, but maybe you should wait and see what the queen comes up with. Hear me out. She wants that dragon something fierce, so I don't think she would do anything to jeopardize that. You don't have to trust her—I don't—but maybe you should wait and see what happens."

"Maybe you're right." When she got home all she wanted to do was fall into bed and read, but she knew she would have to at least be a bit social with her family. Olivia was the last one to know about the dragon egg. If it had been any of the other ones, wouldn't the queen have known about it sooner? Nothing made any sense. She took her glasses off and rubbed her eyes.

"Paisley, don't overthink. You've got this."

"If you say so."

"When have I ever steered you wrong?"

"You're a good friend, Addison." And she was. She was the only friend she had. She didn't want to think about her being a traitor, so she didn't. It was much easier to think it was her aunt, because it being Addison might just tip her over the edge.

❧❧❧❧

"Paisley, stop." Beatrice walked to the counter and starting preparing all three of them a cup of tea. "You're preoccupied today and it is going to hinder your progress." She set the three cups of tea on the table and motioned for them to join her. "Tell me what is on your mind."

"The queen knows I have a dragon egg."

Beatrice arched her eyebrow. "And you think I told her?"

"Actually, no, and she is looking into finding me a trainer." Paisley sipped her tea. Hot just the way she liked it.

"That might not be a bad idea."

"No, but I have recently found out about someone who might be able to train me, but Caroline told me the queen would never agree to it."

"Who's Caroline?"

"She works in the library and the queen assigned her to me."

"Who would you like to train you?"

"I came across a book that dealt with The Goldenmare Triad. What do you know about them?"

"Caroline is right, the queen would never agree to have Rosemary teach you."

Paisley straightened in her chair. "So, you do know about them?"

"I do."

Why did everyone have to be so vague all the

time? "Why would the queen never agree?"

"Let me ask a question first. Why don't you believe it was me that told the queen about your dragon egg?"

"I am not a hundred percent sure it wasn't you, but I have a gut feeling it wasn't." She shrugged and took another sip of her tea. "That's what I am basing it on."

"The Goldenmare estate is located in neutral territory. The queen would have no say in your training. In fact, if any form of military from the surrounding countries entered the neutral territory, it would be an act of war."

"So the estate is protected?"

"Only because of where it's located. It isn't specially protected. The entire country is."

"So, do you know Rosemary or have you only heard her name in passing?"

"What I am about to tell you goes no further than this room. Is that understood?" Paisley and Addison nodded. "I have met every member of the Triad once. So, yes I have met Rosemary. In fact, she was the only one I talked to. Do you know their story?"

"I skimmed over it and just read Rosemary's parts."

"Then I won't ruin it for you. Rosemary would be an excellent teacher for you, but even if you choose her, she would have to choose you as well. She is quite accomplished, but she is picky about who she trains. The choice is always hers."

Paisley finished her tea and leaned back in her chair. "How would I even contact her?"

"You don't. If she wants to train you, she will find you. Do you trust Caroline?"

"I don't not trust her. Though she has been quite forthcoming with the information I am looking for. I get the feeling that she doesn't like the queen much, but there does seem to be something off about her. I can't put my finger on it."

"Not many people do trust the queen," Beatrice mumbled, but Paisley heard her. "Do you know how long she's been working in the library? I was there a few months back and I don't remember anyone by the name of Caroline."

"I'm headed there next. I'll ask her when I get there."

"Fine. I don't think we will get much more done today. You can head to the library and I will see you tomorrow, Paisley."

"Have a good day." They weren't in a hurry so Paisley and Addison set a relaxed pace. For the first time all week she felt a deep sense of peace. It wasn't unwelcome, but it was unexpected. Her newfound peace was shattered when she walked into the library and was surprised that J.J., of all people, asked to speak to her alone. Neither Caroline nor Sydney were present. She'd only talked to him a few times over the royal family dinner, so she didn't know what this could be about.

"Your guard can wait outside."

"No, I trust her with my life. She stays."

He ran his hands through his hair and paced in front of her. "Fine. I can't believe I am doing this. If she finds out, I don't know what will happen to me."

"Who?"

"Lana has always been their favorite, and although I will be king one day it doesn't make a difference. My mom and I don't get along all that well. She feels Lana should be queen. It doesn't matter that Lana doesn't want it."

"J.J., what's this about?" She had a bad feeling.

"I like you. I did the moment I saw you." He waved his hand in the air. "Not romantically. I thought maybe with time we could be friends, but now I see that won't ever be the case. My mother has found a trainer for you. I overheard her talking with her personal advisors and the commander of her personal guards."

"From the way you're acting, I take it that's a bad thing."

"She wants to send you to Kent." When Addison gasped behind her she knew that was a bad thing. "In her mind, everything is already taken care of. You are to leave in five days' time."

"I would fight her before I left."

He shook his head. "They have ways to subdue your powers. Please heed my warning. Leave now. Leave while you can."

"I don't know what to say."

"Don't say anything, and please don't tell anyone what I've told you."

"I won't." He nodded twice, spun on his heels, and walked out the door. Should she trust him? What if this was a trap? She turned toward Addison. "I take it Kent is bad?"

"Yes. Daren Ravspon is the Dragon Master there, and he is a vicious and brutal man. He doesn't have any morals. You would not flourish under him; you would wilt and die. Having him as your trainer would kill your spirit. We have to do something."

"Like what? Is it really feasible for me to pack up and leave? Where would I go?"

"I don't know. There are rumors that he has

mind magic."

"That sounds ominous."

"He can control someone through their mind. The queen doesn't want you to learn from him, she wants you to become her puppet."

"Shit."

"That's an accurate assessment."

"Where is everybody?" They walked around the entire space, but they were alone. She stopped in front of the door to the Royal Archives, but didn't dare enter. She'd already found out what she came here for, there was no need to get caught going into the room. She would have to find a way out of this. Rosemary was out. Alexia was out. At this point, even her family was out. Who could you turn to when there wasn't anybody left in your corner? Addison could only do so much. "Let's get out of here. I'm ready to go home."

"Sounds good to me."

❧❧❧❧

As soon as she walked in the front door, she knew something was up. For one thing, Caroline was sitting on the couch nursing a cup of tea, and for another thing, all her bags were packed and stacked by the kitchen. It looked like a nap was out of the question.

She pointed to her bags. "Anyone care to tell me what's going on?" Her aunt and uncle were seated in both chairs that sat by the fireplace, and her nana was seated in her rocking chair.

Caroline stood up. "I should probably be the one to start. I am not who you think I am."

Straight to the point. That was new. "Really? I would have never guessed that."

Caroline rolled her eyes. "Please sit down so we can talk."

Paisley didn't want to, but one look from Nana had her sitting in the chair across from the couch. "Go on." This felt like history repeating itself.

"My name is not Caroline. It's Kennedy."

Paisley rolled the name around in her mind, until it clicked and she gasped. *It couldn't be.* "Kennedy. As in the Kennedy of the Goldenmare Triad?"

"Yes."

Paisley slumped back in her seat and rested her hands in her lap. Could nothing in her life ever be straightforward? "Why the secret identity?"

"It was the only way I could get close to you. Rosemary was quite adamant that I was to come and get you. I had no idea I would be here for four months." She frowned. "She wants to train you."

"Just like that?" She snapped her fingers.

"When Rosemary gets something in her mind, no one can change it."

It was clear that Kennedy loved Rosemary. Her eyes lit up when she talked about her. Since they were in a Triad she assumed they were all involved. That was intriguing. She herself couldn't handle one woman, let alone two. There was no way she could become involved with both Lana and Alexia.

"I see a question brewing in your mind. Go ahead, ask it."

Paisley couldn't have stopped the blush that trailed up her chest and neck. "Triad. So, all three of you are in a relationship? Together?"

"We are."

"Okay."

"Just okay? Usually people have more questions

than that."

"Yes, okay. I'm a private person and I wouldn't want someone asking invasive questions of me." She rested her head back against the cushion. What now? This was exactly what she had been looking for. She wanted Rosemary to train her and Rosemary had chosen her, but it made one hell of a coincidence. "Isn't this all a bit convenient?"

"I can see that from your point of view, but from mine this has been in the works for months. There isn't a hidden agenda. If you agree, you will accompany me to the Goldenmare estate."

"Just me?"

She eyed Addison. "Yes, just you. Our privacy is important to us we cannot have the location of our home in the hands of just anyone."

"Addison is my personal guard. What do you think will happen to her when they find me missing? I won't risk her life like that." Not to mention her only friend.

"You should go, Paisley," Addison said. "This is the break you've been looking for."

"You know I hate people making choices for me."

"We're not. This is your choice and I think you should take it. Don't worry about me. I'll be fine."

"You don't know that." Paisley turned to her.

"No, I don't."

This felt like K.G. all over again. She closed her eyes and took deep, steady breaths. "This is so messed up."

"Paisley, whatever it is you're thinking, stop. I'm not dead yet. Give me some credit."

Paisley turned to her family. "And what about all of you? What happens to you? They will question you.

What then?" And Jynx. Paisley still had no idea where she was and her aunt hadn't had any luck either.

"We can take care of ourselves. You should go." Paisley held Nana's tear-stained eyes as long as possible before turning away.

Good-byes all over again. Is this what her life had become? Always running away. But she wasn't really running, was she? If she stayed here, she would never live her own life, she would have all her choices taken away. Not to mention Alexia. If she stayed she would never see her or the girls again. "Kennedy, what happens now?"

She jumped up. "Now." She took a piece of paper out of her pocket and handed it to Paisley. "That is a spell that will allow you to shrink your possessions so that you will be able to fit them into your pack."

She eyed the piece of paper doubtfully. "Really?"

"Yes. And don't worry, we can make them regular size again. No problem."

Paisley doubted there would be a *we*, but she slipped the note into her pocket nonetheless. "I need to speak to Beatrice before I go. It's important." She didn't wait for them to object, just followed Addison outside and climbed up beside her on the carriage.

"It's the right thing to do, Paisley."

She slipped her hand through Addison's arm. "Maybe."

"No, it is."

She was just coming to terms with leaving her first family, and now this. Fate was a cruel bitch sometimes. They were both quiet for the rest of the ride to Beatrice's, who opened the door before they reached it and waved them both in.

"You have questions."

Paisley declined her invitation to sit. "Yes, but right now I only have one." Beatrice nodded. "What exactly is a DragonWitch? That is my only question and the only reason I am here."

"Paisley, come now. Surely you've figured it out."

"I don't follow."

"A DragonWitch is just that—a witch that owns a dragon."

She rolled her eyes. "Yes, I figured that out. But, what *is* a DragonWitch? One is surely more powerful than a regular witch. My power will be amplified by the dragon's magic. I know unless I agree to my dragon being bound to another, then it will always stay loyal to me and fight and die for me." Paisley paced in front of the fireplace. It couldn't be that simple. What was she missing? She ran her fingers through her hair, then spun on her heels when it hit her. "Have there been witches in history that have owned dragons?"

"Yes." A smirk played on Beatrice's lips.

"But were all of them considered DragonWitches, or were they just considered witches that owned dragons?" She held her hands out, palms up. "Is there a difference?" She had a sinking feeling there was. "I guess my question shouldn't be what is a DragonWitch, it should be what makes *me* a DragonWitch?"

Beatrice stood up. "What indeed. I can't give you a clear answer. I can only say that you *are* a DragonWitch. They are rare, but there have been plenty in existence. A DragonWitch holds an unbreakable bond with their dragon. It is an unquestionable bond. A witch that owns a dragon is just that, and the dragon would be more of a loyal pet. But a DragonWitch's dragon...even if your dragon was to be bound to another, you would still hold a connection with it. It is also rumored that a DragonWitch can communicate with their dragon through their thoughts. One would not be able to do that with a pet."

"That's not what I was expecting." She slipped her glasses off. "Will the connection be instant?"

"It should be."

"And if it isn't?"

"Come now, Paisley. I don't think you have anything to worry about. I see great things in your future. Great things indeed."

"I think my great things and yours are probably different."

"I wouldn't be so sure of that." Beatrice retrieved a small pouch from the basket atop the table and handed it to her. "Just something to help your travels."

Paisley eyed her but decided against asking how she knew she would be leaving, and slipped the pouch inside her pack beside the dragon egg. Her fingers brushed up against it, which sent tingles all the way to her toes. She zipped her pack and stood up. "I would say until next time, but we both know there won't be one."

Beatrice tilted her head. "I had a pleasure teaching you."

"Really?" Paisley narrowed her eyes. "All I did was weed your garden."

"Oh, Paisley, you did so much more, and in time you will figure it out." Addison helped her on with her pack and they walked out the front door. Paisley didn't bother looking back. Her future was in front of her, not behind.

Halfway home, Addison stopped the carriage, grabbed her by the chest, and dragged her to the ground as arrows whizzed by their head. The carriage took off as the arrows flew in their direction, and Paisley watched in shock as the horses rounded the bend and she lost sight of them. "Shit. Really?" Addison motioned for her to follow and they crawled to the tree line.

Addison picked up an arrow and threw it to the ground in disgust. "Those arrows belong to the Queen's Guard."

"Shit." The thought of killing them did cross her mind, but on the other hand, they were only doing their job—even if that included killing them. She frowned, then shook her head. No, the guards trying to kill them made all the difference. "What do you want to do?"

Addison flung her hand in the guards' direction. "Can't you do something?"

"I can, but is killing them going to send the right message?"

"Who cares what kind of message it sends?"

She was right. Paisley unfastened her necklaces and handed them to Addison. She shook her hands out but nothing happened. Usually there was a gray spark. "Shit."

"What?"

"I don't know." This was a great time for her powers to flatline. *Shit.*

"I think that I am the reason you don't have powers." They both whirled around and came face-to-face with a man in a long black robe. Lined up behind him were six archers who had their bows cocked and aimed at them.

Addison stood up and Paisley accepted her hand. "Who are you?"

"I am me." He laughed and produced a blue fireball in his hand. "You're not as powerful as everyone seems to think."

She didn't feel the need to correct him. Her powers may have been blocked, but she felt an electrical current race through her veins. The dragon's powers weren't muted. She wasn't sure how much she would be able to do, but she would give it her best shot. "People think what they want to."

He pointed his finger at her. "I don't know why the queen is so stuck on you." He raised his hand and Addison stiffened next to her. The archers behind him straightened. As soon as his hand lowered, Paisley threw out her hand. The look of disbelief on his face was almost comical as the arrows connected with the barrier around them and bounced off. Her excitement at one-upping him vanished when she watched Addison fall to the ground, an arrow sticking out of her upper chest.

Paisley knelt by her side. "Addison, hang in there."

"That's all I can do. It was through and through. I don't think it hit anything major, just hurts." She gasped and balled her hand up in a fist.

Paisley's mind was in overdrive. This was a perfect opportunity. They would never get another chance like this one. She leaned over Addison and whispered in her ear. "If you die, they'll never look for you." Thank god Addison was a quick study. She nodded. Paisley ran her hand down Addison's check. "I'll get us out of here quickly." She jumped up. "You killed her!" She screamed, tears running down her cheeks. Tears for K.G., her family, her dad's family, Alexia, tears for everything. "I hope you realize what you've done," she sneered.

"I know what I've done." He laughed, eyeing Addison, who lay still on the ground. "There is no way out of this. Just give yourself up."

"I am leaving and I am taking her body with me to bury. You can't stop me."

"Your father was a stubborn one, too."

She shut out his words and connected with the powers coursing through her body and tapped into them. She grinned and knelt next to Addison and spoke to the man. "You'll regret what you've done today. The last time someone killed a friend of mine, I killed her. Granted, your death won't be as quick as hers was, but it will be just as satisfying, and you will get what's coming to you. The only reason I'm not killing you now is because I have a better use for my powers." She latched onto Addison's arm, waved her hand in the air, and they were engulfed in a gray fog. In an instant, they were transported to her family's living room.

The transition, thank goodness, was flawless and a lot easier than she'd anticipated, which led her to believe her dragon's magic was guiding her own. She jumped up and directed her uncle and nephew to carry Addison's body to one of the bedrooms where they tended to her wounds.

With a final glance at Addison, she walked back into the living room, confident they would be able to save her friend. Kennedy, wearing a pair of black leather pants, long-sleeved white shirt, and purple jerkin, waited for her by the front window. She wore her hair down and finally looked the way Paisley had expected her to upon their first meeting.

Before addressing Kennedy, she walked up to her aunt. "To anyone who asks, Addison is dead. That's what the bastards that attacked us think, and I want to keep it that way. The leader of their group was accompanied by six of the Queen's Archers." She reached for and caressed her aunt's hand. "Can I trust you to get her to safety? She deserves to live a life free from the confines they have put on her."

"I will do my best, Paisley."

She hadn't expected anything else from her. Although she wanted to question her loyalty, she didn't have time. The choice was taken out of her hands and she had to believe that she put her trust in the right person. She nodded, withdrew the piece of paper from her pocket, walked to the pile of her belongings, and recited the spell. In the blink of an eye the pile had been reduced to a square the size of a Rubik's Cube. It would be easy to doubt her actions or even herself, but instead she picked up the cube, placed it beside the dragon egg, then slipped the backpack on. "I'm ready."

Kennedy nodded. "I'll be outside while you say your good-byes."

Paisley ignored the fluttering of her stomach as she hugged each of her family members and then knelt beside her nana's chair. "I'll miss you."

Nana patted her cheeks. "You'll be fine, sweetheart. Just fine."

Paisley kissed her palms, stood up, then kissed her cheek. "I'll never forget you." She turned, and without looking back exited through the rear door. The sweet smell of the wildflowers she had become used to every morning when she woke up calmed her racing heart, and she sighed at what she was once again having to give up. Losing two families in a matter of a few months had to be some sort of record.

"Don't think too hard, Paisley. We need to go." Kennedy stood beside what she could only describe as a beast. The horse was at least a foot taller than Kennedy and Kennedy stood almost six feet tall. Paisley eyed the horse, then Kennedy, before she stepped up next to her.

"I don't particularly care for riding." In truth, she had never ridden before in her life because it didn't interest her, and as beautiful as the beast was, she knew she would sustain quite a few injuries if she fell off.

"I didn't ask if you did." Kennedy cupped her hands and laced her fingers together to form a stirrup. "Hop on. Shadow is a sweetheart."

Paisley knew it wasn't a request, and when she was settled Kennedy climbed on in front of her. Out of instinct, Paisley slipped her arms around Kennedy's waist and tightened her hold. The last thing she wanted was to fall off. Even though Kennedy was virtually a stranger, she was the sole friend she had, if only by proxy, and Paisley was grateful for her presence. Some of her nervous energy dissipated when Kennedy patted her hands, then nudged the horse into motion.

≈≋≈≋

"How much farther is it?" The humidity had been steadily rising all morning and seemed to grow worse as the day went on. Paisley pulled her ball cap low on her brow and a quick look at her watch told her they had been riding for well over six hours with only a few breaks to allow Shadow a chance to rest. The day she didn't have to ride a horse anymore would be the day her ass would thank her.

Kennedy ignored her and instead asked a question of her own. "Has it occurred to you that since you left without the queen's permission you will now be considered a traitor to the crown? Even if you are married to her daughter."

Paisley tightened her grip around Kennedy's

waist when her words washed over her. At one point, she did have a fleeting thought about that, but had never dwelled on it. But it was a big deal. How did her life get so messed up? "Yes. I assume it means I won't be able to go back without facing jail time?"

"Yes, but there is probably something else you haven't thought about." She tightened her hand around Paisley's arms.

That didn't sound good at all. "What? If I don't have to see them again, I think my life will be better off."

"Do you ever want to see your other family again?"

"Of course. What kind of question is that?"

"The only portal that will allow you into your world is in Dangor."

Crap. "I'll never be able to see them again. I didn't even think about that." It never even dawned on her that there was only one portal, and now she had just screwed her chance to ever see them again. "There is no other way?" There had to be another way.

"None that I know of."

Even though she would have loved to have seen them again, she didn't feel the heartache she thought she would have at the news. "It looks like Goldenmare will be a completely new start for me." The last thing she needed right now was to become depressed. They could still be ambushed. She also didn't imagine something like a neutral country would keep the queen out.

First, she would need to practice her magic, then learn how to control her dragon, then she would find Alexia and the girls. Every time a thought of them would enter her mind, she would shove it back as far as it would go. Their safety was her number one priority, and letting herself get distracted by anything might lead to her to lose focus.

Even if she wanted to see them, she wouldn't risk their lives in the process. Everything was too risky. Hell, riding on Shadow with Kennedy was risky. She would have loved the opportunity to at least see her family again, but right now she had to focus on herself, Alexia, and the girls.

She was jerked out of her thoughts when Shadow slowed, then stopped, and Kennedy slid to the ground. Why where they stopping? There was still plenty of daylight left. She accepted Kennedy's hand and landed next to her. After a few stretches, she was ready to go. "Are we making camp here?"

"No. The shack isn't far from here, we'll walk. Do you mind if I ask you a personal question?"

"You can, but I might not answer it."

"Of all the people you could have chosen, why Alexia? And please understand, I don't mean any disrespect."

"Why not her? She's gorgeous, funny, powerful, loving, sexy, strong, loyal, the list could go on and on. But the real reason is because once I laid eyes on her I couldn't stop thinking about her. I was pulled to her from the moment we met. I don't think I could have stopped it even if I wanted to, but believe me, I don't want to. My heart races and my palms get sweaty, and I have to remind myself to breathe every time I see her. I feel safe when she holds me, and loved. I don't want to ever not know that feeling. We're just getting started on the two of us, and I want to give that a chance to flourish."

"You love her?"

"Yes," she said without hesitation. "I can't

explain it and I am not even going to try, I just know it's right. I can feel it." It was an unreal feeling, but she knew she loved her. From the moment she laid eyes on her. She didn't believe in fairytale romances, or love at first sight, but she knew when to admit defeat. Love at first sight was such a cliché.

"The same way you knew it wasn't right with Lana?"

"Yes. Lana was never my choice, she chose me. She just showed up and slapped the bracelet on my arm. The matter was taken out of my hands. After talking with my parents, grandma, Addison, and even Lana, I was willing to give a relationship with her a chance, but then Alexia happened again and whatever I was feeling for Lana burned out and died. I thought perhaps we could be friends, but then she pulled that stunt at the marketplace and she solidified her place in my life."

"Sometimes people do the wrong things for the right reasons."

Paisley tightened her hold on her backpack straps and rolled her eyes. "She was willing to stand back while the guards killed Alexia and her babies. I wouldn't be able to live with myself if I let anything happen to them."

"You won't always be able to protect them."

"Maybe not, but I will die trying." Kennedy didn't seem to be in a hurry to reach their destination, so Paisley just enjoyed the walk. She swung her gaze back around when Kennedy slowed down beside her. Then her gaze locked on what Kennedy was looking at.

When Kennedy said they were heading toward a shack, she had assumed she meant a cabin, but that was not the case. It really was a shack. From the way the building was leaning, it was a miracle it was still standing. Moss and some type of vine she couldn't recognize had grown across the sides of the shack and up onto the roof.

Paisley adjusted her glasses. "It's not what I was expecting."

Kennedy had an unreadable expression on her face. "I don't think it's what's on the outside that will interest you."

"I don't—" Paisley shut her eyes tightly when an all too familiar sound reached her ears and she bit back a sob. "How?" As she wiped the tears running down her face, Kennedy patted her on the shoulder, and she opened her eyes. Kennedy had a big grin on her face and motioned for her to turn around. The sight that greeted her was one she wouldn't soon forget. Alexia stood in the lopsided doorway with a smile on her face, and she was flanked on either side by the girls.

"Go to them," Kennedy whispered in her ear. "They've been waiting for you."

Before Paisley could even take a step toward them or register what was happening, two little girls squealed and ran down the walkway. Paisley crouched on the ground, and the only thing preventing her from falling flat on her back when their bodies collided with hers was Kennedy's hand on her shoulder. They were talking nonstop, but all she cared about was that they were here, in her arms. She inhaled their familiar scent and kissed them both on the head, then pulled back.

"Girls," Kennedy hollered. "Why don't you come inside with me. I have a present for each of you." As quickly as they had come they were gone.

Paisley didn't have the energy to get up, and in truth she was afraid that when she did stand up, Alexia would be gone instead of standing in front of her. Out of the corner of her eye, she saw Alexia flex her fingers and offer her hand. Paisley couldn't speak, but buried her head in her hands and cried.

"Paisley, please stand up, darling. I am much too old to be kneeling on the ground, and I think I deserve a proper hello." Alexia grabbed her hand and pulled her to her feet. She wiped Paisley's tears. "Please don't cry. We are fine."

Paisley hiccupped, then wrapped her arms around Alexia and buried her face in her neck. "I had hope, but I didn't know."

"I know. I know." Alexia squeezed her tighter before pushing her back and wiping her tears again. "I—"

Paisley didn't wait for her to finish before she pulled her down and kissed her. The feel of her lips after weeks without it almost brought Paisley to her knees. The only thing keeping her upright were the arms wrapped around her waist. Paisley pulled back and bit down on Alexia's bottom lip before trailing kisses down her jawline and nipping the spot behind her ear. She snickered into Alexia's neck when she moaned. "I cannot wait to get you alone."

Alexia slid her hands down Paisley's back, cupped her ass, and pulled her close. "Do you have any idea what you're doing to me?" She cut off Paisley's response with another kiss. "I didn't think I would ever feel this way. You have destroyed me for anyone else, Paisley. When you touch me, my magic flares up and shimmers under the surface. I love you."

"I love you, too." Paisley kissed her neck, then licked the same spot. "I thought that only happened with my magic."

Alexia groaned. "We have to stop, as much as I would love to continue this. We have a lot to talk about, there are two little girls who missed you, and I have another surprise waiting for you inside the cabin."

"Shack," Paisley corrected her.

"Whatever."

Paisley held on tightly, afraid if she let go she would never hold her again. She didn't think she could bear it if that were the case, so she held on tighter.

"Paisley, I'm right here and we are not going anywhere."

"Promise?"

"Yes. Now I can make you that promise. We're not going anywhere. I'm not sure how our lives are going to play out, but I don't plan on living them separately. Do you?"

"God, no." She pulled back and clasped her hands behind Alexia's neck. Everything she had ever wanted to see was reflected back at her. Love, caring, understanding, hope, was all shining from Alexia's eyes. It was both a blessing and a curse. Living the rest of her life with her and the girls would be a dream come true, but she knew if that dream ever came to an end because of outside sources, she would burn that country to the ground. That scared her.

It scared her how much she felt for the woman in her arms. She knew it wasn't that easy, but she had hope, and together she was confident they could overcome everything anyone threw at them. She had to, because for her there wasn't another option. Now that she had them, she would never let them go.

Paisley pulled back from her love's embrace, turned away, and raised her arms into the air and stretched. She didn't think she could ever be this happy. Not after everything that had happened up to this point.

Before she could lower her arms, a pair of hands slid around her waist and pulled her back into a warm body. Soft lips slid down her neck and Paisley tilted her head to allow better access. She moaned when Alexia nipped her ear, and laughed when she was spun around and her lips were captured. The kiss offered so much love, trust, and care. Paisley couldn't believe she had made it this far. Thing were so much sweeter than she could have ever imagined.

Alexia kissed the tip of her nose. "Shall we?" She motioned with her head to the shack.

"There is nowhere else I would rather be."

About the Author

Born near Chicago, but raised in Southern Illinois, where she still lives, Shannon spends her free time writing. When she isn't writing, she enjoys binge watching fantasy, science fiction, or true crime shows.

You can contact Shannon at -

Website: smhfiction.com
Email: smh1981@live.com
Facebook: facebook.com/smharrisauthor
Twitter: @smhfiction

Check out Shannon's other books

The Adearian Chronicles - Book One - The Oath – ISBN – 978-1-943353-17-0

Ex-mercenary, Lanis Welsh, is finally at a place in her life where she is content with what and who she is; High Priestess Anya's Protector and Lover. After an unexpected request, she has no choice but to leave Anya's protection in the hands of someone else and travel back to the one place that holds nothing but bad memories. When she is manipulated into signing an oath she has no desire to fulfill, she questions the very truths she has built her life on. As strangers become friends and enemies become allies, Lanis must face the demons from her past. It doesn't take her long to realize there is more going on than anyone could have ever foreseen and nothing and no one can be trusted.

Adearian Chronicles - Book 2 – Revelations – ISBN - 978-1-943353-33-0

What would you do if you were faced with finding and saving the one person who held your heart, but you only had two weeks to do it?

When the unexpected happens and Lanis's world is turned upside down, her and Elson have no choice but to align themselves with two people from a strange land. With new enemies at play, and a Goddess that seems to have forsaken them, Lanis relies on the only people she can; her friends. To fight the demons that plague her daily, she has to separate her love for Anya, from the task she must perform. On top of the unknowns, she is gifted a small black book that changes the way she sees everything and everyone around her. As her world starts to crumble, Lanis must face her fears and the nightmares that invade her dreams. With the hours ticking away, she must come to terms with the fact that she might already be too late.

The Details in The Design - ISBN - 978-1-943353-79-8

Every Stitch tells a story.

Avery Michaels has longed to work in the fashion industry since she was six years old. Now at thirty-two she's fed up with her job as a food critic and signs up with an employment agency that promises to find anyone their dream job.

She is thrilled when she gets an interview with the fashion house of her choice, Catherine Davenport Designs. There's only one problem. For the past six years, Avery has had a massive crush on Catherine, one of the hottest fashion designers of the past two decades.

In the midst of a new job, nosey friends, Catherine's meddling daughters, difficult co-workers, and a dachshund named Polly, Avery also has to contend with a new woman that enters Catherine's life.

From the Start, Avery knows winning Catherine's heart will be no easy feat. When curve ball after curve ball is thrown her way, does she scrap her design or make it work.

Other books by Sapphire Books Publishing

The Dreamcatcher - ISBN - 978-1-943353-67-5

High school is rarely easy, especially for a tall, somewhat gangly Native American girl. Add a sprinkle of shyness, a dash of athletic prowess, an above-average IQ, and some bizarre history that places her in the guardianship of her aunt. Then normal high school life is only an illusion.

Kai Tiva faces an uphill struggle until she runs into Riley Beth James, the extroverted class cutie, at the principal's office. Riley shows up for a newspaper interview, while Kai is summoned for punching out a classmate.

Riley is the attractive girl-next-door-type whom everyone likes. Though a fairly good student, an emerging choral star, and wildly popular, she knows she'll never live up to her older sister. She makes up for it with bravery, kindness, and a brash can-do attitude.

Their odd matchup is strengthened by curiosity, compassion, humor, and all the drama of typical teenage life. But their experiences go beyond the normal teen angst; theirs is compounded by a curious attraction to each other, and an emerging, insidious danger related to mysterious death of Kai's father.

Their emerging friendship is tested as they navigate this risky challenge. But the powerful bond forged between them has existed through past lives. The outcome this time will affect the next generation of Kai's people.

In the Direction of the Sun - ISBN - 978-1-943353-65-1

"The emotions flying between the two women who tell their story here is as dramatic as the Appalachian Trail and as tumultuous as the Atlantic Ocean. These natural elements are a perfect backdrop for the revelations of love which both repel and engage them."
– Jewelle Gomez, author, The Gilda Stories

Steady and smart, Alex McKenzie is settled into a comfortable life in her beloved hometown of Stockbridge, MA. Everything Alex thought she knew about life and about herself changes the moment Cate Conrad blows into town like a warm breeze. Alex falls head over heels in love with the free-spirited artist and sailor but there's one problem: Cate's complicated past makes it impossible for her to open her heart completely and so she does what she's always done— she runs away. Devastated, Alex tries to heal her heart by literally walking away from her life to hike the famed Appalachian Trail while Cate takes to the water. The unexpected turn of events shows Cate and Alex how fragile life is and how love is the all that really matters.

Lavender Dreams - ISBN - 978-1-943353-59-0

When Sarah Chase got on the ferry to Bainbridge Island, she left her lover, her job, and her past behind. She didn't know that in the course of one day she would meet a woman who might be the girl of her dreams, change her career path, create a new family, and find herself in a fairytale mansion with two of the quirkiest little old ladies imaginable.

When Butches Cry – ISBN – 978-1-943353-57-6

Reveling in her contrariness, Traf's got no time for 'good' women who conform. She competes with men, wears male clothing, and steals their jobs. A fighter, damn the consequences, she's totally unsuited to the mundane role of a mid-twentieth century Azorean woman. Traf dreams of going to America where women do as they like, make their own money, and live without the permission of men.

Emotionally damaged by past relationships, Ana is convinced she's hopelessly inadequate. She joins an unprecedented type of private club, a group of women loving women calling themselves Troublemakers. The golden-haired beauty could have her pick of lovers, but her heart yearns for the mischievous butch with dark, brooding eyes. Fascinated by Traf since they were schoolgirls together, Ana knows her crush is hopeless; how could such a cocky, not to mention arousing, woman ever love her?

Gossip, sexism, priests, the US Air Force, and even their families, oppose them at every turn. Battling to exist in peace, Traf, Ana, and the other Troublemakers develop a unique subculture of support for each other, but no one is prepared When Butches Cry.